MEET ME
IN GREECE

A Friends to Lovers Travel Romance

D PICHARDO-JOHANSSON

MEET ME IN GREECE
A Friends to Lovers Travel Romance
© 2022 by Diely Pichardo-Johansson.
Camilo Press

ISBN: 978-1-951400-06-4

Cover Design by Roland Hulme ginger@hiddengemsbooks.com

Developmental Editing by Savannah Jezowski www.dragonpress.com/author-services

Copy Editing by Krista R Burdine iamgrammaresque.com

Formatting by Champagne Book Design champagnebookdesign.com

DEDICATION

This book is dedicated to every wonderful woman who ever accepted mistreatment from a man. May the wisdom of experience break the spell of childhood wounds and lead you to realize you deserve much more.

This book is also dedicated to long-term couples. May the winters of the relationship always blossom back into spring, like an ever-recycling friends-to-lovers story.

<u>And of course, to my ultimate best friend and slumber party companion, my husband David.</u>

In the words of Ezra: Thank you for teaching me about the type of love that can see the best part of us, even when we've forgotten it. Love that doesn't walk away when we show our worst side, because it knows what's real, hiding underneath.

Get A Free Companion Book!

Enhance your reading experience by immersing in the beautiful images of Athens, Mykonos and Santorini. <u>Sign up for my Newsletter to download the companion photo book for this novel</u>. *Meet Me in Greece: An Interactive Photo Book. Worth A Thousand Words Series Book 3.*

Downloading this book is not mandatory to follow the story, but highly recommended for your pleasure.

Get your free book Here.
https://mailchi.mp/b53552c75f09/meet-me-in-greece

PROLOGUE

(About ten months ago)

L ET'S GET SOMETHING OUT OF THE WAY: I'M NOT A GOOD
person; but I'm working on it.

Everyone has heard ridiculous tabloid stories claiming I
clawed another model, backstabbed another designer or used sexual
favors to rise to the top. I shrug off those lies by now. I've received
tons of hate in my life and I've become immune to it.

But the truth is that behind the reputation of being the most
horrible person in the world...

Well, I kind of am.

Yes, I've been *bad*—really bad. The "worsest floozy in Greenyard,
Illinois," as my uncouth stepmother used to call me—and not as a
term of endearment. But today I leave all that behind and commit
to becoming the best possible version of myself.

Under the round silver moon, the crackling fire breaks the
monotone hum of the ocean waves. The golden flames protect me
from the night chill despite my strapless, white minidress—makeshift
wedding attire for a self-vow. Next to me, also in wedding dresses,
my three best friends gather around the firepit. In this symbolic ceremony we do more than commit to a year of introspection and celibacy. We also mark the beginning of a new stage in our lives.

We all have memories to leave behind. Tender Sophia just ended
her engagement. Spiritual Chloe struggles to find in her career the
sense of belonging she never had. And sweet Iris, the writer and wise
soul, puts the rest of our troubles in perspective. Who would have

1

thought her premature cancer diagnosis would bring us together after a decade apart?

The salt-scented breeze plays with my long ombre hair as I read my list of grievances—everything I regret, that I'm ready to let go of.

"I'm not proud of the life I've lived. Even if I haven't done one-tenth of what people accuse me of, the faults I did commit haunt me." I start my confession. "I did compete aggressively in the world of modeling, not always in the most ethical ways. I did sabotage my competition at times—usually because they were about to destroy *me*. And even if it's not true that I've slept my way to the top—" I wrestle with the words. The statement I'm about to read might be the most painful of my life.

Chloe places her hand on my back. God bless this wonderful friend, my champion since middle school. Her touch infuses me with strength, so I resume. "And even if it's not true that I've slept my way to the top, I can't deny it either. Because I never would've been so successful if it hadn't been for Quentin." And here I burst into tears.

Quentin Xenakis, the last American couture designer—who's surprisingly straight. Combining our multiple breakups and make ups over the years, my relationship with him was the longest of my life. The doors he opened for me almost made it worth it that he destroyed my self-esteem and cheated on me with every woman that crossed his path. Last month we broke up yet again, but this time I know deep inside it's forever.

I throw my letter in the fire and the three girls embrace me. As the paper crinkles and blackens, my sobs taper off, but I still can't speak. Iris and Sophia seem at a loss—Chloe is the only person in the world who's seen me cry. The tears caught me off guard too; I didn't even cry the day my stepmom kicked me out of my dad's house at age fifteen.

"Come on! Whoever spread the gossip that you slept your way to the top doesn't know how picky you are with men!" Iris whispers with studied cheerfulness. She's so brave, lifting all of our spirits despite her starting chemotherapy tomorrow.

"Oh my, that's right! You should've seen the guys she used to sneak into our dorm!" Sophia adds, forcing a playful tone. I appreciate my former roommate's effort to join in on the joke despite how prudish she is. "Sleeping with your bosses? *They wish.* Mia Kostopoulos wouldn't give a guy a second look unless he were as hot as a Greek god."

We giggle and I'm glad to break the solemnity of the moment. "Well, I haven't always been that picky about looks," I manage to jest between my tears. "After all, I once kissed *Ezra.*"

Sophia whimpers in disgust and we all laugh. She hates it when I repeat my story of kissing our geeky best friend in high school.

And my weeping resumes, this time bittersweet. *Ezra.* I wish so much he could've joined us tonight. Like Chloe, Iris and Sophia, he's an angel on earth.

Memories from that night on the raised deck behind his house flash in my mind. A star-filled sky and spring-scented air. Ezra's scrawny, late-bloomer body in my arms. His cold hands, his quivering lips. We were at once proud and scared of our audacity; but mostly, we were still so young and innocent—two seventeen-year-olds kissing under the stars.

I pick up my box of regrets to release, and toss old souvenirs into the fire. Every love note Quentin ever sent me. The magazine pictures of me as a skeletal bottle blonde, from when I teetered near the edge of an eating disorder. My father and stepmother's wedding portrait that always hurt me to see. At the bottom of the box lies one more photo; I'm being crowned prom queen. I wear a plastic tiara and my white prom dress, the first dress I ever made myself.

"You're not burning that picture!" Chloe gasps. "It's beautiful!"

"It brings back bad memories." I groan. "The idiot who took me to the prom behaved like a jerk. And the photo reminds me of everything I never want to be again: weak, desperate for love, obsessed with what others think of me."

Chloe scrunches her face. "Okay, go ahead, I'm pretty sure I have a copy at home."

When I drop the photo in the fire and watch the flames consume it, its power over me floats away in sparks and ashes, as if I have been released.

Then, Ezra returns to my mind. I see him again enter the school gym for the prom party—alone. Our eyes meet across the dance floor, and I quietly beg him to brag to our friends about kissing me, but he never does.

How strange it is that two such different men share my thoughts tonight. Quentin, the man who overwhelmed me with attraction—but never loved me. Ezra, someone with whom I lack physical chemistry—but is the only man who's ever loved me for free.

Someday I hope to find a mixture of the two.

At the end of our ceremony, we write in the sand our intentions for this year. As I write my wish, I hope none of the girls looks over my shoulder. It might ruin my practical, no-nonsense reputation.

"I want to fall in love with someone who cherishes me, deserves me and treats me well. Someone I can love *and also* desire."

That's a tall order. Perhaps the hardest pattern I have to leave behind is that I always fall for men who treat me like shit.

I watch the waves crash against the beach and wash over the sand, absorbing the words.

CHAPTER 1

Ezra

D ESPITE A DECADE OF CONTACT LENSES, HIGH-END clothes and fashionable haircuts, deep inside I'm still the biggest nerd in the word—and I won't apologize for it.

So here I am, having lunch at the hippest seafood restaurant in San Francisco, and instead of enjoying the stunning view of the Bay through the large windows, or relaxing in the company of the friend sitting across from me, I have my nose in my laptop. But this time it's for a good cause; I'm helping Ian, my martial arts trainer turned newest friend, with some web marketing basics to boost his business.

"Do I really have to learn all that computer stuff?" Ian adjusts the black and red belt tying his black jiu jitsu gi. "SEO? RRS? *Cookies*? The only 'cookies' I care about are Oreos."

I suppress my amusement. Clearly, I've geeked out enough for one day. "Maybe I should've started by showing you what I mean by branding." I search my files for the new logo I put together for him.

But something grabs my attention. The blonde at the neighboring table just shot me a look way longer than the standard two-point-five seconds. All my brain circuits light up like an awakening control panel.

It doesn't matter that I'm no longer short on female company. After spending my early life as the nerd no woman ever gave a second look, I can't help feeling deep gratitude whenever I get any attention.

I scan the blonde as she crosses her long legs. Not bad. As per rule number eight, I make sure my eyes don't linger too much on her body. Mia's voice sounds in my head, *Compliment her; tell her something nice that is true.*

She has nice blue eyes; I could use that.

Ian forks the last bite of his shrimp salad. "You were showing me something, Cohen?"

"Oh yes." I return my attention to my computer. "Ready to see your new logo?"

"Can't wait." He slides his chair closer. "Your branding Q&A session was so intense, I wondered if we'd just been on a blind date."

I turn my laptop around to show him the logo. It's a sea-blue dragon emerging from golden flames. "Well, here's my latest masterpiece."

Ian's ecstatic expression fills me with satisfaction.

"Do you like it?" I ask.

"Like it? I want to get it tattooed on my face!"

I love this new creative job-slash-hobby. It's so much more fun than plain coding.

"I didn't realize you had such an artistic side?" Ian gapes at me.

I signal to the waiter that I'm done with my sushi plate. "I double-majored in computer science and graphic design. It allowed me to work on both ends of game and app development: the software and the graphics."

"Wow." Ian threads a hand through his wavy black hair. "No wonder you became a gazillionaire!"

When your list of contacts includes the billionaires of Silicon Valley, you learn to be humble about your net worth. Compared to some of my friends I'm a "penny millionaire" worthy of commiseration. "I'm not a 'gazillionaire.'"

"As far as I'm concerned, you are, *desgraçado*." I think Ian just mumbled some cussword in Portuguese. "You just passed on a three-million-dollar offer for an app, and you're retiring at age thirty-three."

I shudder. "First of all, I prefer to call it 'working for fun.' The word 'retire' makes me feel old. And second, I didn't *pass* on the offer for *Squiggles*. I *counteroffered* at five million, hoping they meet me in the middle."

Ian glowers at me. "I hate you so much right now."

I can't believe the blonde is still checking vanilla *me* out instead of dark, hunky Ian. I'm so flattered I want to volunteer to wash her car—or something.

What excuse can I find to approach her table? Chloe's voice whispers in my mind, *Notice what she's doing and offer her some help.* The blonde seems to be writing in a journal. How can I help with that?

As if in answer to my will power, her pen rolls off the edge of the table and falls on the plank floor. I spring out of my seat and pick it up before she can react.

"Here you go," I extend it to her with my brightest grin. Rule number one: *always smile.*

"Thank you!" She beams right back.

"I'm Ezra." I offer my hand, which she accepts.

"I'm Lori."

I keep her hand in mine two seconds longer than the duration of the handshake. Time for strategy number five, courtesy of Iris. *Apologize and compliment.*

"Wow, I'm sorry." I chuckle as I release her hand. "I don't mean to stare, but you have the most beautiful eyes."

Her eyelashes flutter, and she flushes a little. "Oh. Thank you."

Rule number three—Sophia's advice. *Eye contact, but not creepy. One. Two. Three.*

"Well, enjoy your lunch, Lori." I send her one last wink and return to my table.

"Why did you walk away?" Ian asks as I settle back on my seat. "That woman was definitely into you."

"It's okay. She'll come to me."

Rule number seven comes from my princess Mia. *Always leave her wanting more.*

"So where were we?" I ask.

"You were telling me about your double major."

"Oh yes. I took many art classes during college; my girls had the theory that developing the creative parts of my mind helped balance my brainy nature."

"Your famous girls?" Ian's dark eyes are full of questions. "Your four friends from college?"

Warm gratitude fills me. They say that behind every successful man there's a woman; in my case there are *four*. "I wouldn't be who I am today if they hadn't decided to make me their project."

"What do you mean?"

My lips twitch at the memory. "I used to have an extreme case of social awkwardness—growing up, more than one pediatrician tried to label me with Asperger's or autism. My girls socialized me by having me memorize social cues and what to say in every situation." I point at the logo he just claimed to love so much. "They also coaxed me out of my scientific, algorithmic brain and got me into art."

"How did that start?" Ian leans forward, seemingly intrigued by my story.

My standard response tells all about how Sophia, a painter, encouraged me to enroll in a photography class with her. But in all honesty, the work started long before that. "My friend Mia, whom I've known since middle school, used to police my outfits all through high school and college. Not only did she teach me how to dress, but she taught me everything I know about color coordination, which has helped me tons with web and app design."

As with every time I talk about Mia, nostalgia spreads inside me. I wonder what she's doing right now.

"Hey."

I lift my eyes from the computer screen. As I predicted, the blonde is by my table. "I'm on my way out. I just wanted to say thanks again." She lays a Post-it on top of my empty dessert plate, twinkles at me and paces away.

I pick up the Post-it; it's her phone number.

"You evil genius," Ian snickers. "Social awkwardness my ass."

"You should've met me a decade or two ago." I slide the note into the front pocket of my shirt. But for some reason, after thoughts about Mia leaked into my brain, scoring this number doesn't feel that rewarding.

I shake the thought away. "Let me show you how your logo will look at the top of your new website."

Over coffee I use the logo to whip together a staging homepage and promotional materials, relishing Ian's reborn enthusiasm. I'm still going as we settle our separate checks—Ian refuses to let me pay his despite our disparate incomes. Then, a text message dings on my phone.

I grin at the sight of Iris' name. "Speaking of my girls!"

The message is a video-chat link and a text that reads, *"Hi, Ezra! Can you please join us at the weekly call?"*

I begin to reply that I'll call her in an hour when a second part of the message pops in. *"It's important. It's about Mia."*

My thumbs freeze at the screen keyboard and apprehension fills me.

Worry must show on my features because Ian asks. "Everything alright?"

"I don't know." I frown as I text back, *"Give me a minute."*

I close the laptop and spring from the table to indicate that the meeting is over. "We're going to need to regroup later, if you don't mind." I return the laptop to its case.

Ian rises too. "I hope everything is okay with your friends."

"I'm sure everything's fine. Just something about Mia, but it sounds important." Why do I have to overreact to anything that involves her? I signal Ian to follow me.

"Mia." He repeats the name in his smooth Brazilian accent as we stroll in the direction of the restaurant exit. "That's the friend you just mentioned, the one who taught you how to dress and color-coordinate, isn't it?"

Pride fills me, and I can't help but brag. "She's good at it. She's an up-and-coming fashion designer now."

"Wait a minute." Ian stops walking. "You're not talking about Mia Kostopoulos, the former model, are you?"

I forget my princess was once kind of famous. "Yes, that's her."

Ian inhales through closed teeth. "The last model I dated used to say, and I quote, 'Mia Kostopoulos is a soulless, cruel diva who clawed her way to the top.'"

I snort a laugh as we approach the valet parking stand and extend our tickets. I wait until the attendants have left to resume talking. "I'll tell you a secret, but you have to promise you'll never tell anyone." I look over my shoulder to make sure nobody is eavesdropping. "Mia will make you believe she's a witch, but deep inside, she's a softy, and the nicest person you'll ever meet. I've known her for over twenty years."

He shoots me a disbelieving glance "Rumor has it she once put sulfuric acid in some competing model's beauty cream to ruin her face and swipe a contract."

I crack up at the memory. "That's not true, I was there. We were sixteen and goofing around in summer camp. It wasn't *acid*. She put *Vaseline* in Kelly Jones' acne cream, to make her break out. And Mia didn't even know Kelly was her competition for that makeup ad audition. The prank was meant to punish Kelly for being mean to our friend Chloe."

We pace while waiting for our cars. It's a cool October day in San Francisco and the air smells of sea fog and pot. "The world is still not used to women who have both beauty and brains, and it's a natural human tendency to demonize what we can't understand. The media has vilified Mia; smart as she is, she happily rides that for publicity."

It's true Mia is the woman everyone hates but who hides a heart of gold.

The opposite of me. I'm the "nice guy" everybody loves but who hides the darkest secrets.

"Mia has always been my hero, because she doesn't care what anyone thinks about her," I add as the valet approaches with Ian's Nissan. "She was the most popular girl in our high school, yet she unapologetically hung out with two of the biggest weirdoes in the class: our friend Chloe, the goth girl with a witch for a grandma, and me, the class nerd."

"It sounds like Mia's quite a gal." We stroll toward his car.

"She is." It must be my remaining social awkwardness; I don't know why I have to overshare, but I blurt, "I used to have the biggest crush on her."

Ian scrutinizes me with a suppressed smirk. "Uh...judging by your starry eyes right now, something tells me you still do."

I almost bust a gut. "Oh, you're hilarious, Ian!" I slap his rock-hard back and wave him off. "Mia is like a sister to me. You're one hundred percent wrong!"

Ian shoots me one last skeptical look before entering his car and I step toward my arriving Maserati.

Well, he's *ninety-eight* percent wrong.

* * *

Ever since Iris started a yearlong treatment for breast cancer, Mia, Chloe and Sophia have stuck to their promise of video-chatting with her every week. I join in from time to time, but I've never been as good as the girls are at keeping up with programs. They've all been following some insane cleansing year Iris lays out in her famous self-help book *The Self-Vow*, about how to reboot your life with meditation, healthy food and celibacy. I tried it and lasted three days.

The moment I find a place to pull over, I tap the link Iris texted me and join the call. The image of Chloe and Sophia together in Chicago alternates on the screen with Iris' in Florida. Iris is a tough gal. Not even months of chemo and recent radiation have taken away her spirits.

"Look at your hair, Iris!" I cheer at her carpet-like scalp fuzz.

"I know!" She beams. "But it's so uneven, and the texture is like steel wool—I'm not ready to give up my wigs yet." As quickly as Iris' glee appears, it vanishes. "Ezra, we need your help."

I make a mock military salute. "For you, my ladies? Anything! Do you need me to get someone killed? I know a guy." I'm only half-joking on both statements.

"Well…Good thing murder is illegal, because I wish I could ask you to assassinate someone." Chloe purses her lips and wrinkles her pointy nose as if something disgusts her. "Quentin Xenakis."

My visceral reaction is instant. Hot blood washes over my face. My chest tightens and a twinge of nausea rises even before my brain retrieves his image in my memory. But the strongest sensation is my eyes burning as if my contact lenses had turned to dry potato chips. "Please don't tell me Mia took him back—again."

"Not yet." Sophia sighs. "But he's getting ready to attack."

Quentin Xenakis, a.k.a., *the Unmentionable*. Or as I prefer to call him, *Mr. X*—his super-villain name.

If someone invented an app to measure evil, that man would render the app non-functional, due to him reading off the charts.

I suspect his vileness would score so high, it would freeze the cell phone's operating system—maybe even crack the screen and set the phone on fire.

Mr. X is the Devil.

Wait, I take that back. That's insulting to the Devil.

I run a hand up my face and rake it through my hair, while speaking from between my teeth. "What is he plotting now?"

"Oh, he's plotting something, we can tell," Chloe plays with her armful of quartz crystal bracelets. "He invited Mia to show her designs in some...big deal fashion event overseas that implies they have to work together for weeks. And you're not going to believe how transparent his plans are," Chloe gets closer to the camera. "Coincidentally, this fashion week is hosted in the precise place Mia has always wanted to visit: Athens, Greece."

I frown. "I didn't know Greece had a fashion week."

Iris raises her re-growing eyebrows. "Our point exactly. This smells of fabrication."

Quentin Xenakis is the worst thing that ever happened to Mia—and he's happened about half a dozen times. The on-again, off-again boyfriend who on a good day simply cheats on her and on a bad day also leaves her demoralized and ruins her health. It takes her forever to bounce back, yet the moment she's finally dating a good guy, he reappears with promises he never fulfills.

"Come on, Mia is too smart to fall for this again." I scowl at the screen. "She's been doing so well."

"And that's what makes it so dangerous," Iris takes over. "Mia thinks she's finally over him and this time it will be different."

I grunt. "That is like a junkie saying. 'Hey, I'm finally clean from heroin—let me celebrate by shooting up *just a little*." I roll my eyes.

"We need you to talk some sense into her," angelic Sophia begs. "You're the only one who can speak to her in person."

I live in San Francisco and Mia lives in Los Angeles. Yet in the past few years, we've spent more time with Iris in Florida or with Chloe and Sophia in Chicago, than with each other—and that's a shame. I could blame our disconnect on how busy we both are, and how much I travel, but there's more.

I tend to avoid Mia. If she's out of sight, I'm okay. But after we get together, it becomes too painful to say goodbye. So I spare myself the distress by seeing her as little as possible. I guess I shouldn't beat myself up for that. It's impossible not to keep a special place in your heart for the girl who taught you how to kiss.

The memory flushes my entire body and fills my skin with goose bumps.

Maybe Ian was only *ninety* percent wrong.

CHAPTER 2

Mia

M Y FIVE-INCH PLATFORM STILETTOS DEMAND ALL MY concentration to avoid landing on my face with each step. I'm dying to take off these zebra-print heels and trade this uncomfortable dress for jeans and a T-shirt. But when you're a fashion designer negotiating a contract with a Beverly Hills boutique, you have to dress the part.

I sit behind my ebony desk in my black, white and silver minimalist office. Today I'm wearing my signature outfit for negotiations: a little black dress with an asymmetrical neckline that hints at my shoulders and collarbones while leaving my famous cleavage to the imagination. Short but not too short; and tight enough to reveal my curves without being slutty. Finally free from the blond dye that took forever to grow out, my brown hair is twisted into an elaborate up-do.

Miss Beverly Hills Boutique, Madame Buxton, is a Devil-wears-Prada-wannabe with short gray hair, an impressive business suit and a flashy Balenciaga bag—so big I could hide in it. Next to her perches her sidekick: an impeccably dressed—and just as bitchy-looking—unapologetically queer assistant. It takes effort not to crack up every time I glance at his thin mustache, curled at the tips. It took excruciating work to convince them to meet me here in my *atelier* instead of at their office. My staff and I have a ton riding on this.

"Ms. Kostopoulos," Madame Buxton eyes me from head to toe, as if searching for something to criticize. "Why would my boutique want to sell your designs? In your words, what makes your line special?

You have two minutes." Despite her impossible, red acrylic nails, somehow she manages to snap her fingers. "Go!"

I take my time, crossing my leg and leaning back in my art-deco chair. I'm not intimidated by her archetype. I have women like her for breakfast.

Well, not literally.

"The magnificence of my collections cannot be expressed in words." I answer with an air of self-importance. "I will have to show you my designs and let them speak for themselves."

"Oh no." She taps her red claws on the desk—I bet she's used them more than once to scratch the face of a competitor. "You first have to earn the privilege of my time. Tell me what's special about your line. Now."

I wish I had the ease with words that my friend Iris, the writer, has. But I don't. What makes my designs special? That my Chloe line strives for fair trade and eco-friendly materials? That my Sophia line flatters and celebrates curvy women and raises awareness against eating disorders? That a portion of the earnings from my Iris line go to breast cancer research? That a percentage of all I sell supports local animal shelters where I volunteer as a cat foster-mom? Unfortunately, those things I'm most proud of wouldn't impress this lady.

And I have the feeling that, no matter what I say, Madame Buxton will only use it to scorn me.

I ring a crystal bell on my desk, the signal for Marcia and Trent to step in.

Trent, my junior designer slash aspiring business partner, comes in. He shoots Madame Buxton's sidekick an appraising look before he sets our catalogues on the desk.

Then Marcia, our assistant and part time model, enters the room carrying my luxurious silver tea set on a tray. "Good afternoon, Ms. Kostopoulos." She does a respectful curtsey and bows her head so low I clear my throat to let her know she's overdoing it. "Here's your tea, ma'am." She advances toward my desk, tray in hand.

I fixate on the box of teabags on the tray and make my voice glacial. "Is that *ginger* tea?"

She freezes and feigns a terrified expression. "Uh…yes, ma'am. Just like you requested."

"How many times do I have to tell you idiots, I want *ginseng* tea. Not *ginger*."

As we rehearsed, Marcia trembles and her features contort in dread. Our little routine is helping her practice for auditions. She's a striving actress working as our model until she gets her big break.

"I'm so sorry!" Marcia begs with a feeble voice. "Please forgive me, it will never happen again!"

A faint high-pitched "meow" gets my attention and I look down. Oh shoot. I knew I'd forgotten something! One of Lucy's kittens is crawling out from under my desk. By the tabby patch on its back it must be Fuzzball.

I know, I shouldn't name my foster cats, but they're so cute I can't help it.

I clear my throat to dissimulate the sound of the meowing kitten and use the side of my shoe to gently slide Fuzzball back to his mom. God forbid Madame Red-claws sees them. Then, I rise from my chair and glower at Marcia as I stroll in her direction, swinging my hips. "Listen to me." I enunciate each word slowly. "I have zero tolerance for inefficiency. I did not become a goddess of design by putting up with less than absolute perfection." I flicker my eyelids to signal her to get ready, then slap my hand over the tray, sending it crashing onto the ground.

Marcia quivers, staring at me like she's afraid I might hit her.

I lift one finger. "Give me one good reason why I shouldn't fire you right now."

"Please, don't fire me!" Marcia pretends to cry. "I'm a single mother. I have bills to pay and children to feed. Please have mercy!" She sobs a little too dramatically and I widen my eyes to send her the message to stop over-acting. Behind us, Trent makes an explosive breathing noise and I fear that any moment he'll burst into laughter, exposing our charade.

"Get out of my sight." I spin on my heels—which takes super-human balance—and return to my desk where I now find Fuzzball *and* his sister Twinky venturing out. I pretend to drop my pen off the desk. When I bend to retrieve it, I return the kittens to the basket where their mom is nursing the rest of the litter.

Marcia picks up our indestructible silver tea set. The tray shakes in her hands as she backs away. "I swear this will never happen again!" She darts out of the office.

Once Marcia is gone, I snap my fingers and Trent jumps to my side, faking a slight tremor. "Yes, Ma'am?'

I wave my hand in the direction where Marcia exited. "Escort what's-her-face out. She's fired."

Trent flinches. "But…"

I send Trent a warning glare and he stops. "Nothing justifies incompetence."

Trent swallows. "Yes, ma'am." He walks to the door backward.

"And on your way back, get someone with brains to bring me a proper cup of tea, understood?"

"Yes, ma'am. His voice a whisper, Trent keeps bowing his head on the way out, never showing his back to me.

When the door closes, I heave with studied exasperation and straighten my dress. "I apologize for that display of ineptitude. Where were we?"

Madame Buxton and her assistant gape at me, but the glow in their eyes reveals our little theater achieved its purpose. She now believes I'm every bit as cold and evil as she is—and now she respects me.

She taps her red claws on the desk. "You were about to show me some of your designs."

I press my lips to stop them from curving and signal them to follow me to my *atelier*.

* * *

An hour later, Marcia, Trent and I celebrate the successful negotiation.

"Wasn't my performance amazing?" Marcia grins.

"Oh, stop bragging." Trent flips a manicured hand, then pats his artfully tossed blond tresses before turning to me. "So, happy hour after work to celebrate?"

"Sorry, guys, I can't!" I remove my painful shoes and exchange them for flats, then untie my hair. "I'm swamped getting ready for the trip to Greece. I can't even take a lunch break today."

"I'm so excited about that trip!" Marcia clasps her hands, then wags her eyebrows and elbows me. "I have a strong feeling you and Mr. Xenakis will return to the US reconciled!"

I shudder. "Don't even joke about that! After everything he's put me through?" Marcia doesn't even know a sliver of my history with Quentin. I pick up Fuzzball and pat him, hoping he'll help neutralize the bad memories.

"But that's what will make the best story to tell your grandchildren!" Marcia insists. "You're like Carrie Bradshaw and he's your Mr. Big. No matter how many times you deny it, you belong together!" She turns toward Trent. "Right, Trent?"

"Don't care. Keep me out of this." Trent flicks his wrist.

Before I can answer, my phone blasts into the *Squiggles* theme song. That annoying tune that sounds like *Baby Shark* and *Crazy Frog* bred a Christmas Carol. It's one of those tunes that latches onto my brain like a leech, and I hate it but can't stop humming it all day—precisely the reason why a *certain friend* installed it on my phone for his ringtone as a prank.

I return the kitten to his mom and grab my phone. It has been so long since this particular friend called me that I stare at the screen, unable to believe the name on it.

Ezra.

I answer. "I must be hallucinating. This can't be really you."

19

"Hello, Princess."

The playful voice makes my heart jolt in joy. "Excuse me while I sit down, I'm about to pass out!" I flop onto my office chair. "*You* are calling *me*? Did someone die?"

"Oh, come on!" He chuckles. "I call you all the time."

"Uh…no. Having the girls Skype me on the rare occasion when you go visit them doesn't count. Neither does texting me GIFs and links to funny videos." I spin my chair in a half-circle and Trent and Marcia's curious faces enter my view. I wave my hand to dismiss them. "So, what's up?"

"Nothing. I was just in the neighborhood and wondered if you wanted to meet for lunch."

"What?" I fake a gasp. "What have I done to deserve this honor?"

"Oh, come on, Mia, don't turn into my mother. If when I finally call, you spend an hour getting after me for never calling, then don't be surprised if I never do it again."

Now, that's amusing. Poor Mrs. Cohen would die if she knew Ezra was comparing me to her. When Ezra and I were kids, she never liked me, convinced that my bad influence could corrupt her saintly son.

Not that she was wrong.

"Okay, okay!" I check the time on my computer. It's almost noon. "I wasn't planning to take a lunch break, but how to say no to this special occasion? How far away are you?"

"Well… I am—"

My office door opens and Ezra peeks his head in. "Not too far away."

At the sight of him, a squeal of delight escapes my throat. I drop my phone, leap out of my seat and throw my arms around him, shrieking and jumping up and down. It's stronger than me. In Ezra's presence, I often regress to the twelve-year-old girl I was when we met. God forbid Madame Buxton see me now.

Ezra surprises me by lifting me and spinning me around causing

20

my screeches to turn into laughter. Gosh, when did he get so strong? This was the scrawny little boy I used to boss around.

"It's so good to see you, my favorite nerd!" I kiss his cheek, prickly with fashionable stubble, and only then realize Marcia and Trent are staring at us.

Marcia gawks, while Trent raises one eyebrow with arms crossed, toe tapping on the floor. "So…" He clears his throat. "Are you going to introduce us?"

I can't believe my staff doesn't know Ezra, but I guess I hadn't hired them yet last time he visited my office. "Marcia, Trent, this is my friend Ezra."

"Oh!" they say at once. Marcia's eyelashes flutter and Trent takes a step back.

"Nice to finally meet you!" Marcia steps forward and shakes his hand with enthusiasm. "After everything Mia has shared about you, I didn't expect you to be so…" The unsaid words hang in the air as her eyes devour him.

"Ditto!" Trent shoves Marcia away with his shoulder to claim Ezra's hand in an enthusiastic handshake. His appreciative look shows he's currently consulting his gaydar to figure out his chances of scoring with Ezra.

"Don't let my dashing fashion sense fool you," Ezra jokes as Trent releases his hand. "Deep inside I'm still the hopeless geek of her high-school stories."

Why are Marcia and Trent making such a big deal about Ezra? I have to peel him out of their grip to get back to our lunch plans.

"So where should we go?"

"Anywhere you want, Princess. My treat."

"Hm." I consider it. "I have a place in mind. Should we take a taxi?"

"That won't be necessary, my lady; take a look at the new toy I drove here." He opens a picture on his phone and shows me a flashy blue convertible Maserati.

I've never been into fancy cars, but I fulfill my duty as a friend and ooh and aah over the picture as we walk toward the elevator, with Trent and Marcia following behind.

Clearly more impressed than I with the Maserati, Marcia asks with a forced casual tone. "So… Ezra. What do you do for a living again?"

"I used to do game development; then I moved into app design. But I'm about to retire."

"Retire from what? Don't ask me." I tease him, poking his side. "My friends and I joke that we've never seen Ezra work. Nobody knows how he's managed to get paid so well."

"Ha, ha, very funny." Ezra points at the stairs. "I'll go get the car from the valet. Do you want to test-drive it?"

"Nah," I wink. "I'd rather be chauffeured around."

Ezra's devilish grimace makes me wonder if he's about to stick his tongue out at me. He sends a wave in my direction and takes the stairs.

"Wow!" Marcia fans herself. "I wouldn't mind taking a bite of that cake." She shimmies, then returns to the office.

What's Marcia talking about? Ezra looks fine—especially compared to the time in high school when he weighed less than me and wore telescopes for glasses. But there's a long distance between that and saying he's worth a "wow".

While I wait for the elevator, a suspiciously quiet Trent keeps me company.

"So…" Trent drops the nonchalant words. "Are you *absolutely* sure you and that guy are only friends?" The doors open and we step in.

I snort, then push the button for the lobby. "No doubt!"

As the elevator descends the two floors Trent's pressed lips and high eyebrows tell me he's not buying my answer. "I'm sorry, my dear." He clicks his tongue. "I've seen this movie and read this book before. There's no way a reformed hussy like you can be friends with a hottie like that and tell me you've never tried to jump his bones."

I have the perfect stock answer for that; same reply I've used to shut up dozens of people before. As we cross the lobby toward the building exit where Ezra waits for his car, I call him up. "Hey Ezra! Trent asks how come I'm immunized against your sex appeal. Should I tell him or should *you* tell him?"

Ezra spreads a hand. "Be my guest."

With a smirk, I turn to Trent and announce, "This is the guy my college best friends and I used to send to the store for Midol and tampons."

Trent winces and shivers while raising a hand. "TMI!"

Ezra and I crack up. He's the only man I know who has zero squeamishness about discussing menstrual cycles—the girls and I cured him of that.

Ezra circles my shoulders with an arm. "I loved those ice-cream-binging, PMS slumber parties we used to have with Chloe, Iris and Sophia." He bats his eyelashes at Trent before dropping his usual line. "Our periods were synchronized."

Trent squeezes his eyelids shut and waves both hands with a grunt before walking away. Ezra and I giggle our way to the car.

I study Ezra as he gives a generous tip to the valet who brought his car. Trent is so wrong. I would never, ever jeopardize my friendship with Ezra by treating him as anything other than my friend. Our bond has survived many challenges over the last two decades. It outlived a separation when he went away for college, and the crisis that made him return. It endured being roommates for a while. It held on every time I've done something crazy—like taking Quentin back—against his wise advice. It even carried on when Ezra dated one of my former girlfriends who then broke his heart.

Oh, and of course, there's also that little thing that happened our senior year of high school. Our friendship survived the biggest challenge two friends could ever confront.

"Princess?"

Ezra's voice brings me back from my musings. He holds the car door open for me. I smile and get in.

Yes. It's a small miracle that my friendship with Ezra has survived so much. And I will never risk losing him again.

CHAPTER 3

Mia

E ZRA, LIKE MY GIRLFRIENDS, IS THE TYPE OF FRIEND I MAY NOT see for years, but we reconnect as if no time has passed. The ride to the restaurant flies in a blink as we catch up.

He's done amazing. Every person I know has some version of that *Squiggles* game app series he created. I do, as well, but I stay away from it like it were cheesecake. That darn addictive game always leaves me humming the silly music and hallucinating the colorful, jumpy shapes all day. After making a fortune in advertisement on it, he's selling the rights to *Squiggles* for a chunk of change. Like Chloe would say, it must be his good karma. Because, in truth, Ezra's my definition of an intrinsically good human being.

Contrary to me.

As he drives, Ezra tells me all about his new "work-for-fun" project. Applying what he learned about advertisement through *Squiggles*, he plans to become a high-end consultant to help businesses with their online marketing.

That reminds me of an earlier conversation. "Hey! Maybe you'll finally come through with your promise to revamp my web marketing plan!"

"I know; we're way overdue for that." He winces as we leave the car. We then stride to the restaurant entrance under the LA midday sun. "I've just been traveling so much."

I envy Ezra for that. He can work from anywhere in the world, so he thinks nothing of jumping on a plane. One time he packed his work computer and "hopped to Thailand" because he needed inspiration for the graphics of some video game. Who would've thought the roles would be reversed between us in so many ways? I used to be the rich world traveler, the years I modeled. And now I'm the one who's penny pinching and homebound. I once carried the title of partier and floozy and he the badge of nerd; and now here I am following a celibacy vow, while he lives the high life.

The Tex-Mex restaurant I chose offers a cozy place to talk, with soft ambient music and perennial Christmas lights. It's also the first place I could think of where my picky friend could find something to eat.

Our waitress, an ample middle-aged woman, seems unable to take her eyes off Ezra as she hands him his lemonade.

He reads her ID tag and beams at her. "Thank you, Gloria. You have such a beautiful smile."

Our waitress flushes and giggles like a schoolgirl. "Oh, thank you!"

The girls and I used to joke that Ezra was a form of artificial intelligence we were programing with endless algorithms. Teaching charm to that awkward boy so he could someday get a girlfriend seemed merciful at the time. But we never imagined that, after heartbreak, he'd use the knowledge to become a bit of a player.

After Gloria takes the order for his nachos and my quesadillas, I become aware of Ezra's attention on me.

"What?" I ask.

"I can't believe you just ordered something that's not a salad!"

"Yup! I'm not a model anymore, I get to eat now!" I pinch my expanding hips and moan. "And it shows."

I bet he's going to give me the automatic answer the girls and I taught him.

"What are you talking about? You look great!"

Called it. "It's okay, Ezra." I chuckle. "I knew I'd gain weight when I quit smoking."

He scrutinizes me. "Your healthier lifestyle shows. You're glowing. You look…amazing!"

I might've taught Ezra his flirty responses, but I don't remember teaching him that intense look. His eyes slide over my body and the sincere spark of approval in them makes me blush.

I reprimand myself. This is not a guy complimenting me on a date. This is Ezra. The closest thing to a brother I have. Heck, he's one of the closest things to a *sister* I have.

"Look who's talking! You look awesome!" I rest my elbow on the table and my chin on my hand, studying him for the first time since his arrival. Gosh, he's changed quite a bit over the years; but so gradually I hadn't noticed. He's gotten some fashion sense at last, after I tortured him for two decades, criticizing his outfits. Those *Dolce and Gabbana* jeans fit him like a glove. The eighties-inspired light blue blazer he wears over a white collared shirt brings out his eyes. He flaunts casual chic with his sleeves rolled up, a touch of studied stubble and tossed dark brown hair—much better than the blue-spiky hair he sported for a while.

Beyond the fashion statements, his overall looks have also improved. Even after ditching his glasses and braces he's always been *not bad—but not stunning*. He has nice blue eyes, but they're just slightly off balance, one seeming bigger and higher than the other. Or maybe it's his nose, a bit longer than close-up modeling would allow. Or maybe it is our usual joke about how his head is too big for his body.

Which, by the way, that proportion seems to have improved since he gained weight.

Wait, is he wearing padding under that blazer? I don't remember him having such built shoulders.

The waitress checking on us interrupts my thoughts. Once she leaves, I charge. "Okay, let's get real." I stir my iced tea. "Why are you here?"

"What?" He fakes a gasp. "Who says I need a reason to visit one of my best friends?"

I shoot him my cut-the-crap look and he seems to get it. Bit by bit, his shoulders drop; his jaw tightens and his eyebrows knot. "The girls sent me to talk some sense into you."

I know where he's going, but if he's here to nag me, I'll make him work for it. "What do you mean?"

"Hanging out with Mr. X again?" He squints and tilts his head from side to side. "Do you think that's a good idea?"

I can't blame him and the girls for feeling defensive. I, myself, am a little scared. But this is an opportunity I just can't pass up. I speak with more confidence than I really feel. "It's different this time."

"Uh…I think I remember you said the exact same words last year."

"This time it's true. I'm stronger than before." I mean that. The past year, between Iris' diagnosis and reuniting with the girls, my life has been transformed.

I sip on my iced tea then wince. "Yes, it's going to be awkward seeing him again. But this is a huge professional step for me. I bet the girls didn't explain it." I lean forward on the chair. "Quentin is starting a designers' mastermind and bringing his VIP members with him to Greece for three weeks." My enthusiasm rises. "And in a huge lucky break, his apprentice had to cancel due to a family emergency and now he's offered the spot to me."

Ezra's voice is flat. "How lucky. Because, of course, it's impossible that he made up that part."

"Come on!" I look up to the ceiling. "Do you think Quentin would mix his personal life with work?"

"Mr. X?" Ezra snorts. "I wouldn't consider it beneath him to put together the entire event just to lure you there."

I restrain my eyes from rolling. Over the years Ezra and the girls have made Quentin into some legendary evil figure. "This isn't new; Quentin spends a month in Greece every fall. It's his way to remain connected to his roots." Like my father, Quentin's parents are from Greece. "Do you have any idea how expensive it is to bring a designer to an event like this? Besides. The itinerary!" I straighten in my seat and clasp my hands together. "First, we're attending *AXDW*! Athens Xclusive Designers Week! *The* fashion event of Eastern Europe! And I'm taking his apprentice's place and competing for a New Designer Award!" I clap quietly.

Ezra's pressed lips advertise his skepticism, but he says nothing.

I give him a wide-open-eye look. "And then after the week in Athens, we're going to a huge charity fashion show in *Mykonos!*"

"*Charity*? Yes, this smells bad." He folds his arms with a scoff. "Like we didn't know Quentin Xenakis would never do anything charitable if it didn't provide him some benefit."

I brush aside his comment. "And then we're going to *Santorini!*" I pretend to scream while no sound comes out.

"What a coincidence; exactly the places you've always said you want to visit," he deadpans. He leans forward and gets his face closer to mine. "Again. Too good to be true."

"It's too late to cancel. I rearranged my entire world to leave someone in charge of the business. And Marcia and Trent would kill me. They get to come along as my *entourage*." I reach across the table to hold his folded arms and shake him lightly. "Do you have any idea what a networking opportunity this is?"

"Two words." Ezra drills me with his blue gaze. "Diet pills."

I flinch at the memory of those low times in my life when I let Quentin feed me amphetamines to lose weight. I release his elbows. "That's ancient history. I haven't touched an Adderall in years."

"I don't know what's worse, that the bastard got you hooked on speed and nicotine—or that he brainwashed you enough to halluci-nate you had weight to lose."

My shoulders back, my chin raised, I sustain eye contact. "I will not make myself into a victim by blaming him. I made a poor decision at the time and take responsibility for it. And now things are different."

We lock eyes for a long moment and then he exhales through pursed lips, unzips his laptop carrier and gets out his computer. "Time for emergency Plan B." Ezra types at incredible speed and, seconds later, turns the computer toward me. Sophia, Iris and Chloe appear on the screen. Iris holds a sign that reads "Intervention." Dread and gratitude mix inside me as I recall that time they found the diet pills in my purse.

"My dear…" Chloe takes a deep breath. "We need to talk."

* * *

Ezra and I have finished our lunch and ordered dessert and coffee and my video intervention still goes on. By turns, my friends attempt to convince me to cancel the trip.

"Mr. X is bad karma; a bad mojo bomb." On the screen, Chloe twists her long black hair in her fingers. "Mia, I love you. But getting near that man again is proof you enjoy playing with fire."

She has a point about my taste for tempting danger. But who would think I'd ever see these friends trying to protect me? I'm usually the grounded cynic protecting *them* from their innocence.

Take my dear Chloe, a quartz-rubbing, mantra-chanting hippie who doesn't so much as check her mailbox without first aligning her chakras. Back in our school years, when she, Ezra and I were inseparable, I considered her my life guru. Yet in the past couple of months, she's shocked us with borderline reckless decisions. She dove head-first into a relationship with a guy who's clearly incompatible with her—an ultra-conservative medical researcher and retired Army Captain—and things have been moving scarily fast between them.

Or take my sweet former roommate, newly-engaged Sophia. The prudish Midwestern girl I had to defend from scammers and who's slept with a grand total of two guys in her life.

And then Iris, the introverted writer who gets so absorbed ruminating over new stories that she literally runs into walls.

And of course, there's my beloved brainiac Ezra, with an IQ of like a thousand but when he's engrossed in his phone doesn't notice if the room around him is on fire.

It's adorable that these four believe they're here to protect *me*.

"Guys, thank you. But I'll be fine," I repeat for the hundredth time. "What do you think is the worst that can happen?"

Iris clears her throat. "That's not hard to imagine, if you remember history."

The flashback from a year ago makes me nauseous. At a fashion show, I ran into Quentin and his latest supermodel girlfriend, acting inappropriately affectionate as if to rub her in my face. I'd bragged so much that I was over him, but seeing them together hit me harder than I expected. I went home and cried in hiding. Later that night, he knocked on my door. We locked eyes, then he kissed me and I was back under his spell, almost an exact repeat of every other time we broke up. It resembled hypnosis.

Just for a moment, fear rises in me that my friends do have a point.

Ezra seems to have noticed my doubt. The slowing of his movements suggests he's about to change strategies. "Mia, do you remember when Crystal broke up with me?"

Rage rises inside me at the memory of my former nemesis "Crystal Meth"—nickname courtesy of Chloe. After toying with Ezra for three years, she shattered him by rejecting his marriage proposal and moving to London with some rich guy. The worst part? *I* introduced them, when she was still my friend and colleague at the modeling agency. Before she started spreading rumors about me and doing everything she could to sabotage my career.

I return my attention to Ezra. "I wanted to murder her—still play with the idea sometimes. You were devastated."

He nods. "I was miserable. And remember what you did when I planned to throw myself at her feet and beg her to take me back?"

My lips curve at the memory. "I became your voice of reason?"

He snort-laughs. "You practically imprisoned me in my own house. You hid my car keys, confiscated my phone and camped out in my living room."

"You did what, Mia?" Iris cackles so hard her wig falls back.

I giggle, remembering that weekend. "For three nights I slept on his couch with one eye open so I could stop him if he tried to sneak out to go see her." I grimace. "That was a little over the top."

"But I've been forever grateful for it!" Ezra's fingers reach for mine on the table. "If I had carried on with my plan, I would've been humiliated, because she was already with that other guy."

I join my other hand to his and savor the familiar pleasant feeling. See? Trent is so wrong. Ezra's touch brings no sparks, just peace. "I get your point. You thought you were thinking rationally at the time and you weren't. But there's a big difference. You were still hung up on Crystal. I'm over Quentin—completely over."

Contrary to you. Because despite his claims, I've always suspected he never forgot Crystal. That's why he hasn't had a serious girlfriend since. Eight years and counting.

"Guys, this time is different," I insist, meaning it. I point at Iris' image and reference one of the passages in *The Self-Vow*. "Quentin's power came from my own weakness. And I'm stronger now."

"Dang it," Iris grumbles. "I guess I don't have anything else to add." Her eyes move around, as if she's exchanging looks with Chloe and Sophia, searching for a new strategy. They shrug lightly, apparently resigned to my decision.

The girls say goodbye and Ezra disconnects the call. His knitted brows speak of deep worry.

Trying to lighten the mood, I pat his forearm. "Come on, Big Nerd, do you need more proof that I've changed?" I raise my palms. "I ordered freaking quesadillas!"

His frown relaxes, so I go on, counting on my fingers. "I quit smoking and vaping; I rarely drink now. Do you remember how I used to be?"

He eases back in his chair and his lips twitch.

I throw my arms in the air for dramatic emphasis. "Not to mention I'm a freaking nun now! Did you ever imagine the floozy Mia Kostopoulos would be celibate for almost eleven months?"

Ezra's expression falls. "Wait. You what?"

CHAPTER 4

Ezra

MY DEAR MIA HAS NO VERBAL FILTERS. SHE OCCASIONALLY cusses like a sailor, and enjoys scandalizing Sophia with sex talk. She's shocked *me* many times in the past with her frankness—and still nothing tops this news today.

All this time, when the girls talked about their cleanse year, I've assumed Mia was only humoring Chloe, Sophia and Iris about the celibacy part. "Are you serious?"

"Dead serious! I'm proud of myself for keeping up with it!" She picks up her clutch and rises from her chair and I grab my laptop carrier and imitate her. She giggles as we leave the restaurant. "Who would've thought? Mia Kostopoulos celibate? The ultimate tramp who made it to the top by screwing her boss?"

"Stop it." I flinch when she quotes my ex-girlfriend Crystal's words.

She makes a dismissive wave. "I'm fine. High school got me used to hateful gossip about me. And Roxanne, my stepmom, gave me a thick skin." Despite her casual tone, her cheerfulness appears forced. "The thing is, this vow has worked wonders on my self-esteem and self-respect." She winks. "Since, let's admit it, Crystal did have a point. I am a reformed slut."

I hold her wrist to make her stop walking. "Please, never again use those words to refer to yourself."

"Double standard alert!" She pokes my chest. "Why should it

bother you when I joke about being a tramp, or a floozy, or a slut—when you've bragged about being a man-whore for years?"

Touché.

"See?" She spreads a hand as we approach my car. "Why do we still believe that sexual experience is a badge of honor for a man and a stigma for a woman?"

"I would never double-standard you," I clarify, sincerely. She had enough of that from her own father. "I've always admired how unapologetic you are about your life choices." I open the door for her and she enters the car.

Mia turns unusually quiet as she clicks her seatbelt. When I take the driver's seat, she turns toward me, biting her lower lip. "Can you drive me somewhere?" she says. "There's something I need to show you that may explain why this trip is so important for me."

Her expression reminds me of that time in tenth grade when she told me she planned to run away from home, so I'd better listen. I agree with a bow of the head and turn on the engine.

* * *

It's my first time entering Mia's high-rise apartment, but I've seen it enough through video-chat that it seems familiar. Everything, from the kitchen to the ultra-modern furniture, is black and white, but colorful abstract art brightens the walls. She signals me to follow her to a closed room.

"It's costing me a kidney to rent a two-bedroom apartment here, but I needed space for this." She opens the door and the scent of thread and fabric in the air transports me to her seamstress grandmother's house.

The place seems like a miniature version of Mia's work *atelier*. Design sketches plaster the walls. A sewing machine sits on a long table, next to a pair of scissors and a sketchbook, hinting that the surface doubles as drawing table and workspace. All sorts of rolls of fabric and ribbon sit carefully stacked in a corner of the room.

But the headless mannequin in the room monopolizes my attention. I know nothing about fashion, and even I can tell that the dress it displays must've taken a ton of work. It's an airy, one-shoulder white gown that vaguely resembles a Greek tunic. It seems made mostly of silk satin, but also lace and feathers, giving it transparency at strategic places. Gold and turquoise embellishments trim the shoulder strap and the empire waist.

"I've been working on this dress for two years," Mia's eyes fix on the mannequin. "At first, it was just a hobby—indulging in the fantasy of working on *Haute Couture*. Later on, it became an obsession."

Having Mia as a friend has certainly added to my fashion vocabulary. I get that she refers to the highest-end, most expensive branch of fashion. The odds of a designer getting to that level are infinitesimal—lower than making it in Hollywood or in professional sports. "Didn't you say once that the industry of *Haute Couture* is becoming an extinct art? That only a couple hundred people in the world can afford it?"

She dips her chin and her fingertips brush the dress without touching it, as if afraid of ruining it. "Most designers, me included, are better off sticking to mass production. But Haute Couture is far from being dead. It's an art form. It's homage to a lifestyle of enjoyment and accepting only the highest quality standards. For a designer, it's the closest thing to an ideal of perfection."

The reverence in her eyes makes me keep quiet, respecting the moment.

"We were talking about double standards?" she explains. "Sexual double-standards are just one facet of the power struggle. We live in a world that still uses the B word to refer to a woman with strong opinions—the same opinions they would celebrate in a man. A world that either demonizes female power, or considers it mutually exclusive with femininity. This dress is my answer to that. It's not only my highest creation, but also my tribute to strong, free, women in history—the so-called 'Bad Girls' of their times."

She launches into a vivid explanation of every detail in the dress. How the gold and turquoise belt and trim are inspired by Cleopatra; how the lace and ruffles are an homage to Madame De Pompadour; how the feathers are a nod to cancan dancers. "And of course, my biggest inspiration was the Greek goddess Aphrodite, the archetype of female desire." She moves her hand in circles around the dress. "She's a symbol of our God-given right to seek love and passion in our lives—a right society has condemned for centuries."

Wow. I always considered fashion design a superficial industry. I never quite grasped that, like any form of art, it could be used to make a statement.

"Ezra. If I could deliver one message to the world, it would be to end the double standards. To encourage women to embrace their power and sexuality, reject the labels of 'bad girl' or 'good girl' and just follow the true passions in their hearts."

I'm speechless. I've never seen this deep side of Mia before.

"This is my biggest offering to the world as an artist and deserves to be shown to as many people as possible." She turns toward me. "My designs may never make it to the catwalks of Paris, Milan, or New York. But now, I found an event that has the attention of the whole fashion world." She paces away from the mannequin. "And what an amazing coincidence that it happens to be AXD, *in Greece*, the birthplace of the myth of Aphrodite—and of my paternal ancestors." She points at me with an open hand. "Do you understand why I can't let my fear of Quentin stop me from this opportunity?"

Damn it. How can I refute this argument?

We stroll out of the room. Once she has locked the door, she signals me to follow her to the compact living room and we flop into two surprisingly comfy modern chairs shaped like giant white tulips.

"I get why this is so important for you," I mumble with reluctance.

"But I can't shed this gut feeling that Mr. X plans to warp your mind again. Couldn't one of the girls go with you?"

"For three whole weeks? Impossible." She shakes her head. "Chloe just came back from Italy and can't take time off again from her holistic practice. Sophia is in the middle of wedding planning. And Iris has chemo every three weeks."

I groan and swivel my chair. "Someone needs to be there, like your watchdog."

"Yes, like—" She stops abruptly. Shadowed by a frown, her beautiful whiskey-colored eyes study me with caution. "Would you…" She bites her lower lip the way she used to do in middle school when trying to solve a complicated math problem. "Would *you* like to come with me?"

The unexpected invitation takes me by surprise. I stop swiveling in the chair. "Go to Greece with you?"

She gives a slow, tentative nod. "I mean…if you're so worried, come and camp in front of my hotel door. Kind of like I did for you when you broke up with Crystal."

My pulse picks up pace. "Just for the sake of brainstorming. Is that even possible?"

She considers it. "Well, you're officially my online marketing advisor. I could get you a staff badge, like I'm doing with Marcia and Trent."

The idea appeals me. If I can't convince her to cancel the trip, the second-best option would be to support her if she's tempted to forget the past.

Mia squints and chews on her lip as more thoughts spark. "You're so good at photography, you could help me by taking pictures of my designs on the catwalk for my website. Maybe even capture them in a few gorgeous locations for my online catalog."

I'm not sure about that. As much as I enjoy it as a hobby, it's been a while since I practiced any photography that requires complex lighting. "Do you want me to go?" I ask, tense.

She folds her arms and leans back. "Only if *you* want to."

Despite her answer, her huge golden eyes beg me to consider it.

Quentin Xenakis' image jumps in my mind and my stomach tightens. My eyes turn dry, as if wanting to spit out my contact lenses. I feel the humming in my skin announcing my pores are snapping back into acne-producing mode—as if I'm reverting to the hopeless guy I used to be so many years back.

"It's really short notice," I finally mutter. "I'm in the middle of negotiations to sell *Squiggles*…"

A flash of disappointment crosses Mia's features. "Of course. It was a long shot."

I study her as she wriggles her hands, frowning. Is she more worried about facing Mr. X than she lets on? I rush to add, "But let me look into it and I'll call you."

* * *

I'm still dwelling on the question the next morning as I drive the hypnotic six-hour stretch between LA and San Francisco for the second time in twenty-four hours. Walter Tolstoi, the developer buying the rights to my app series, emailed me a counteroffer earlier and I haven't even opened it. I'm so worried about Mia's wellbeing that I hardly care about a four-million-dollar deal.

Needing to clear my mind I invite Ian to come over my place to watch the football game and have a beer. The girls taught me that's the way to treat guy friends—even if I don't care for sports and don't intend to drink.

But I must not be doing a good job socializing today, because Ian immediately notices my absentmindedness about the game.

"O-kay. You haven't said a word since I got here. Something's bothering you," he stirs from the bright yellow sectional. Somehow his Brazilian accent sounds stronger at the end of the day. "Spill it. What's on your mind?"

Maybe having four women as my best friends for years has caused irreversible damage in my brain. I'm dying to vent to someone. And Heaven knows none of my girls can hear this.

I use the remote to lower the volume of the large screen TV. "Do you remember when you asked if I still had a crush on Mia and I told you I was one hundred percent over her?"

"Yes?" Ian's lips twitch but he presses them together.

Avoiding eye contact, I pull threads from the hem of my old Minecraft T-shirt. "Well. Maybe I wasn't accurate. Maybe I am more like… *eighty-six* percent over her."

Amusement dances on Ian's features. "And the other fourteen percent?"

"That part is not the real me."

At his puzzled stare I add, "Let me explain." I draw in a lungful and search my mind for an example. "I believe people are like computer programs. Let's say WordPress web pages." I straighten in the black La-Z-Boy. "When you make revisions to a webpage, old versions don't disappear. They're stored as backup and you can revert back to them."

Ian's creased forehead shows his confusion. "Okay?"

"In the same way, I believe we all have younger versions of ourselves trapped inside us."

A light of understanding on Ian's face encourages me to continue. "Inside me there's an old version of myself—at age seventeen."

"I see." Ian sips his Heineken.

"That seventeen-year-old kid inside me? No stretch of your imagination will ever help you picture the mess he is," I continue. "As a teenager, I was the geekiest late bloomer in the world, with the worst case of acne you've ever seen. I was rail-thin and had shark teeth, and glasses as thick as icebergs."

With a chuckle, Ian scratches the back of his heavily tattooed arm, exposed by his short-sleeved T-shirt. "No one who sees you today would guess that."

I brace myself internally for the next confession. "Well, that boy is still smitten with Mia."

The announcers narrating the game ramble on in the background. I keep my eyes fixed on the ceramic figurine on my side table, a monkey having a beer. "That guy is no longer me, the adult I am now," I clarify. "So, I've had no problem being around Mia as her friend all these years. But once in a blue moon, I have to watch out for that seventeen-year-old version of me peeking his head out. I don't beat myself up about it; that boy will never forget Mia. After all, she was...."

"She was what?" Ian leans forward.

The deepest self-consciousness invades me, like I'm regressing to that younger me. "She was the first girl I ever kissed."

Ian's eyebrows shoot up. "Really?"

I reach for my root beer and take a long, cold sip while I psych myself up. This must be the first time in my life I'm sharing this story in detail.

"It was the end of our senior year in high school. Mia was failing math and science and needed good grades on her final exams or she wouldn't be able to graduate with us. I offered to tutor her."

The memories I've been suppressing shower over me, filling my soul with bitter-sweetness. "She aced the math test, and thanks to that passed the class. So, I want to think she felt thankful toward me that night—better that than saying she felt full of *pity*. We took a break from studying science and went on the raised deck. While we chatted under the stars, I found myself venting about being unpopular; and about the shame of never having kissed a girl. And out of the blue she...she kissed me." My chest tightens and overflows with emotion at once.

"Then what happened?" Ian prompts, as if he's riveted with my story.

"She took me by the hand to my room and we made out for a while."

41

"Only made out?" Ian's intense scrutiny brings thoughts of a human lie detector.

Shyness surges inside me, making me blush. "Well…" My eyes dart away. "We might've done some exploring of bases."

I finish my root beer in one large gulp, then I set it down and meet Ian's eye contact.

"Do you understand how surreal that was? Mia was one of the popular girls, and I was the biggest nerd in the school, bullied all the time." I stop, remembering that Ian has bullying stories that make mine seem like funny cartoons. You think being teased in school is bad? Try being harassed in jail.

"Wow. No wonder Ezzie was starstruck with Mia," he comments.

I give him a blank stare. "Who's Ezzie?"

Ian makes a dismissive gesture. "It's getting too long to say 'seventeen-year-old-Ezra' over and over. So, I'm going to name that guy trapped inside you 'Ezzie' for short."

Typical of no-nonsense Ian, the master of leverage.

"So," Ian puts down his empty beer. "Did *Ezzie* ever consider asking Mia out after…" He waves a hand near my face and then my torso. "Whatever you did to crawl out of your cocoon?"

"No." Between my three years with Crystal, the relapse curse of Quentin Xenakis, and Mia's near-instant rebound boyfriends, we've never been available at the same time for long.

"Why not?"

I search for the most truthful answer I can give. "I admit it, even the adult me finds Mia very attractive. But why would I risk losing something rare and precious, my deep love for my friends, for something there's no shortage of—sleeping partners?" I pick up the drinking chimp figurine, a present from my girls on my twenty-first birthday. It referenced our ongoing joke about my secret childhood dream of having a pet monkey. "Ian, you have no idea how important these four women are in my life. If something happened between Mia and me and then we broke up, things would be forever awkward.

The girls would feel obligated to take sides—and you can bet their loyalties would be with her. I would lose not only Mia, I'd also lose my other three best friends."

"What if things *did* work out?"

I shake my head as I set down the figurine. "I know Mia and myself enough to know the chances are remote. I wouldn't even try." I'm not kidding. As much as I love Mia as a friend, I've seen her harsh side. And she and I have very different tastes and life views.

Ian fiddles with a rip in his jeans and seems to mull over the words for a moment. "Any reason why this is bothering you more than usual today?"

"Well…" I rub my temples, trying to understand my worry. "Mia has invited me on a work trip to help shield her from her evil ex-boy-friend. My gut is telling me that I should go, but I'm not sure I can trust 'Ezzie' with the task."

Ian rises from the sectional and signals me to come closer. I leave my seat and pace toward him.

Before I realize what's happening, he's slammed me on the car-peted floor and has a knee on my stomach.

"Ow, ow!" I tap on the rug signaling surrender.

He releases the hold and springs from the floor. "Ezra, what's the most important rule in jiu jitsu?"

I scramble back to my feet. "Distance management."

He nods. "Either you are all the way in—" He wraps my neck in a chokehold with is arm. "Or all the way out." He pushes away from me, out of reach, before I can hit him. "When you make the mistake of being undecided, within arm's length of your opponent, that's where you get hurt."

I rub my sore neck. "My brain is too algorithmic for metaphor; you need to be more explicit."

"You have to make up your mind." He holds my head and pierces me with his dark eyes. I fear for a moment he'll hit me with his forehead. "Either you're all the way in with her, or all the way out. No wobbling in the middle." He releases my head and paces away.

My eyes wander to the ceramic monkey as I consider his words—speaking of crazy dreams I've had to let go of. "Maybe you're right. Maybe I need to close this chapter with Mia and move on with my life."

Ian strikes a blow I fail to block, but he stops short of hurting me, his elbow barely an inch away from my nose.

"Maybe this trip is something you need to do to give Ezzie closure."

He has a point. I owe more to Mia than she'll ever know. Perhaps this trip can be my last offering of friendship, so I can pay my debt to her. And then, I can put this to rest.

I pick up my phone and search for Mia's number.

CHAPTER 5

Mia

"I'M SO GLAD EZRA'S GOING WITH YOU! THAT'S AWESOME!" On my cell phone screen, Iris claps. I haven't seen her glow like this in ages. Now that she has finished the worst of her chemo and radiation, she's finally recovering her luster. Though she still has the something-tuzumab maintenance infusions every three weeks. "Are you traveling together?"

Dragging my rolling garment bag behind me, I roam the airport gate in search of a free chair. "No, Ezra's flying from San Francisco."

I find two empty linked chairs and claim them, so I can use one to set my matching Louis Vuitton garment bag and tote—the few remnants of luxury I kept after I broke up with Quentin. I checked most of my luggage and shipped all my other designs ahead of time, but I would not trust anyone else with the Aphrodite dress. "Having Ezra there won't be fun," I joke as I sit down. "It will be reliving those high school parties when the teachers assigned him to tattle on anyone hiding cigarettes or booze."

Under my cool tone, I'm overjoyed that Ezra's joining me. Not only do I appreciate having an extra layer of protection from Quentin, but also, I need all the help I can get to prepare for the New Designers Awards on such short notice.

"I wish so much I could go too!" Chloe chimes in from the screen. "I've always wanted to go to Athens! Max and I love ruins."

Speaking of Chloe's new boyfriend, the classic paintings behind her advertise she's not in her tiny apartment overlooking Willis

Tower, but instead in Dr. Maxwell Steele's suburban house. "Are you in Maxwell's house again, Chloe? You seem to be spending so much time there lately."

A grinning Maxwell appears behind Chloe and hugs her from the back. It's hard to reconcile him with the somber man Chloe used to describe. "Well, girls, get used to the view. I finally convinced her to move in."

Sophia and Iris cheer and congratulate Chloe but I flinch internally. *Already?* I hope Chloe doesn't get her heart broken with this guy.

"You spilled the beans, Max! I was easing into that topic!" Chloe beams at him and pecks him on the lips.

By "easing into that topic," she means with me. I'm the most protective of all the friends and the last one to give her blessing to a guy. Only since they set a wedding date have I started trusting Sophia's fiancé, Trevor.

Maxwell has come to remind Chloe of somewhere they're going, so she excuses herself and leaves the call.

"Aw! Aren't they adorable?" Sophia sighs. She's delighted that Chloe paired up, because now she's no longer the only one of us who ended her year of celibacy prematurely. "Well, Chloe and I are already set. I guess one of you two is next." Sophia drops the comment with an innocent smile, batting her eyelashes. "Your vows end in little over a month. You should start browsing guys already!"

"Well don't look at me," I snort. "My chances of meeting someone on this trip are remote, especially with Ezra following me around like a chaperone or a pesky little brother."

Silence falls for a second and Iris and Sophia seem to exchange a look through the screen.

"Speaking of that *little brother* title. I've always wanted to ask you something, Mia. And if you guys will be traveling together for weeks, I guess this is the best time." Iris removes her long auburn wig and scratches her fuzz-covered scalp. "Is there something going

MEET ME IN GREECE

on between you and Ezra? You always seemed to have such a strange relationship."

"What do you mean?" I frown.

"Remember all those nights when we the five of us met at my place to study? You two were always in your small little world together."

Has the chemo affected Iris brain or something? "Uh…what?"

"And all the touching and rubbing with any excuse!" Sophia adds.

"What are you two talking about?" I protest, folding my free arm.

Iris makes a high-pitched voice, apparently imitating mine. "*Ezra, braid my hair. Ezra, paint my toenails. Ezra, rub my shoulders.*"

Sophia bobs her head with zeal. "Ezra, I'm itchy; scratch my back. Ezra, I'm cold; come sit on the couch with me under this throw blanket."

"Oh, come on!" I look up to the airport's high, industrial-style ceiling. "Ezra used to braid your hair too."

"Never mine." Sophia twirls her index.

"Uh…he braided mine *once* in four years." Iris imitates Sophia's hand movement. "He brushed Chloe's a handful of times. Definitely not every Friday like in your case."

My mind travels in time to our study-slumber parties. Some lonely times, in between break-ups with Quentin and rebound relationships, I might've used Ezra's affectionate nature as a nicotine patch for a man's touch. "Ezra was just this…big teddy bear always available for cuddles. And he was…so *non-threatening*. It felt good to know there was *one* guy in the world I could snuggle with under a throw blanket on a couch and he would not get handsy with me."

"Sometimes I saw it as another example of how you like to play with fire, like you *wanted* to provoke him," Sophia comments, tentative. "Are you absolutely sure there was never anything between you two?"

"Not you too, guys!" I groan. "I've had enough questioning from Marcia and Trent this week!" I shift in the chair with a sigh. "I love

Ezra to death, but I could never see myself dating him. He and I are like an old couple who's been together forever and know all of each other's stories—there's absolutely no mystery, no spark, no passion."

"I don't know," Sophia tilts her head. "The best part of marrying Trevor is that I'm also marrying my best friend and favorite travel companion."

"Well, you tell me, Sophia." I move the phone closer to look her in the eye. "Were you thinking about *friendship* when you first met Trevor?"

Sophia's blush is evident even through the tiny screen image . We all know the story about the overwhelming physical attraction that first drew her to her fiancé. "Not…really."

I bow my head and spread a hand. "That's what I want. It's not too much to ask that the man in my life makes my toes curl when he kisses me." Determined to end the drilling with humor I drop my hand and add, "And if memory serves me right, Ezra is the worst kisser on the planet."

Mission accomplished. Sophia squeezes her eyes shut and raises a hand. "Stop it! You know it creeps me out when you talk about having kissed Ezra!"

"Between his shaggy haircut and his clumsy technique, it was like kissing a Golden Retriever that was trying to fish a treat from my throat with his tongue."

"Stop it!" Sophia covers her ears with her hands.

"I had to keep my eyes closed the whole time not to jar myself with the sight of the giant zit on his nose."

"Okay! I'm out of here!" Sophia leaves the call.

I giggle at my victory, but Iris doesn't join me. Her expression reminds me of the day she first noticed my unhealthy weight loss. "Mia, that's not nice."

I dry a tear of laughter off the corner of my eye. "It's okay, Ezra doesn't mind that I joke about it." That's what I admire so much about

Ezra. He cares so little about being cool that he becomes a new standard of coolness wherever he goes.

"Why did you even kiss Ezra in the first place?"

Iris question makes my glee vanish instantly.

"I've told you!" I flick my wrist. "The guy was heading to college and had never kissed a girl. He desperately needed help." I play with the jacket zipper on my comfy velour tracksuit. "And you had to be there to know how much teasing the poor guy got from the school bullies, saying he was gay. I wanted to give him a chance to brag to everyone about making out with one of the popular girls."

"Really?" Iris narrows her hazel eyes.

I nod. "I even gave him a hickey so he could show it around. And I even let him get to second base. *I* got to third base—"

"Okay!" Iris closes her eyelids. "I've had enough too. Goodbye!" She ends the call.

I should be amused, but I'm not. A memory jumps into my mind. Avril Lavigne's music plays at the school gym, decorated with gold and purple balloons, white Christmas lights and cheesy farewell banners at prom night. Ezra enters the party wearing a gray turtleneck sweater, concealing the proof of where my lips had been. I wonder why he decided to hide it. Then our eyes meet across the dance floor and the love and gratitude in his gaze makes me want to cry.

I relive the bittersweet rawness of that moment. Then, Trent and Marcia approach, dragging their luggage, and I stow my memories away.

* * *

I have European flying down to a system. I take the red-eye flight, set my watch to the time zone I'm heading to and go to sleep when that watch says it's bedtime. This routine used to involve knocking myself down with scotch, and maybe Valium. But now I take one

49

Ambien and a melatonin—the latter is Chloe's favorite trick to adjust daily rhythms. I'm proud of turning into such a squeaky-clean girl!

Granted, dozing off on planes is never ideal, and some jetlag will still fog my mind the next day or two. But this routine is the fastest way to sync myself up with the new time zone.

Next to me, Trent and Marcia chat nonstop, giddy with excitement like schoolgirls on a field trip. I signal them to leave me alone by wearing my face mask and noise cancelling headphones and go to sleep as soon as the plane takes off.

I wake up shortly before the plane lands to have time to brush my teeth, get dressed and do my hair and makeup—all of which takes effort since the cramped airplane bathroom has no room for all my beauty products. I'm in networking mode now and have to be ready for any photography. Not to mention I'm about to re-encounter a cheating ex, and the best revenge is to look gorgeous. This embroidered azure knee-length dress of my own design infuses me with self-confidence, reminding me of my accomplishments.

I'm a little apprehensive about facing Quentin again. Until now all my communications about this trip have been through his assistant, Paul. I haven't seen Quentin in almost a year. But I don't share Ezra's fear that Quentin may try to lure me back. Only recently have I acknowledged that he's been over me for years and it was me who insisted on chasing him over and over again.

Once at the airport, my heart jumps in excitement at the sight of Greek alphabet characters all over the signs. It's really happening! I'm in Athens. The birthplace of my paternal grandparents. Being here makes me feel a connection to my father for the first time in ages. Pride in these roots is the one thing Roxanne, my stepmother, could never take away from me.

"Kostopoulos. Miss Mia Kostopoulos."

A uniformed man holding a sign with my name brings me back from my musings. It's a limo service, a small luxury courtesy of Quentin. "That's me! I'm Mia Kostopoulos." I wave.

Trent and Marcia squeal in delight as we follow the driver. They bounce in their seats the entire trip, pressing buttons and touching everything they find in the back of the limo, barely letting me take in my first impressions of Athens. All I retain from the trip is highway traffic signs in Greek (1).

The driver takes us straight to our hotel, where Quentin is holding a brunch reception for his VIP guests and their entourages, while they wait for their rooms to be ready. We drop our luggage at the lobby, which seems as lavish as the limo ride, but everything is out of focus for my jetlagged brain. Then, we join the rest of the party at the rooftop hotel restaurant.

Quentin always travels with a gazillion people, from assistants, to adulators, to models. I used to be one of those groupies until I lost him to another model—more than once. It's barely noon and the alcohol already flows, so Marcia and Trent abandon me and make a beeline for the bartender.

I stroll around and scan the crowd, both scared and hopeful I'll run into Quentin, so I can get it over with. I have no doubt he's history, but seeing him will likely open old wounds of hurt female pride.

The sight of a group of young models chatting makes me feel old. They're all so beautiful, and cool and catty. I wonder which one is dating Quentin. One of them lights a cigarette, and as the smell hits me, the urge to smoke takes me by surprise. Ugh. Keeping the healthy lifestyle away from home might be harder than I thought.

"Don't even think about it."

I search for the source of the familiar voice. Like a savior angel, Ezra stands some distance away, leaning on the rooftop railing. His smile is playful but his eyes send me a serious warning. He must've read the cigarette craving in my expression.

"Hey! You made it before me!" I advance toward him and greet him with a hug, then study him. He wears the go-to outfit I taught him to rely on for informal events. Dark jeans, blue-gray sweater, and navy jacket, to create a monochromatic silhouette that emphasizes his height. He looks good, and seems to fill out his clothes better than I remember. His eyes look bluer, and surprisingly bright and rested today. "Why do you look like you just woke up from a refreshing sleep?"

"Because I did. My flight arrived yesterday. I wanted to sleep off the jetlag so my mind would be fully sharp for my mission today."

I beam. "My new marketing plan?"

"No. Mission Blocking Mr. X." He uses two fingers to point at his eyes, then at me.

I chuckle. "You are over-worrying. If Quentin were really after me, he'd want me alone—he wouldn't have invited you to this reception."

"He didn't. I found out about it and added my name to the guest list."

"You did what?" Oh shoot. I hope this doesn't mean what I think it does. I hook his arm and move out of earshot of the young models while lowering my voice to a whisper. "Ezra, please tell me you didn't hack the hotel registry."

His face remains blank and innocent. "Miss, I have no idea what you're talking about."

I punch his arm and glower at him, but I also want to laugh. I taught him to say that to fool the teachers when they interrogated him about my latest troublemaking. I look over my shoulder. "Ezra, don't joke about this. You promised me you'd drop the hacking business for good. It's a miracle you didn't get into real trouble back at Stanford."

"Please don't nag me," he grumbles. "Hacking a few hotels was the only way to get first dibs on cancellations and find a room on such short notice. And I had to make sure I'm nearby when Mr. X tries to pull his tricks."

We pace away, arms still hooked. "What do you mean by 'tricks'?"

"I bet you I can predict what's going to happen today. Mr. X will find a way to put you in the hotel room closest to his suite."

"He will not," I contradict. "I'm staying in this hotel; Quentin is staying with his VIP group in a house he owns here in Athens."

Ezra snorts. "Then I bet all my bitcoin that 'someone on his staff' is going to 'screw up' and they'll have to transfer you to stay with him."

"You're so paranoid!" I shove him away with my shoulder and he shoves me right back.

"So…you guys whisper secrets to each other and get handsy while you walk around arm in arm…but you're *not* a couple, just friends. Right?"

Trent approaches us, holding a mimosa in each hand. His uneven eyebrows and flat tone advertise his sarcasm.

I let go of Ezra's arm and accept the mimosa from Trent. I puff dismissively, then, point at Ezra with my thumb. "Me and this guy a couple? Nah. I'm not his type." I take a sip. "He's into ditzy blondes."

"Yeah, and I'm not her type either." Ezra waves Trent off. "She only dates narcissistic jerks who treat her like garbage."

Ouch. Not funny—because it used to be true.

"Uh…Mia. I need your help here!" Marcia arrives with Paul, Quentin's assistant. The lines creasing her forehead hint something's not right.

"Oh, here you are, darling!" Paul greets me with an air kiss on each cheek. For that, he has to stand on his tippy toes because he's quite short. I can't believe he still works for QX Designs. I hired him myself when I was Quentin's girlfriend because I didn't trust him having a female assistant.

"I'm sorry." Paul checks Ezra out with the corner of his eye as he talks. "The hotel messed up our reservation. So, I hope you don't mind, there's a tiny chance you and Marcia will have to stay with two of the models."

I tense up. It was already a stretch sharing a room with Marcia. "Actually, I do mind. I have a ton of luggage. And a lot of work to do in the evenings."

"I told him that," Marcia frowns. "I don't mind sharing the room with other models, but I know you're very particular about that."

Paul flourishes a hand. "Don't sweat it. We'll figure something out."

As Paul walks away, Ezra pulls me aside. "Called it."

"Do you really think this is a scheme?" I whisper.

"Wait and see. Mr. X is going to charitably offer you to room with him and his friends at his house."

I stare at Ezra in disbelief. "How can you know more than me about Quentin's thought processes?"

"How can I break this gently?" He rests a hand on my shoulder. "I know it doesn't look like it to you but—" He winces in fake apology. "*I am a man.*"

I shake my shoulder free and pace away from Ezra, looking for a table in which to drop my barely touched mimosa. Suddenly I've lost my appetite. My heart beats a tad faster.

Is Ezra right? Did I underestimate Quentin's desire to derail me?

"Hello, my dear!"

Speak of the Devil. The sound of Quentin's voice behind me makes my stomach plummet.

I slowly turn around to face him. He looks exactly the way he looked a year ago—he never seems to age. Chic silver strands and slightly more angular features are the only difference from the man I met thirteen years ago. He's still striking, but it's a relief to confirm I feel absolutely nothing for him. The cigarette tempted me more—and was probably less toxic.

Still, my insides knot and I have to make an effort to keep my voice indifferent as I offer a handshake. "Hello, Quentin."

Instead of shaking my hand, he holds on to it. "Paul had mentioned you were coming straight from the airport, but I can hardly believe it. You look amazing."

I disentangle my fingers from his. "Thanks, but I do feel quite tired. I wouldn't mind checking into my room already. Paul mentioned there's an issue with my reservation?"

"Don't worry about it. We'll figure something out." He keeps his eyes on me and something blazes in them that fills me with dread.

Paul's high-pitched reply feels rehearsed. "Maybe we can move Ms. Kostopoulos to the house with us."

Oh my God, Ezra is right.

I was an idiot coming here. Even if I have no intention of falling for Quentin's attempt to lure me, this will make for a very uncomfortable trip.

"No, that won't be necessary." God bless Ezra. He seemed to have disappeared, but he now steps forward like a bodyguard ready to rescue me. "I was just telling Mia she can stay with me."

CHAPTER 6

Ezra

THE MOMENT QUENTIN XENAKIS ENTERS MY SIGHTLINE MY
eyes turn dry and itchy and the rapid blinking begins. My
corneas reject the contact lenses, as if my body's trying to get
rid of them along with any other layer of fake coolness I've acquired
over the years. My skin tingles, threatening to break out. If I'm not
careful, I might start slouching and fidgeting and my voice may
acquire a nasal tone.

In short, the nerd trapped inside me struggles to break free—
like Hulk bursting out from inside Bruce Banner. That only happens
when something makes me insecure to the extreme. Life and death
business meetings; women way out of my league…

And Mr. X.

Despite that, I manage to force a calm tone. "Mia can stay with
me. There's plenty of room in my suite."

The tall and slender man resembles a mixture of John Stamos
and Michael Douglas in their prime. The only hint of time passing
on Xenakis is a few more silver strands in his shoulder-length hair.
If anything, his facial lines make him look even more irritatingly
smashing.

I flash back to the first time Mia introduced us. That thirty-six-
year-old man seemed incredibly worldly in our twenty-year-old eyes.
I noticed the way she looked at him and I can't explain the instant
hate I acquired for him. Maybe a part of me predicted how much
he'd make her suffer over the years.

And just maybe, Ezzie—the kid trapped inside me—peeked out and felt terribly jealous.

Keep it together. I scold myself. I have to focus on my mission. I'm only here to stop him from derailing Mia.

"Ezra, isn't it?" he offers me a handshake.

"I'm surprised you remember me," I force a pleasant voice. We barely interacted a handful of times during the years Mia dated him. After the second time he broke her heart, she got the memo that I despised the guy and avoided mixing us.

"I never forget a name or a face. Though I must say you've changed quite a bit. I'm glad you're willing to host Mia and help rectify our stupid mistake."

I would've bought his act of friendliness if he didn't cling to my hand while making this weird eye-contact that's equivalent to a cat spraying to mark his territory.

He finally releases my hand and ushers us to a table, but he keeps studying me. "I remember Mia mentioned once your business was thriving. What exactly do you do, again?"

"I did game developing and app design for years."

"*App design.* How marvelous." Despite his words, his smug air tells me that he hardly considers what I do as design compared to his work as fashion mogul.

Mia chimes in, "He's done very well; he's retired now."

"Retired this young? Good for you!"

There it is. The condescending tone, like he's congratulating a kid with special needs for eating his soup without spilling.

Ugh. I'd be happy to spell out my successes to him, but bragging has never been my nature. Not to mention that my net worth is probably nothing compared to his. "I have a few income-generating products—"

"He created eighteen apps, including *Squiggles*, named by Times Magazine as the most addictive video game app series in history," Mia chimes in, her chin up.

I send her a grateful look. "And had the luck of investing wisely a decade back…"

"He owns a slice of *Facebook*, *Instagram* and *Snapchat*. Not to mention he was a bitcoin mining pioneer." Mia boasts again.

Normally I would feel self-conscious, but I'm glad she's doing it for me. Whatever it takes to get street cred in front of this guy.

Mr. X gives me a cold smile. "Excellent. It's very kind of you to take time to come help Mia." He seems to be fishing for why I am here if I don't need to get paid.

Feeling a bit more comfortable, I reply, "I'm here mostly for friendly support. But I'm also helping Mia with her online marketing and lending a hand as informal photographer."

"That's very generous of you, but unnecessary. Just relax and enjoy your stay. Mia can use my staff and equipment for anything she needs."

Bastard. He knows I'm here to block him and is trying to get rid of me. "It would be my pleasure. Mia mentioned the event at Mykonos benefits breast cancer research, and that's a cause we support strongly on behalf of our mutual friend Iris. I look forward to joining you on the islands, after the AXD event."

A flash of anger crosses his expression, but he recovers quickly. His voice remains terse. "We'll be happy to welcome you."

My hand irks to slap his, resting on Mia's elbow. But luckily, Mia frees herself. "Well, Ezra, let's go then. I could use a shower and some rest." She rises from her chair and I follow suit. She sends Mr. X a forced grin. "Nice catching up, Quentin. I will see you tomorrow at rehearsals."

Mr. X insists on one more handshake and this time I feel a notch more confident as I sustain his weird eye contact.

We walk away and Mia clings to my arm as if I were a piece of driftwood she's holding onto after a shipwreck. Under the forced indifference of her fashion persona, I sense her worry. She's too proud to ever admit it, but she might be realizing my concerns make sense.

Filled with renewed strength and commitment, I tighten my grasp to send her my reassurance.

Mr. X might be relentless, but when it comes to protecting my princess, so am I.

* * *

The taxi ride gives Mia and me a chance to process what just happened at the reception, as well as get the first impressions from Athens. Only when Mia points things out to me do they become real. A view of the Parthenon perched on top of the Acropolis (2). A peek at a street market where sellers advertise colorful fruit, nuts and olives (3). Traffic signs and street signs in Greek in an unending procession.

I love how here in Greece they're constantly honoring their heritage. Everywhere you look buildings embrace the Greco-Roman architecture. The same goes for our hotel lobby, which boasts extra-high ceilings, Ionic columns and crown molding engraved with the Greek key (4).

"Fancy!" Mia wags her eyebrows at me.

"Everything cheaper was already booked," I grumble.

After registering Mia as a guest, we ride the elevator to my room with the porter wheeling a cart piled high with Mia's luggage.

The space we now share is a good-sized room with two queen beds, two nightstands, a desk, a dresser and an armoire. Yet the moment the porter unloads Mia's two huge suitcases, a large purse and a garment bag, it seems much smaller than before.

"When you said you had plenty of room, I hoped it meant you'd rented a suite where we could each have separate quarters."

I tip the guest service attendant and drag her luggage to her side of the room. "This was the best I could find. Everything is booked because of the fashion show." I set the larger suitcase on top of a luggage rack against the wall.

"It's okay!" She sets the garment bag on the bed and unzips it. "It's not like we haven't been roommates before."

Well, we've roomed in together in the past, but never under these conditions. Those months we shared a townhouse in our junior college year, we had separate bedrooms and bathrooms. Not to mention Sophia as a buffer.

Mia doesn't waste one minute. She prioritizes hanging the Aphrodite dress, then unpacks the rest of her clothes. Apparently, a big part of the trip's appeal consists in wearing her own designs and hoping the media notices her. She carefully stretches each piece, smoothing them out with her hands, before she hangs them in the closet. Every time she's in front of fashion, she shows as much reverence for it as if she were performing a religious ritual.

As she unpacks, I work on setting up the charging station for my electronic devices that I neglected to assemble yesterday. There's not enough space on my nightstand, so I drag the room desk next to my bed. "If I had any doubt Mr. X is plotting something, this mess-up with your room confirmed it." I comment.

"I agree." She removes a purple silk dress from her luggage. "I should've confronted him, but I have to keep a good relationship until after the New Designers Awards."

I find my multi-outlet charger and set it on top of the desk, then unpack my electronics. "When is that?"

"It's the second day of AXD."

As we work side-by-side setting up our halves of the room, Mia tells me everything about this event. Athens Xclusive Designers Week, AXDW, dedicates one day for new talent. Young designers present a mini collection of ten outfits each and compete for three prizes. The winners receive important awards including media attention and participation in other international fashion weeks.

"I only have a couple of days to get ready. Since I'm filling in last minute for someone else, I'm not aware of all the details."

I unroll charging cables. "Haven't you been in touch with the event directors?"

She hangs a black and white block dress on a hanger. "Not directly. Quentin's assistant, Paul, has been dealing with the organizers. Tomorrow we're having a catch-up meeting for me and will be working all day to get my models ready."

Done unpacking her clothes, she turns her attention to a beauty bag. "I wish I could've also participated in the Mykonos fundraising show, but that's a whole different league."

"What do you mean by 'a different league?'"

"To apply to participate you needed to raise a minimum of fifty thousand dollars for the charity, either from sponsors or by your own donation."

"Ouch."

"Exactly."

She carries the beauty case to the bathroom. Curious, I step closer and stand outside the door to watch her set up her cosmetic and hair styling products. Soon every inch of the vanity is covered. From a curling iron to a professional make up kit, it's more stuff than I've seen in my life.

"Did you pack Sephora in that bag?"

She chuckles. "Why are you surprised? You know me."

As she talks, she keeps setting materials on the counter. Anti-aging serums, eyelash curlers, sheet masks, eye creams, moisturizers, anti-frizz hair drops…The embarrassing fact that I know what they are gives testimony to my years hanging out with four women.

I hide my amusement behind a stern expression. "Hey! You didn't leave me any space."

"Yes, I did!" She points at a remote corner of the double vanity that holds my razor, toothbrush, travel-size toothpaste and tiny shaving cream.

"And where am I supposed to keep my contact lens products?"

"Oh, I forgot." She moves her block of beauty supplies literally one inch. "Here. I made you more space."

I put on a theatrical display, complete with huffs and grunts and eye rolls. But the truth is that I'm inexplicably happy. Seeing her stuff next to mine feels pleasantly intimate.

Am I pathetic?

On her way out of the bathroom, Mia winks and nudges me away with her shoulder. She then returns the bag to the closet floor, kicks off her shoes and flops onto my bed.

"Uh. Excuse me, miss." I clear my throat and fold my arms. "That's *my* bed. Yours is the other one."

Defiance flashes on Mia's face as she props herself up on her elbows. "And why is that?"

"Because I spent last night there. And because I already set up my charging station."

I point at the desk next to the bed. Plugged into the surge protector, my work MacBook Pro, personal MacBook Air, iPad and iPhone charge alongside my Apple Watch, AirPods, camera and wireless headset.

Mia sits on the bed and studies my charging station raising an eyebrow. "It seems like the Apple Store threw up in here."

"Ha ha, very funny." I push her shoulder and she drops against the pillows. "My work depends on being connected. I can't play around with battery charging and surge protection, especially considering that European outlets are different from American ones."

Mia sits up again. Holding her chin, she frowns at my multi-outlet charger where all power cords attach and I stand, folding my arms, my back straight and my head up. I'm proud of my sophisticated equipment and I dare her to find anything to criticize about it.

"Aw!" She clasps her hands. "Look at all your devices, sucking power at the same time. They remind me of my cat Lucy."

"What?" I have no idea what she's talking about.

She flutters her eyelashes. "They look like kittens nursing together!"

Never again will I be able to look at my charging station and not think of a mother cat nursing kittens. I have to bite my lips not to laugh. "Out of my bed. *Now.*"

She gasps with fake indignation. "That's something no man has ever said to me!"

"Well, there's a first time for everything." I grab her wrists, yank her out of the bed and swing her to the other bed, where she lands giggling.

Her beautiful face, flushed with laughter, hurts me. There's not a shred of self-consciousness in her as she stretches in bed, her lustrous brown hair spread over the pillow. She's not even aware of her skirt clinging up her thighs teasing me with a glance at her soft skin. God, I'm so deep into the friend zone I hardly exist as a man for her.

Not that it bothers me.

"Well, I had a chance to catch up on sleep last night, but I imagine you might want to take a nap before tonight's events."

"I'll sleep when I'm dead." She springs up from bed. "But I definitely could use a shower after twenty-four hours of travel."

As she heads to the bathroom she grabs the hem of her dress and starts lifting it.

"Whoa, whoa!" I squeeze my eyes shut and lift a hand. "Room sharing rule number one. No stripping in public."

She puffs air. "After so many years as a model, changing in front of a legion of people, I'm cured of any modesty."

I keep my eyes closed. "Don't care. For the duration of this trip, you're only allowed to take your clothes off in the bathroom. And no prancing around the room wrapped in a towel either. Go get whatever outfit you're going to wear and take it with you."

She releases an impatient groan. "Okay, okay."

I open my eyes in time to see her stomp to her closet. From there she picks out some clothes and takes them to the restroom.

Then she returns to me and throws her arms around my neck. It catches me off guard and I have to step back and hold onto her so as not to lose my balance.

"Thank you for letting me stay here, Big Nerd. It means a lot to me that you came on this trip." The tenderness in her voice moves me.

Tentative, I slide my arms around her. "Don't mention it."

"Oh no. It's a bigger deal than you think." She hesitates. "This trip is bringing out the old me; the one who loved partying and drinking, and smoking and hooking up. The me from those years when I forgot who I really am. Your presence here reminds me of my best version."

I'm a little choked up. Trying to keep my cool, I cover it up with humor. "Well, it's only fair. When we were kids, you taught me to misbehave; now I can return the favor by whipping you into good behavior."

Her musical laugh makes my chest flutter.

"I'm glad you're here to keep me on track." She buries her face in my neck and whispers, "I love you, Big Nerd."

I'm not ashamed to admit I'm fighting a little moistness in my eyes. I tighten my embrace. "I love you too, Big Airhead."

Her hair smells like honey and roses. Having her tucked against my neck must be one of the most delightful sensations I've enjoyed in my life. So is the awareness of her hands sliding down my back. Her soft, warm body molds into mine so easily. It feels so different from the rib-lined rail she became during her years of starvation as a model. I dwell in the blissful delight for a moment.

And then something twitches below my belt.

At once, it all acquires a different connotation—the heat of her body against mine, her breath near my ear, her fingers sliding inside my jacket to better caress my waist. A sharp image enters my mind of what I'd like to do with her. And it's too X-rated to belong to underage Ezzie.

Needing to escape the intensity of the moment, I gently push away from her. "Okay, okay you got what you wanted. You can keep your things on my side of the bathroom vanity."

She stamps a big kiss on my cheek. "You're the best." Then, she releases me and walks away, leaving me in a haze.

"Wait. Forgot my underwear." She pivots, returns to her luggage and rummages through it.

From the bag, Mia removes a lingerie collection just as impressive as her clothes. A black lacy pushup bra with a matching thong, soft pink lacy briefs, golden satin bikinis, a balcony bra, another thong...

The string of drool dripping from the corner of my mouth is my first clue that I've been staring. I wipe it as I jerk my head away. "Are you planning to take that shower this year? Or should I jump in first."

"I'm coming, I'm coming! Geez!" She carries something to the restroom—I assume her underwear, but I've stopped looking.

Please, just get in that shower. I need a few minutes to gather my thoughts and my hormones.

Still, Mia comes out of the bathroom one more time. She stands in front of me and by her mischievous expression I know nothing good will come out of her mouth.

"Yes, Mia?"

"I couldn't help notice that the sight of my underwear upset you," she whispers. "I promise I'll do my best to hide it from you."

I glower at her. "Thank you."

She strolls back to the bathroom and as she does, she works on un-hooking her bra from outside her dress. "And I promise I'll also hide my vibrator."

"Mia!" I squeeze my eyes shut and shudder. "Room rule number two. No oversharing!"

She dissolves into giggles. Right before she crosses the bathroom door threshold, she succeeds at unhooking her bra and pulls it out from one of her dress sleeves, then drops it on the floor. Soon the sound of running water fills the room, mixed with the sounds of her humming in the shower.

She didn't even close the door all the way.

I stumble to my bed and drop onto it, and cover my head with a pillow, trying really hard not to think about her naked in the shower.

Shit. This is going to be a long trip.

CHAPTER 7

Mia

AXDW is the official fashion week in Greece, which happens twice a year in the spring and the fall. It showcases Greek designers along with top international fashion houses. Every season, AXD welcomes more than 25,000 visitors, including buyers and international press and media. I love their philosophy, *Fashion with conscience*. The event supports a different charity or social cause every season. Last time proceeds went to rescuing stray dogs. So my style!

Last night, Ezra and I barely made an appearance at Quentin's welcome dinner and returned to the hotel early. I've come a long way from my days of drinking and partying until the wee hours. After a restorative night's sleep, I'm ready to face the hectic next three days of fittings, rehearsals and hair and makeup tests with the models.

My mini-team and I wait for instructions at the historic venue of Zappeion Hall. The gorgeous building imitates an original Greek temple, down to bright red walls and gold-leaf trim on the white fluted columns and ceiling reliefs (5 a-d).

As usual, Quentin is running late, so we gather in a small group and chat with some of his staff. Ezra's getting tons of attention from the young models, who flutter around him, raving about *Squiggles*. Marcia and Trent fish for information about what's really going on between Ezra and me; to prove we're just friends, we've been relentless in teasing each other.

As the ultimate torture, I've just stolen Ezra's phone and sent a

FaceTime request to his mother in the States, to have her confirm the story I'm telling.

Mrs. Cohen's crankiness might have something to do with the fact that I forgot about the time difference and woke her up in the middle of the night. But, also, she's never hidden that she considers me trouble. "This young lady could have killed my Ezra!" I love her cute New Jersey accent, which she never lost despite decades living in the Midwest. And I love how she always calls me *young lady*. I so need that today, when these young models make me feel so old.

She points at my image on the screen. "She fed him cupcakes behind my back when he had a life-threatening allergy to eggs, gluten and dairy!"

I snap my fingers. "But I proved he had outgrown his allergies! He survived!"

Ezra's trying to recover his phone but I keep swinging it away from reach.

"You got him hooked on sugar!" Mrs. Cohen shoots me a narrow-eyed glare. "And he did end up in the hospital the following week anyway."

I grimace. "How was I supposed to know he was allergic to the dye in blue frosting?"

"And a few years later, in high school, she gave him a horrible asthma attack by offering him a *cigarette*!"

"You should be grateful!" I spread a hand. "Thanks to that scare he never smoked again."

She barely pauses for breath. "…And she also gave him his first beer!"

Arms folded, shoulders dropped, Ezra grumbles. "More like my first six-pack."

I wrap my free arm around his waist. "And thanks to the horrible hangover he had the next day, he never became a drinker. See? I was his guardian angel!"

Ezra seizes my proximity to swipe the phone from my hand. "Love you, Mom! Talk later." He disconnects the call.

But I achieved my purpose. By now the models have dispersed and Marcia and Trent have no doubt that Ezra and I are anything but a romantic couple.

"Thank you." Ezra glowers at me. "As much as I love my mother, thinking about her is the last thing I need when I'm surrounded by sexy models." He rolls his eyes and huffs as he drops into a folding chair.

Giggling, I hug him from the back and kiss his cheek. "Next time, I'll ask her to retell all the adorable stories about your child-hood obsession with monkeys. That will teach you not to mess with me again!" Despite my levity, guilt twinges inside me. Did I really call his mother in revenge for his teasing? Or did I want to show off our connection and mark my territory—because the models' ogling him bothered me?

"Uh, excuse me, Mia." Paul strides up to us, his arms full of clip-boards. I don't like his expression at all; his frown lines are breaking through the Botox.

I lift myself away from Ezra, hands lingering on his broad shoul-ders. "Yes, Paul?"

Paul casts a glance around the room and whispers, "Mr. Xenakis and I would like to talk to you."

Ezra straightens up. "And this is about...?"

Paul seems to debate whether to include Ezra. He signals us to follow him to an empty conference room and points at a couple of chairs.

Paul's scowl is giving me nervous indigestion. I take a seat while Ezra remains standing behind me, like a bodyguard.

Paul fidgets. "There has been a hiccup, but please don't panic."

If someone doesn't want me to panic, they should never tell me not to. "What's going on?"

"There was a misunderstanding." Paul hunches, as if bracing

himself. "Only Greek born designers are eligible for the New Designers Awards. You don't qualify."

My heart drops to the pit of my stomach. "And you learned that just *now*?"

"We found out a few days ago, but until this morning we still hoped they'd make an exception for Mr. Xenakis."

"There has to be a way to fix this." Ezra chimes in. "Who do we have to talk to?"

Paul shakes his head. "We've done everything possible."

My neck muscles are so tense I'm starting to get a headache, but I keep my voice icy. "Can't we claim my Greek roots? My grandparents?"

"They also have a limit of two years to consider you a New Designer. Your company is older than that, so that's another disqualifier."

"And you didn't even know *that*?" Ezra snaps. "Did you even read the requirements before getting Mia's hopes up?"

Maybe I'm still in denial, because I'm not panicking as much as I should. Instead, my attention focuses on Ezra's transformation. Nothing remains of my even-tempered friend; the man in front of me is a lion about to attack.

Ezra takes a deep breath and clenches his fists. "I can't believe your boss is doing this!" he roars, trembling. "I can't believe he made Mia come all the way here for nothing!"

For nothing. The first twinge of disappointment bubbles inside me.

"It's not for nothing!" Paul retorts. "She'll have a chance to network. Even if her designs are not shown…"

"Her designs *will* be shown, *damn it*!" Ezra interrupts him with a thundering voice. "Mia did not come all this way to sit in an audience and watch other people's shows."

I should lash out now, but I have trouble closing my mouth and taking my eyes off Ezra. I hardly recognize this guy. He's determined. He's loud. He's bossy.

He's kind of hot.

Ezra pokes his finger on Paul's shoulder. "*Your* negligence caused this mess and now *you* are going to fix it! Understood? And go tell your boss I expected more from him."

Ezra grabs my elbow. "Don't approach us again until you've fixed this." As he stomps away, he practically drags me out of the room with him.

"I can't believe his nerve!" he mumbles in between cusswords as we stride back to the Zappeion Hall lobby. "I bet you Xenakis never thought he could get you that spot! It was just a bait to bring you over, so he could plan his attack!"

I hope he's wrong. If I had one shred of respect left for Quentin, it was for his professionalism. "If his intention were really to lure me back, then it would make no sense to make me furious."

I can barely focus on my words; I'm mesmerized by Ezra's hardened eyes, which now seem much more symmetrical than before. Somehow, his tightened lips make his nose appear more elegant. His features' appeal has risen about a dozen points.

I yank my eyes off him. "Can we sit down for a moment? My legs feel wobbly after this bomb."

He slows down and shifts direction toward the atrium, where workers have been setting chairs in preparation for an outdoor show (6). He indicates for me to take a seat first.

"I suspect this is a scare," I muse. If Ezra can anticipate Quentin's movements, maybe I can, too. "I bet Quentin will magically find a last-minute solution to appear like a hero."

"But time is running out! Unless you work on your fittings and rehearsals today, you'll never be ready in time!" He sits next to me.

"I'll work overnight to get ready, nothing new." I study Ezra's unrecognizable face. "Quentin craves drama and loves making his team run on adrenaline, chasing impossible deadlines. I'll start pan-icking if they haven't found a solution by five o'clock."

"If they haven't found a solution by five o'clock, heads will roll." Ezra removes his blazer and hangs it on the back of his chair. His short-sleeve shirt reveals a pair of strong arms, very different from the strings I remember. How come I didn't notice them last night? Did he wear long-sleeved pajamas?

Beyond my control, my hand squeezes his bicep. It must be his tension, but it feels unexpectedly hard. "Hey, since when do you have muscles?"

He frowns, confused at my change of subjects. "I have a new jiu jitsu trainer at the gym and he's been pushing me to a new level."

"A trainer? A *gym*?" I gape at him. This is the guy who used to fake asthma attacks in seventh grade to get away with skipping PE class.

"Yes!" He chuckles as if my surprise amuses him. "It's amazing how much extra time I have since I quit gaming."

"Quit *what*?" My jaw must be hanging lower than my boobs right now. "Who are you and what did you do with my friend Ezra?"

He bursts into the exact same goofy laugh he had twenty years ago—opening with a little snort and ending in a high pitch wheeze.

"Okay. There you are. What a relief." I press a hand to my chest. Where did this come from? For a moment there I felt kind of…turned on by this side of him I'd never seen before.

"Let's go for a walk." I rise from my seat and Ezra imitates me. Luckily, I went for comfort over glamour today and wore flats, along with my work uniform of a jersey wrap dress.

As we stroll toward the stone steps, I glance at Ezra from the corner of my eye. "Did you *seriously* quit gaming?"

He holds my elbow as we descend the steps. Somehow today I like his touch more than usual. "Well, 'quitting' is a strong word." He snickers. "I've been following the advice in Iris' book and taking it one day at a time."

My eyes widen with surprise. "Didn't you say you quit the Self-Vow program after three days?"

"The celibacy part? Hell yeah." He snorts, then his shoulders lower. "But I learned from the other chapters. Every morning I tell myself that, for just the next twenty-four hours, I'm quitting videogames, along with my other two addictions—potato chips and ditzy blondes." He winks and the usual playful gesture seems unusually flattering. "Half the days I give in and game-binge for an hour or two before bedtime. But that's way less than before."

"Heck it is!" This guy used to game for so many hours in a row that one summer in middle school he ended up in the ER with dehydration and low blood sugar.

Ezra seems to find my bafflement hilarious. "You think you know me, but maybe I've changed a little in the past twenty years. He holds his index finger and thumb together. "Just a little."

As we pace down the most beautiful street, lined with jacaranda trees bursting in purple blossoms, I meet an Ezra I've never seen before (7). It's refreshing to hear him talk for real, taking off the goofball persona he wears around me and the other girls.

He's picked up some fascinating hobbies since our roommate days. As we stroll gorgeous marble streets (8 a-b), he recounts interests as diverse as reading about Kabbalah and practicing Brazilian jiu jitsu. The conversation continues during lunch and I can't believe my picky-eater friend just ordered *moussaka*. Or that my couch-rooted-gamer pal has clocked such extensive travels. I marvel, basking in envy, as he talks about Thailand, Tibet and Indonesia. And I thought going to Paris and Milan was a big deal.

We haven't heard back from Paul yet by the end of lunch. Killing time, we explore the colorful streets, shops and cafes of the historic neighborhood of Plaka (9). I love how Athens, despite being a capital, retains some small-town vibe. It must have something to do with the warmth of the vivacious locals, engaged in animated conversations in impenetrable Greek.

Midafternoon, we realize we forgot Ezra's blazer and head back to Zappeion Hall. On the way, we stop for the most traditional Greek snack, yoghurt and honey. I rarely have full-fat yoghurt, but this intense tangy flavor is worth it.

It's almost five by the time we arrive back at the Zappeion Hall. The topic of our flowing conversation has shifted to Ezra's commitment to remain unattached.

He laughs at my theory that he never got over Crystal. "Are you kidding? Crystal is ancient history!"

Can I believe him? "I've beaten myself up sometimes, for having been the one who introduced the two of you." I study him as he finishes the last of his yoghurt. "Then how come you've never dated anybody seriously since then?"

He gives a dismissive shrug. "I'm not sure I could ever tie myself to one woman. It would be boring to have the same person with you every night." A slight tension in his voice hints he's not convinced of his words. He avoids my eye contact as he throws his empty yoghurt container in a trash bin.

"Well, you're still catching up from life adventures, but I had a head start on you." I sigh. "It was getting tiresome having to get to know someone over and over again. Taking the self-vow has been a welcome break."

His intense gaze seems to try to read me. "This cleansing year has been great for you, hasn't it?"

I nod. "This is the first time in my life I love and respect myself."

"My Big Airhead!" He stops walking and surprises me by wrapping me in his arms. "Everybody who matters loves you and respects you. You're finally catching up."

I circle his waist and enjoy his embrace, but something has changed since last night. I'm more aware than ever of his strong arms, his hard chest, his masculine scent.

An inappropriate thought catches me off guard. What would

happen if I slide my hands down to his buttocks? Would his lower body feel as shapely as the top?

Oh dear. This year of celibacy must be really catching up with me. I can't believe I just had a dirty thought about *Ezra*.

"There you are!" Paul approaches us and I resent it when Ezra releases me from his arms. "Mr. Xenakis needs to talk to you. He's found a solution for the issue."

Ezra and I exchange a look.

"Ms. Kostopoulos and I were about to return to our hotel." Ezra folds his arms, which I admit makes them look even more appetizing. "This better be good."

Paul shoots him a glare, then moves his head in a circular motion. "Only that Mr. Xenakis is willing to sacrifice part of his own time to allow Ms. Kostopoulos's designs to show."

Startled, I stumble back. "Do you mean…me sharing his show?"

Ezra must've noticed my lack of balance because he holds my arm. "Is this good or bad?" he asks between his teeth.

"Good! Really good!" My pulse speeding up, I pull away from Ezra to trail after Paul.

CHAPTER 8

Mia

Ezra strides by my side as Paul leads the way across long hallways.

"Quentin has a show devoted only for himself the last day of the event," I explain in a whisper.

"So you'd get more attention." Smart as he is, Ezra's quick to catch up. "Instead of sharing the spotlight with a dozen other designers you're sharing it only with Xenakis."

"His show will have tremendous press coverage." I'm still processing the generous offer—almost too good to be true.

"Can he be more obvious?" Ezra growls. "He planned it all so he could be the hero in your eyes."

Oh, yes. *That's the catch.* The realization clicks into focus. In one deft move, Quentin pushes me back into the uncomfortable position of being indebted to him. Of having the world question what I did to earn his help.

Paul guides us behind the stage where a catwalk has been set up. In a dressing room Quentin works on fittings with his models before a dress rehearsal. His voice resounds on the walls as he barks orders to a stylist. He wears his signature all-black work outfit and his usual displeased expression. Adrenaline floods my bloodstream. I used to work so hard to rip a smile out of him. Even a minimal word of approval.

The moment Quentin sees us arrive he signals us to follow him away from backstage and into a conference room. He settles at one end of the long table and summons me with flick of his chin.

I stroll toward him with Ezra right behind me, feeling like I've been called to the boss's office—but I still don't know if the purpose of the meeting is to offer a promotion or to fire me.

"Did Paul explain my proposal?" Quentin's breath smells of cigarettes. His dark, hypnotic gaze fixes on me and he ignores Ezra's presence.

I nod.

"Are you interested?"

Is this how Eve felt the day the snake tempted her with the forbidden fruit? If I say no, I'd be throwing away the opportunity of my life and admitting I came on this trip for nothing. But saying yes would imply I swallow my pride and treat him like my savior for years to come. It's déjà vu from those years with Quentin. Everything good he did for me came with a big price tag. I almost liked it better when he behaved like an a-hole.

I exchange a look with Ezra but he just shrugs. He's not going to nudge me one way or another. I draw in a breath and bow my head once, accepting the deal.

Quentin leans back in his chair. "I'm glad we've been able to resolve this issue. I'll let Paul discuss the details with you." He rises from his seat and steps out.

"Okay, we have a lot to plan." Paul claims a chair next to me and opens a folder. "Since Mr. Xenakis' show happens Sunday, the last day of the event, we have more time. I'll be arranging for your fittings and rehearsals to happen Friday and Saturday."

Paul removes a set of Polaroids from the folder. Through my mind fog I recognize them as pictures of the ten designs I brought for the fashion show. He separates out three of them. "These are the looks he's chosen for the show."

"What?" I frown, confused. "Aren't we going to show all my outfits?"

"We wouldn't have time for that in the four minutes he's allotting to you."

I jolt in my chair. "Four minutes?"

Paul's impatient tone shows he believes I should be on my knees, thanking them. "He's eliminating two of his designs from the show and shaving time in the final walk just to squeeze you in."

The disappointment that floods me doesn't allow me to feel anger—at least not yet. I stare at the Polaroids on the table and realize the Aphrodite dress is not among them.

"Wait." I search the folder until I find the picture of the dress and place it on the table in front of Paul. "This is the most important design I need to show."

"Oh, I'm sorry, that's not possible."

"Why?" Ezra nearly growls.

Paul uses a pen to drum on the picture. "He's already showing a white wedding dress at the end of the show, so this one would be a duplicate."

"What? No!" I shake my head with force. "This is not a wedding dress."

"It doesn't matter." Paul clicks his tongue. "It's white, it would steal attention from the final model."

All the stress and anger I've been holding inside for the past hours simmers and reaches a boiling point. "No! I will not accept this! That dress is the main reason I came on this trip!"

Paul drops the pen and crosses his arms, then swings his whole body side to side. "Well, dear. Mr. Xenakis is doing you a favor, so you don't have much of a say here. Take it or leave it."

The words feel like a slap. In a moment I relive my entire history with Quentin. Always settling for his love breadcrumbs. And often, having breadcrumbs left me hungrier than having nothing.

"You'd better watch your attitude!" Ezra points a finger at Paul. "You two screwed up big time with Mia and I won't allow you to shorthand her."

Paul wags a finger in circles. "Let Ms. Kostopoulos make this call. It's her fashion career on the line."

Silence falls for the longest time. My heart leaps up and grabs me by the throat, stopping words from coming out. Ezra is right; this whole trip has been a trap. But it wasn't planned to lure me back. Its purpose is to humiliate me.

I keep my voice icy. "I'll get back to you."

I grab Ezra's arm and he gets the signal. He springs from his chair to help me get out of mine and then walks me out of the conference, throwing glances over his shoulder at Paul until we're out.

"Unless I hear back to the contrary, we'll assume you'll be here Friday at eight for fittings." Paul's voice reaches me right before we go through the door.

Ezra and I stride in silence across the building to the exit, only stopping at the atrium to pick up his blazer. With time, my boiling anger turns into lava about to erupt. As we descend the marble stairs, the first words come out in a strangled whisper. "*Four minutes.* All he's giving me is four freaking minutes and I don't even get to choose which of my designs to show."

"I want to murder the bastard!" Ezra grumbles as we cross the front lawn on the way to the street. "He appears like your knight in shining armor and then steps out and lets his minion deliver the bad news? He didn't even have the balls to tell us in person so I could give him a piece of my mind!"

I walked myself into this trap. Now my choices are to call this trip a waste of time and money or accept next to nothing while still owing Quentin a favor.

As furious as I am with Quentin, I'm mostly outraged with myself for falling for the trap again. This feels the same as every time Quentin promised that "someday" we'd formalize our relationship; that he'd introduce me to his mother. Damn it, that he'd at least give me a freaking key to his place. Instead, I only got leftovers of his time and his life.

Ezra rambles curses against Quentin as he hails a taxi. "I can't believe his nerve!" He opens the taxi door for me, and I climb inside, then he slides in next to me and slams the door with more force than necessary. "And of course, rejecting the offer would be passing on a chance for huge publicity. There's no right answer here." He extends the card with the hotel address to the driver.

All the suppressed memories from when I started my career as a model surge inside me. All the anger I swallowed as person after person insinuated I'd only succeeded because I was sleeping with the boss. Every single time Quentin did something like this: raising me to the sky just so it hurt even more when he dropped me and I crashed to the floor. I've been such an idiot.

My anger and frustration reach a point of explosion and I'm afraid I'll terrify the taxi driver by screaming or yelling cusswords. But no. Something much worse is happening. The worst. The one thing I never allow in public.

I'm about to cry.

No, damn it! I wipe a tear running down my cheek with an angry swipe. This isn't me. I didn't even cry each time Roxanne kicked me out of my dad's house.

Worry flashes across Ezra's face. "Oh, Princess."

In a blink, he's taken me into his arms, and that's my undoing. I burst into tears, and sob and wail like the ridiculous, weak and soft woman I never wanted to become.

And like the annoyingly perfect, sensitive man the girls and I trained Ezra to be, he holds me across his chest and lets me cry on his shoulder.

CHAPTER 9

Ezra

I'M A LITTLE FREAKED OUT. NOT BY THE TEARS—DURING college Sophia, who can cry on cue, trained me to see them as natural. What shocks me is their source. As many times as I played the role of supportive "girlfriend" when one of my girls had a shattered dream, I've never seen Mia cry before. Even each time she broke up with Mr. X, if she cried, she did it in hiding.

We ride in complete silence, me holding her against my chest, as the taxi winds across Athens to our hotel. Only the occasional quiver of her breathing hints that she's still crying. Yet I no longer feel disturbed, but in eerie peace. A latent caveman in me feels more attracted to her than ever—as if I'd been born for this job to hold her and protect her.

"I'm just furious because these stupid tears won't stop!" As the taxi arrives at the hotel, she lifts her face off my shoulder and swipes her eyes with her long sleeve. "And now my makeup is a disaster."

The nice young taxi driver says nothing, but he extends a pack of Kleenex in our direction."

"*Efaristó*." Mia thanks him and accepts a couple of tissues.

I pay the taxi with a fifty Euro bill without waiting for change, then rush to help Mia out.

"Sorry, but when Quentin refused to show the Aphrodite dress, he hit the deepest nerve," she murmurs as we cross the lobby toward the elevator. "He always knew how to tackle my weaknesses."

"It's okay to cry; it's good… energy cleansing," I blurt, quoting Chloe, since I don't know what else to say.

Mia blows her nose with the tissue. "Good, because I'm not done."

Hours later, Mia has attacked the mini-fridge in the suite and is curled up on top of her covers, sipping white wine. Luckily, she's moved from self-pity back to anger.

"I want to kill him!" she repeats with a grunt, then punches the pillow.

"A fast death would be too merciful." I refill her glass. "Let's castrate him instead—*slowly*."

"To hell with him! I don't need him." Mia fidgets and jiggles a foot. "We're in Athens, the perfect backdrop for my Aphrodite dress. We'll take beautiful pictures of it among the iconic ruins, then we'll use them for our own online campaign." She sets her glass on the nightstand, jumps off her bed and stomps to the closet where the dress hangs, still wrapped in protective plastic. She picks it up and admires it for a moment, then turns to me. "You would come with me to the Acropolis and be my photographer, wouldn't you?"

That has to be the wine talking. "You probably need a permit or something."

"Tourists take photos all the time. No one can stop us." She hangs the dress back in the closet, grabs her phone from her nightstand and texts someone. "Marcia can be our model and I'll ask Trent to get some photographic equipment. We'll meet as soon as the site opens, to beat the crowds."

I bow my head. Whatever it takes to cheer her up.

She returns to sit on the edge of her bed, facing me. "Now let's figure out a way to punish Quentin!"

If I learned anything during the years with my girls, it was about the healing benefits of dissing an ex. "Let's put Vaseline in his beauty cream to give him acne—like we did with Kelly at summer camp."

Mia's lips bend a little. Good, I'm making progress. I clap once.

"Oh, I know! Let's send the *gaslighting virus* to his computer like we did with that mean math teacher, junior year."

Mia lights up. "Oh that would be perfect! I would love to see Quentin pulling his hair plugs out when his cursor keeps jumping to a different line."

"Or when his computer keeps changing the words he types."

We guffaw together and I'm grateful the worst of the storm is over.

Mia tosses her phone aside and moves over to sit on the edge of my bed, next to me. She kisses me on the cheek then circles me with one arm. "Thank you. It's so good to have you here. I love you, Big Nerd."

I embrace her too. "And I love *you*, Big Airhead." I catch a whiff of her honey and rose scented hair and Ezzie swoons inside me. Ugh, I'm so pathetic.

Trying to break the moment with humor, I burst into the old Rascal Flatt's song, "I will staaaand by you—"

"Please, stop!" Just as I intended, Mia laughs and releases me. "Ezra, the only thing you do worse than dancing is singing."

I'm glad to see her back to herself.

She sobers up. "Now, seriously, I still have to make a decision about Quentin's fashion show."

She leans on me; I wrap her in my arms and tuck her against my side. Her hand casually resting on my thigh makes my whole body tingle. I savor her closeness as we muse in silence for a moment.

"Just to play devil's advocate." I can't believe I'm about to say this, but I wouldn't be a friend if I allowed my own bias to get in the way of Mia's success. "What would happen if you accepted his proposal? Or better, why not counteroffer and ask for more?"

Tension creeps back into her muscles as she lifts her head off my shoulder. "I would owe him just another favor."

"And would that be *so* bad?" I release her from my hold.

She retrieves her wineglass and finishes it in a large gulp, then sets it on my nightstand. "It wasn't only Crystal, you know. For years people accused me of succeeding as a model just because I was sleeping with the boss."

With a moan, she crawls on the bed and flops back onto the pillows.

I debate whether to remind her that she just climbed into *my* bed, but decide against it. Instead, I twist around and hold her elbow. "It's all bullshit jealousy. I was there." I shake her lightly, then lean toward her to poke her nose with the tip of my finger. "It was your hard work that made Xenakis notice you. You earned your success."

"Hard work means little without connections, you know." She rubs the tip of her nose as if my touch made her itchy. "They do have a point. I never would've gotten as far as I did if it wasn't for all the contacts I made while dating Quentin."

She stretches her hand toward the wine bottle and I read her signal; I refill her glass and hand it back to her. She continues, her eyes fixed on her goblet. "Quentin made me his top model, the face of his collection. He took me to Paris, New York and Milan. He paid for my nose job and my new boobs." Her eyes turn shiny again and I realize she's about to resume crying.

Without thinking, I climb in bed with her and grab her free hand. "You didn't need any of that."

"Well, Quentin believed I did. Not to mention the twenty pounds I had to lose, or all the laser hair removal. That was excruciating!"

She takes my hand to her leg and I startle at the touch of that silky skin. "Feel that? No hair!" She moves my fingers up to her thigh. "No hair there either. Do you have any clue how many painful laser sessions I had to endure to become the ideal model? The inhuman, hairless freak Quentin wanted me to be?"

I'm really trying to be a supportive friend right now. But her exquisite thigh under my palm messes up my operating system. I would do anything to keep exploring the rest of that skin. "He made you get laser removal…everywhere?"

She bobs her head. "That and teeth whitening that gave me terrible sensitivity. And lip plumping injections. So painful." Her voice cracks. "Sometimes I wondered why he was with me if he wanted to change me so desperately."

Tears reappear, so I embrace her. I want to tell her I never wanted her to change. I loved her natural nose. I loved her old, smaller breasts. I loved every inch of her exactly the way it was. "Why did you ever put up with him? I never understood why such a strong, smart woman like you kept gravitating to a-holes." My voice sounds hoarse and ragged. "Xenakis took the gold, but he wasn't the only one! How about Brad, the idiotic beef blob that took you to senior prom. Or what's-his-face the narcissist underwear model." The memories hurt today as much as then.

Silence hangs between us for a moment as she stretches her arm to set the wineglass next to my charging station. When she speaks at last, her voice is tentative. "One time a shrink suggested that jumping from jerk to jerk was my way to punish my father and stepmother."

I process the words, remembering her struggles as a teenager. The mother who abandoned Mia when she was twelve in exchange for her own freedom. The verbally abusive stepmother who made her life miserable, and the father who couldn't be present for her emotionally—because she reminded him of the woman who'd left him.

"It would make sense," I reflect. "You grew up hearing them demonize your mother and demand such high standards of good behavior from you."

She dips her chin. "Every boyfriend I ever had became my desperate attempt to soothe that pain," she continues, "an effort to get the attention Dad denied me, and the affection Mom took away from me—even if my only source of affection was letting a guy get to second base. Every man was a cry for help, 'Please someone tell me I do matter!'"

For the first time I understand why an intelligent woman like Mia could've made the same mistakes over and over again with Xenakis.

She has her own version of Ezzie trapped inside, making bad decisions. She's still the teenage girl suffering Dad's rejection.

She nestles into my side a little deeper and I squeeze her a little tighter. Tomorrow I'll have to do something to punish Mr. X, I don't know what. Maybe I'll throw a rotten egg at his door. Or post a YouTube video ridiculing him. I might send the gaslighting virus to his computer.

But tonight I'm completely booked. All I want to do is hold my princess in my arms and give her the love and acceptance she's sought in the wrong places all her life.

CHAPTER 10

Ezra

I'M FLOATING BETWEEN DROWSINESS AND CONSCIOUSNESS AND something feels unusual in a good way. I'm spooning someone in bed, but my sleepy brain can't remember whom. It's not the first time I've woken up next to a woman and, for a moment, can't recall who she is or where I am.

But it's different this time. For starters, I have no hangover, like I'd expect to have if I brought home a stranger from a club last night. Next, this feels way too natural and pleasant. Her soft body molds to mine oh so perfectly, like we were both made out of play dough or gel. It's difficult to imagine she hasn't always been here.

But there's another clue that refutes the theory that I'm waking up next to last night's hook up—a less poetic one. If I'd gotten lucky barely hours ago, I should be calm and soothed from the waist down. That's not the case right now. I'm horny, unsatisfied, restless...

And so, so hard.

Through layers of fabric, Ezra Junior presses against the woman's buttocks, and she rubs against me. Dang it, it feels so good. My hand caresses a thigh that's unbelievably smooth, then travels to cup a firm, full breast. And I'm torn because my upper half feels so blissful I don't want to move, but my lower half is dying to get busy with this delightful stranger. I want to get rid of all these clothing layers between us and confirm the rest of her is as silky as her thigh. I want to taste that skin that smells like honey and roses.

Wait. Honey and roses?

A truckload of adrenaline dumps into my bloodstream.

Oh shit. This is Mia.

I jerk up straight in bed. Still in yesterday's clothes, Mia stretches out like a kitten. Her closed eyes and relaxed features hint she's still asleep.

My heart drums in my chest. This cannot be happening. Did I just fondle and grope *Mia?*

And did I really enjoy it *so* much?

And now that I know who she is, why is my lower half turning more restless instead of calming down?

I scramble out of bed and stumble to the carpeted floor, bringing the top cover with me.

Mia mumbles a protest and rolls around, while feeling with her hand for the missing blanket. Then, as I rise from the floor, she opens her eyelids and the beauty of her golden eyes blinds me. She smiles weakly. "Did we fall asleep in your bed?"

I clear my throat and steady myself. "Yes. I guess."

She giggles. "Hopefully I didn't take advantage of you last night?"

Something weighs heavier between my legs. "Very funny."

"What time is it?" She yawns.

I glance at the alarm clock on the nightstand. "It's not even 4:00 am yet."

Her eyelids droop. "I hope you don't mind I stay here. I'm too tired to move to my bed." She stretches and wiggles, pulls her dress up over her head and drops it on the floor.

My lungs stop working. "Why did you take off your dress?" I try not to stare at her lacy push up bra.

"It itches." She yawns again. "Wake me up by six to go to the Acropolis, would you?" She turns around and before she pulls the blanket back on, she gives me an eyeful of what her thong doesn't cover.

I'm glad she's dozed off again because I can't conceal my body's desperate state.

This is bad. Really bad. Inside me, Ezzie is waking up. But there's someone new. A very adult man who's desperate to get this woman in his bed *for real*.

I grab my phone and my computer from the charging station, then a pillow. I tiptoe to the bathroom. Using the pillow to soften the hard, cold floor I sit with my computer on my lap and desperately search for plane tickets from Florida to Athens.

It's about ten pm in Florida, so I send a FaceTime request to Iris' phone.

"What? Who? Where?" she mumbles as her baby-hair covered head fills the screen. She's always gone to bed earlier than anyone I know.

I don't waste times in greetings. "Iris, when is your next infusion?"

She rubs her swollen eyelids, struggling to wake up. "Uh…in ten days."

"That works." I make a quick calculation. "What were your plans for the next week?"

She blinks grogginess away from her hazel eyes. "Uh…Not much. I was just planning to write."

"Pack your laptop. There will be plenty of time to write at the airport and during the flight."

Another time, I would've cracked up at Iris' puzzled face. "What flight?"

"How quickly can you pack? If I send an Uber to pick you up at five, you can make it to the Miami airport in time to catch the 10:30 am flight to Newark and then you can be here in Athens by—"

"Whoa, whoa, slow down!" Iris straightens in her bed. "Why am I coming to Athens? What happened?"

What can I answer? That Mia's assigned chaperone needs a chaperone for himself? That I'm failing at my job of keeping Mia out of trouble because now *I* want to become her trouble? "Iris, do you remember that time when you called me at midnight and begged me to rescue you from a dumpster and not ask any questions?"

"I know, I owe you a bunch." She scratches her fuzzy scalp. "But your best chance to convince me to go is to tell me exactly what's happening." Iris shifts and brings the phone closer. "Ezra. What's really going in between Mia and you?"

Damn it. I should've known Iris is too smart not to realize that what I'm asking her to rescue me from is myself. "Nothing. Nothing's going on." *Unfortunately.*

Iris moves around to sit against pillows. "For real! I've waited fifteen years to hear this answer. What really did happen that time you and Mia kissed in high school? You always joke about it and claim you were just goofing around and it meant nothing...is that true?"

"We ...might've changed a few details." I draw in a lungful and fidget on my pillow seat. Am I really about to break the wordless pact of silence Mia and I made fifteen years ago?

I rise from the floor, pick up my electronics and tiptoe out of the bathroom and the room. After gently closing the room door behind me, to avoid waking Mia, I move to a small seating area down the hallway and settle in an armchair.

After I've shared the uncensored version of the night Mia kissed me, Iris scrunches her face like when she's thinking hard. "So, when Mia says she only kissed you to free you from the stigma of having never kissed a girl...that's not true?"

I sigh. "It might be true for her, but not for me."

I didn't share this with Ian. Not even Chloe, the third leg in our tripod, knows this. But it's liberating to say it aloud—to transfer it from the realm of imagination and dreams into the real world. "Iris, how can I explain how life changing that night Mia kissed me was for me? My first glimpse of a sexual experience happened with the most beautiful and popular girl in the whole school. It revolutionized my self-esteem."

Iris' head jerks back. "This is far from Mia's version that she gave you a hickey just so you could brag to the school bullies."

"Brag? I never told anybody! It was too unbelievable for me to digest, let alone share." It's all coming clear as I speak. "I felt empowered in a new, different way. I knew that for other people around I was nothing but the class geek—but I'd received something all the popular boys coveted and had no chance of winning."

I'd had *her* in my arms, even if only for an hour. Something must not have been so bad with me after all.

A new sharp understanding fills me, how much I owe to Mia. No wonder I've never forgotten her. No wonder I'm ready to kill or dismember Xenakis if he ever dares hurt her again.

"So now you're afraid being alone together can bring back your feelings toward her." Iris' words are not a question, but a statement.

I swallow and nod. "Just putting it into words I understand better. Maybe I'm just confusing gratitude with other feelings."

"Then, let's do something," she offers. Her eyes send me reassurance through the screen. "Give yourself a day or two to settle down. If you still need me after that, I promise I'll come."

I bob my head on automatic pilot. But inside I'm not sure I can withstand Mia's proximity for an hour—let alone three weeks.

CHAPTER 11

Mia

M Y ANCIENT GREEK ANCESTORS WERE DEFINITELY MY kind of people—they appreciated strength, brains *and* beauty. The impressive bedrock where the Acropolis rests is high enough to flaunt the gorgeous white marble temples while offering protection against attackers (2).

The morning teeters between brisk and chilly as Ezra and I climb a surprisingly challenging hill and pass the Greek theater on our way to the Acropolis (10). I've carefully re-packed the Aphrodite dress in my Louis Vuitton garment bag, which I miraculously got away with passing off as a purse—large bags are not allowed for security reasons. Ezra carries a backpack stuffed with basic photography equipment, while Trent is in charge of borrowing the rest from Quentin's team, since the AXDW events don't start until tomorrow.

We can see all of Athens from the top of the hill. From our vantage point, I inhale the sight of the Mount Lycabettus and the white chapel of St. George sitting on its top (11 a-b). Among the Acropolis ruins—close to twenty-five-hundred years old—I love the temple of Athena Nike, with its long and elegant white ionic columns (12 a-b). But my favorite building is the Erectheion, where female sculptures, the famous Caryatids, act as columns in an awesome display of feminine power (13 a-b). The sculptures seem to scream, *Hell yeah. We women have held up the roof over men for eternity—and the world knows it.*

"I'm afraid we underestimated how crowded the place would

be," Ezra comments as he unpacks his backpack, resting it on top of a column stump.

"Where the heck are Marcia and Trent?" I grumble, staring at the time on my phone. "Soon, this place will be so packed we won't be able to move, let alone shoot pictures. And I still haven't figured out where Marcia can change."

In fact, I'm grateful for these convenient worries that consume my entire attention. They ensure I have no mental space left to dwell on any lingering attraction toward Ezra.

What on earth came over me yesterday? The only thing stranger than me crying myself to sleep in Ezra's arms is the unthinkable moment that happened earlier—when I felt madly attracted to him. And what was that sudden need to revisit my relationship with my father? Today I can't shed this sense of vulnerability that opened in me last night.

We decide our backdrop will be the Parthenon—of course. Who would settle for second best when we can have the most famous Greco-Roman building in the world? (14 a-b) Ezra has set the camera on the tripod and captures photos. Later, he plans to overlap several images to airbrush people out of the takes. But a gray cloud inches toward us, and I'm already losing hope that we'll get our pictures today.

"This is not going to work," I mutter, staring at the time. "I miscalculated how early Marcia and Trent could peel their hung-over asses out of bed."

Ezra leans over the camera and peers through the lens. "Well, I'm in no hurry. I don't mind some time admiring this stunning marvel." He rotates the camera my way and snaps a picture of me, then winks. "And the Parthenon is not bad either."

My knees wobble a little at the sight of his mischievous smile and I reprimand myself. Like I don't know he's just reflex-flirting. "Very funny." I force my eyes off him and up to the sky.

Luckily, he moves the camera back and returns his attention

to the temple. "Did you know that the Parthenon's symmetry is an optical illusion?" he asks. "It's actually curved. And the columns are slightly wider in their mid portion."

"Get out of here!" Thank God my nerdy, fact-quoting Ezra is back. I relax a little and study the columns. "It looks perfectly straight!"

"And that's the point." He leaves the camera and stands next to me to appraise the building from my point of view. "The ancient Greek architects did that to balance the distortion of perspective, so the columns appeared completely straight. In a way, the architects faked perfection."

Hearing Ezra geek out about something returns the world to normal. I tilt my head to take in the Parthenon image. "Isn't that like everything in life? What we see is distorted, depending on where we stand."

His expression sobers as he nods. "And perfection is just an illusion. The closest thing to appearing perfect is being imperfect on purpose."

Frowning, I nudge his shoulder with mine. "Since when are you so deep and philosophical?"

He chuckles. "There must be something contagious about being in the birthplace of the greatest philosophers of all times. Aristotle, Socrates, Plato…"

"But tell me about faking perfection! That's a model's life story." A text from Quentin pings on my phone—speaking of fake. He says he wants to talk about his offer, but I delete the message without reading the rest. Feeling blue, I walk away and sit on a weed-covered stone step.

Ezra strolls toward me and settles a few feet away, on a stone low wall. "Are you okay?" Ezra has avoided mentioning my meltdown, but his worry shows in the eager way he studies me.

"Just a little bruised in my self-esteem. Maybe it's being surrounded by young models again." I sigh. "Not long ago I was one of them, radiating youth and sensuality… And now I'm a woman approaching her mid-thirties. By fashion world standards, I'm as ancient as the Parthenon."

"Nonsense!" he snorts. "Not one of the models we've seen comes close to being as beautiful as you."

I resist the urge to roll my eyes. "The girls and I created a monster when we taught you how to flatter a woman."

"I'm not flattering you." He uses a matter-of-fact tone. "You *are* the most beautiful woman I know—model or not."

His gaze caresses me, and heat rises inside me, as if someone has dialed up my thermostat.

"Okay, let's stop the BS." I shake myself. "I wasn't the most beautiful model even when I was younger—heck, I barely met the height criteria. I had to sweat bullets at the gym to build muscle in my flat butt—"

"It never was about your measurements," he interrupts me. "Or making your nose a millimeter shorter, or your breasts a cup size bigger. You had—" He stops, and his voice softens. "You *have* a unique beauty, an inner light people can't ignore. And we all gravitate toward you because we want more of that. More of your confidence. More of your unstoppable nature. More of your energy."

His blue eyes fix on mine paralyzing me for a moment. Waves of electricity flow from his pupils to mine, then spread through my veins like a drug.

Panic surges through me. Am I turned on—by *Ezra*? "Stop it." I squeeze my eyelids shut so I don't have to see how handsome he looks right now. "I regret having taught you all those automatic responses."

"This is not an automatic response."

"Of course you'll say that." I lift a hand, then open my eyes. I can't keep my voice from rising. "You have to stop that reflex of saying what a woman wants to hear. Your shenanigans don't work on me."

His head jerks back. Then his countenance darkens as if a veil had fallen over it. "I would never use shenanigans on you."

The gray cloud has caught up with us and now compromises the blue sky we need for our photo shoot. "I'm afraid it might rain; let's get out of here." Ezra avoids my eyes as he disassembles his workstation. His lips compress and his brows knit as he stows the camera away and folds the tripod.

Damn it, now I can't shed the worry that I might've hurt his feelings. "I'm sorry; I didn't mean to let the harpy out." I advance toward him and rest my hand on his arm. "Big Nerd, let's make a new deal."

He stops repacking the light ring to give me his attention. "Yes?"

"For the remainder of this trip, I don't want you to be my self-esteem booster. I want you to be my brutally honest judge that makes me give my best. No flattering, no sweet-talking. We can only speak the absolute truth."

He bows his head. "I can do that."

I raise my hand and crook my little finger, inviting him. "Pinky swear?"

I knew I could get him to crack up with that. His somber expression breaks as he hooks his finger with mine. "Pinky swear."

Relief washes over me as we re-create our childhood ritual. Once more, I can see him not as a silky seducer but my friend—a friend too valuable to risk losing.

The first drops of rain make us rush to finish re-packing Ezra's backpack and we take the path back to the street level.

"Mia, I think you should talk to Xenakis and negotiate his offer."

Ezra's change of subject takes me by surprise. "Why do you say that?"

"You asked for brutal honesty, and this is it." He adjusts the strap across his shoulder. "You should grab any publicity you can get. And it doesn't matter what people think of you." He throws a hand in the direction of the Parthenon behind us. "It's an optical illusion, anyway. Everyone will see what they want to see. *You* taught me we should never let others' opinions of us influence what we do."

"My indifference was fake," I admit in a reluctant mumble. "Of course I cared about what people thought of me." I glance at him with the corner of my eye. *Contrary to you.*

I had no merit for being good-looking, and therefore popular in high school; I didn't choose my genes. Yet he'd been cursed with the thick glasses, the acne, the weird allergies…I couldn't understand how he rose from bed every day and faced the bullies harassing him. He was my hero for not caring about their constant rejection.

That was why that fateful night, studying at his house, when he told me how bad he felt about being unpopular, I couldn't help it. I had to show him the part of him I saw and he didn't see.

A deep surge of nostalgia overcomes me, and for a moment I become that seventeen-year-old girl panicking because she kissed her best friend and now he's hiding from her. The girl who spent three days hoping her phone would finally ring and it would be Ezra asking her to the prom.

I immediately push the memory away.

We've arrived at the complex exit and Ezra flags down an approaching taxi. We get in just as the first drops of real rain start to fall.

CHAPTER 12

Ezra

L UCKILY, THE DRIZZLE DOESN'T LAST. BY MID-MORNING THE clouds disperse, but there's no point returning to the Parthenon, now crowded to mythical levels. Instead, we move the shooting location to the ruins of the Temple of Olympian Zeus, an impressive collection of intact fluted columns with Corinthian capitals (15 a-c).

Despite the beauty of these ruins, they soon prove the wrong place for our session. The columns are too tall to capture whole in the pictures, and the modern traffic around us limits our options for shooting. But the veto becomes final when Mia declares that the temple's yellowish hue doesn't complement the white dress as much as the ivory Parthenon did.

We re-pack our equipment and stop at a modest family restaurant for *gyros*, the traditional Greek pitas filled with meat, vegetables and feta cheese. The place offers outdoor seating, but we sit inside to avoid the chilly breeze.

Marcia and Trent continue to probe for evidence that Mia and I might be sleeping together. Today that doesn't feel funny, especially after Mia shut me down when I expressed how beautiful I've always thought she is. Thank God she did, before I said something to compromise our friendship. I must've gone delusional for a moment.

Maybe she's trying to compensate for her rejection with humor, but she's behaving like a royal pain in the ass right now. As I answer questions from Marcia and Trent about my years in game and app design, Mia rests her arms on the table and her head on her arms and pretends to snore.

I roll my eyes. "I get zero respect around here!"

She raises her head from the table and blows me a kiss. "You know I love you, Big Nerd!" She tosses her thumb my way as she addresses Marcia and Trent. "But seriously, when this guy starts talking about computer stuff, he's better than general anesthesia at putting me to sleep."

I gasp in fake offense and bump her shoulder away. "You didn't complain about that in tenth grade when you wanted me to hack the school and change your grade!"

"You hacked the school's computers?" Marcia gapes at me with veiled admiration.

"He refused! And I still haven't forgiven him for it!" Mia gives me a playful punch in the arm.

Trent rubs his jaw with narrowed eyes. "So, Mia…you hold decade-old grudges against him and you annoy the hell out of each other." He raises one eyebrow, then deadpans, "And you're absolutely sure you're not a couple?"

My phone ringing interrupts us. A glance at the screen shows Walter Tolstoy is calling. Oh shit.

"Excuse me, guys." I wave my credit card at the waiter and signal him that I'll cover the check. Then, I rise from the table and head toward the exit. "Walter, I'm so sorry."

"What the hell, Cohen? Don't you answer your email anymore? You were supposed to call me last night."

I step out of the restaurant to a narrow street that's almost a dead-end alley. What can I answer? That last night I fell asleep with a goddess crying in my arms? "I'm sorry. Between the time difference and how busy I've been here…"

"Listen, this offer is time sensitive. We have a huge campaign we need to launch next month."

A twinge of scruple pulls inside me. "I may need some guarantees that you won't be using this software in unethical ways."

"You're the freaking moral police now or something?" He snorts. "You sell it, you kiss control goodbye."

The twinge grows into a whole-body tingle. "I'll finish reading your offer tonight and will call you tomorrow." I disconnect the call and ponder for a moment. How much damage could this program do in the wrong hands?

"Okay, what are you up to?"

Mia's voice pulls me out of my musings. She stands next to the restaurant entrance with arms crossed.

"What are you talking about?" I stow my phone in my jacket pocket.

She paces in my direction. "I know that face. It's the face you had after stealing cupcakes behind your mother's back." She stands in front of me. "I repeat. What are you up to?"

Hanging around someone who has x-ray vision for my thoughts is tricky. "Nothing. That's just the guy who's buying *Squiggles* from me."

She scrutinizes me. "Honestly I've never understood how you make money with that app. The free version gives so much, almost nobody gets the paid one. And no one ever watches the ads—you just have to ex them out. Why are people offering you millions of dollars for it?"

"Remember that time you asked me to send the gaslighting virus to our math teacher and then made me swear silence?" I wrap my arm around her shoulders and stroll back to the restaurant. "Well, today I'm cashing my silence card."

Her eyes enlarge. "Oh! Is it *that* juicy? Now I need to know."

"Sorry, too late," I chuckle. "My silence card is already cashed."

We arrive at the table and I focus on paying the check, to stop the conversation.

"So…" As we walk out of the restaurant, Marcia grins so wide I can see her back teeth. "What do you guys plan to do the rest of the day?" Despite the plural, her eyes stay fixed on me.

I can't help it; she just gave me a look longer than two seconds, so I have to smile back.

Before I can answer, Mia steps between us. "Actually, Ezra and I have some places to check out for photo sessions, you're free for the rest of the day." She hooks her arm through mine and drags me away. My pulse quickens. The pressed-together lips, the flaring nostrils, the darkened eyes. If my facial scanning skills still function, this means one thing.

Is Mia *jealous*?

We catch a taxi to return to the hotel. After the car drives off, Mia elbows me. "Were you seriously flirting with Marcia, my employee? Are you trying to make things awkward between us forever if you two hooked up?"

"I didn't mean to. It's automatic gratitude flirting." I wince in apology. "You know me. I still can't believe it when a woman gives me attention."

She frowns, arms folded, and tilts her head. "In summary, you have a low bar."

Melancholy surges in me. *Of course you would settle for anything,* Ezzie whispers inside me. *Because the woman you really want is off limits.*

But is she *really* off limits?

My brain circuits light up with hundreds of potential hypotheses. Has Mia taken me for granted? Does she need me to rattle her a little? Why does it seem like the worse I behave, the more attention she gives me? Is Chloe right, and Mia can only feel attraction to jerks?

Let's test that last hypothesis.

I rub my stubble. "Do you want the politically correct answer or the shenanigan-free one?"

"The real one, of course."

I give Mia my best version of a rascal's smirk. "Yes, I have a terribly low bar. I would sleep with ninety-seven percent of the women I meet."

My answer has the intended effect and Mia huffs and groans in indignation. "Sleaze!"

But the chemistry between us spikes. There are seventeen signs of arousal in a woman, and Mia currently shows at least half of them. My pulse speeds up.

As we arrive at our hotel room. Mia studies me with a new intensity. "So, you're serious that you never plan to settle down."

Can she see through my act? I turn my eyes away from her and empty my backpack. "Oh, I most likely will someday—Mom will kill me if I don't give her grandchildren." I plug my camera into the charging station. "But I have no delusion that it will be anything special. I'll just pick a woman who's nice enough and good in bed."

Next to me, she pokes my side, reclaiming my attention. "That's the least romantic thing I've ever heard."

I shrug and go for at least some truth. "I'm a computer geek who's made a living with logical algorithms. I've never understood the need to fabricate a different type of love to call it romantic feelings. In life you have women you like, and love, and admire—your friends—and you also have women you'd like to screw. If you're lucky, you may find one who's both things at once." *Like you.* "The end."

She bites her lower lip. "Well, can you keep a secret?"

"I already have enough dirt on you to blackmail you for life, so go ahead," I joke, setting the empty backpack on the bed.

There it is again. Her face the day she asked for my help running away—flushed cheeks, enlarged eyes, sucked in lips. "I've always felt obligated to play devil's advocate when the girls talk about finding a soulmate. But lately I've seen how happy Sophia is with Trevor, and the way Chloe's glowing since Max entered her life…" She hesitates before concluding, "I want that."

I never would've guessed in a million years. "I thought you didn't believe in all that…fairytale stuff."

"Maybe by taking the other side you've allowed me to ask myself what I really want." She pauses. "And I do want to be swept off my feet in love."

I don't answer and I don't move. I barely dare to breathe, not to break this moment of confessions. Corralled between my bed, my charging station and a wall, I'm more aware than ever of her proximity.

"I want what Chloe and Sophia found," she continues. "I want a man I'm passionately attracted to, but also respect. I want a man who blows me away in all aspects—physically, mentally and spiritually."

My mouth tingles with a hunger to taste hers. What would happen if I kissed her right now? If I guided her to my bed and showed her I can be that man she wants? That man who could blow her mind with passion, yet still treasure her and cherish her?

"That's why the self-vow makes sense to me right now," she resumes talking. "It's teaching me to raise my bar and refuse to accept less than I deserve."

Oh. The celibacy vow.

I release the breath I've been holding and every ounce of wishful thinking leaves me with it.

"And you deserve the best, Princess." I give her arm a gentle squeeze and step away from her tempting scent.

I guess that's my answer. I'd better stow my hunger. I'd better remember that the best gift of love I can offer Mia is to keep my hands off her.

CHAPTER 13

Mia

MAYBE IT'S TRUE THAT THE GODS OF OLYMPUS—temperamental brats who take pleasure in torturing mortals—live around here. Or perhaps, seeing Ezra flirt with Marcia made something snap in my brain. The fact is that the last two nights I've turned in bed for hours, fighting a gravitational pull to Ezra's bed. I've yearned to cross the few steps separating us, sneak under his blankets without waking him up and enjoy his warm, hard body next to mine. Though the *other* longings I've had would require me to rouse him.

Thank God for the celibacy vow that gives me purpose. I cling to it like the last lipstick in Sephora after my favorite shade is discontinued. And thank goodness for the inaugural events that keep me entertained all day. AXDW is more than a series of fashion shows; it's a festival that includes music concerts, photography exhibitions, charity galas…. Here I feel like I found a sample sale on payday.

The New Designers Awards begin the second morning. I have no desire to attend them since I won't be competing. Instead, we transport our mini-crew to the Agora for another attempt at photographing the Aphrodite dress.

Ezra calls the Agora "the original social media." It used to be Athens' public market nearly two thousand years ago. Like *Facebook* or an *Instagram* newsfeed, it was both a sales place and the social center of the city, where you'd go to find friends and catch up with news. Also there, the famous philosophers—the original influencers—would share wisdom with their followers.

Little remains of the buildings that formed the Agora—the *stoae*. But in the early twentieth century, the American magnate Rockefeller invested a big chunk of change into building a replica of one of them, The Stoa of Attalos (16 a-b). The harmonic complex of dozens of white Doric columns surrounding an open hall is, in theory, the perfect place for the Aphrodite dress. However, at the end of a daylong shoot, I don't like what I see in the digital images.

While Trent arranges for the truck to pick up our borrowed equipment, Marcia uses the museum restroom to carefully remove and repack the Aphrodite dress. Meanwhile, Ezra and I disassemble the set and he FaceTimes ruins-lovers Max and Chloe, who are dying to be here with us.

I bring Chloe up to date on the events of the past days. "Now Quentin keeps sending me messages, asking to meet with me to 'discuss other options for his fashion show.'" I fold a lightbox.

"And I'm convinced that's an excuse to get Mia alone." Ezra points the phone toward an authentic ionic column on display to show it to Chloe (17). "But I say we should go talk to him and try to negotiate a better deal."

"But I refuse!" I chime in. "I don't want to owe Quentin any more favors."

"I agree with Ezra," Chloe replies. "In this instance, accepting a favor from Mr. X might be a charity act and help him neutralize his bad karma. Besides, you don't want to have to call this trip a waste of time, do you?"

"I give up!" I sigh, accepting the phone back from Ezra. "If I can just take decent photos of my dress among the ruins, I'll be satisfied."

"Didn't you get the pictures you wanted?" Chloe asks.

"There's something I don't like." I set the phone down on a stone relief and retrieve the camera to review the pictures on the tiny LCD screen. "This building looks too fake."

Ezra disassembles the fan we were using to create wind. "Of course it's fake, it's a reconstruction."

"But the whole point of taking these pictures was to show the authentic ruins in the background."

He studies the photos over my shoulder and his warm breath near my ear sends goose bumps down my neck. I truly annoy myself right now.

Maxwell's bass voice sounds on the phone, "For striking ruins, you should check out the Hephaestus temple, nearby. You can see it from the Agora."

"Wait. Hae-phes-what? How do you spell that?" Ezra reaches from an iPad in his backpack on the floor.

"Hephaestus. H-e-p-h…"

Ezra runs a search and soon is immersed in something on his screen. When that guy gets into his electronics, he's unreachable.

I wrap up the conversation so Max and Chloe can go to work—while it's afternoon here, they're just beginning their morning in Chicago. When I approach Ezra to return his phone, he's still glued to his iPad.

"Did you find out where that temple is?"

"Not yet. I got sidetracked by the fascinating story of the god Hephaestus. Listen to this!" Ezra seems transformed into an energetic kid. "Hephaestus was the ugliest god in Olympus: lame, gruff and unpopular."

I strap the camera on. "Oh, in summary, he was *you* in high school!"

My intention was to tease him to make him mad, but Ezra agrees with enthusiasm. "Exactly! But listen to the best part! He manages to scheme and leverage his way into marrying the super-hot *Aphrodite*!"

"What?" That doesn't make sense. My awesome goddess who is the inspiration for my dress? My heroine married so low?

"Yes! This is the perfect underdog story for every man who

dreams of scoring a goddess out of his league!" Ezra is blinking a thousand times a minute.

I peek over his shoulder to read the iPad screen. "And…she eventually cheated on him a million times."

"Wait! Don't ruin this moment!" He raises a hand. "Can you imagine how happy that must've made Hephaestus? Can you imagine spending eternity as an ugly minor deity nobody likes—and then have such a goddess accept you?"

Gloating pleasure fills me. "Aha!" I snap my fingers. "You just contradicted your low bar theory! You admit that scoring a 'goddess,' the woman who steals your breath away, would be much better than settling for just anyone."

He freezes, and his expression shows more guilt than surprise. "Perhaps…possibly?" He averts eye contact and repacks the iPad. "Let's find that temple. Mythology stories are stupid anyway."

"Well, great session, guys!" Marcia returns from the restroom and hands me the dress in the garment bag. "Should we go?"

She's shooting Ezra appreciative looks again, so I step forward to block him from her view. "Actually, I have some website related work I have to discuss with Ezra."

"Oh well, if you're not planning to return to the hotel yet, then you can take care of this." Trent hands me a clipboard. "The truck driver should be here any minute to come pick up this equipment." Without waiting for my answer, he hooks Marcia's arm and guides her to the road. They throw glances at us over their shoulders and, between giggles, I catch a few words from Trent. "Childhood friends—yeah right."

"Oh great. Now we're stuck here until that truck shows up?" I set the binder and the garment bag next to the folded light boxes.

"That's okay. Let's keep looking for the Hephaestus temple."

While keeping an eye on our equipment, we stroll around the long open building, flanked by columns instead of walls.

"Mythology stories are not stupid!" I resume the conversation Marcia and Trent interrupted.

"Yes, they are." He paces while scanning the horizon. "Titans devouring their own children? People turning into bulls, and cows, and geese? Neurotic gods and goddesses behaving worse than reality TV stars?"

"It's all metaphorical." I search the landscape around us, surprisingly green for the fall. "Every god or goddess represents an archetype—a recurrent symbol in literature and psychology. A recycled energy in history."

He returns his eyes to me. "I studied archetypes for videogame creation: there's always a hero, and a villain, and a wise man, and a character who's the comic relief…"

I nod. "Athena, the patron goddess of this city symbolized intellect and strategy. When the ancient Greeks invoked her, they tapped into that part of themselves." I reach for a different example. "Ares the god of war, represented our anger, that warrior inside all of us we could invoke as needed. See? We're all made of many different parts and subpersonalities."

"I've always said that!" His narrowed eyes show deep interest. "Like we have many different software programs we can access. Or different operating systems we can call upon."

"You got it!" I'm so proud of my Big Nerd for finally getting a metaphor. I hold the camera, strapped to my neck, and review the pictures. "And that's why it's so important for me to do justice to Aphrodite. She represents the free woman who's unapologetic about her passion. The woman who's strong and doesn't need a man to protect her—but refuses to resign her femininity."

"Being feminine can be a woman's biggest strength." He reflects on my words. "You've never disarmed me more than in the past few days, when you've showed me that vulnerable side you always keep hidden."

His gaze seems to grasp me, keeping me rooted in place. There it is again. That weird optical phenomenon where his features re-arrange, making him look more handsome than I ever noticed before. The temperature inside me rises.

A gasp from Ezra interrupts the moment. "Mia, look at that!"

I turn and follow the direction he indicates and my breath hitches. Among the greenery peeks a gorgeous, nearly intact marble temple. If love at first sight exists, this is it (18). "Yes!" I nearly scream. "That's where I want my Aphrodite dress photographed!"

CHAPTER 14

Mia

E ZRA RECLAIMS THE CAMERA AND USES IT TO CHECK THE building in close up. "It's perfect! It's smaller than the Parthenon so we can get it all in one shot. And it's even better preserved (19 a-b)."

"And it's *real*! It's not a reconstruction!" My voice rises to an excited shriek.

"We can get pictures from a distance. It's surrounded by nature instead of traffic!" Ezra's breathing speeds up.

I jump up and down, clapping. "And the marble tone goes so well with the dress. I love it! I love it!"

He puts down the camera. "If we start right now, we can get the natural sunlight and then catch the golden hour right before the sunset. The photos would be spectacular!"

A horn blowing gets our attention; the pick-up truck driver waves at us from the street. While Ezra heads to talk to him, I retrieve my phone from my pocket with trembling hands and search for Marcia's number. Wait, didn't Trent say they'd set their phones to airplane mode to avoid roaming charges?

Desperate, I send voicemails and texts asking Marcia and Trent to come back. "Agh! They're not answering!"

Ezra's using Google translate on his phone to communicate with the truck driver, but by their serious faces I suspect the news isn't good. "What's going on?" I ask, approaching them.

"The driver can't take us much closer to the temple; most of these roads are pedestrian or have restricted access." Ezra fills me in. "He says our best bet is to get there on foot."

"On foot?" I glance at the temple, which seems quite distant from here, then at the pile of equipment still lying on the Stoa floor. Dread fills me. "We won't be able to set up all this before we lose the light!"

"My GPS says it's closer than it seems. We can do this!" Ezra straps the camera to his back and grabs a fan and a folded light box. "Bring the dress and the bag with the hair and makeup stuff; I'll run back for the rest."

I hang both bags on one shoulder to free my hands while quietly reciting some of my Greek-Orthodox childhood prayers. As I grab more equipment to carry, I invoke my Greek ancestors—even the gods of Olympus. If we can't pull this off, I'll be devastated.

"You're American, aren't you?" A petite brunette with a pixie haircut approaches me while I try to juggle a camera tripod and another lightbox. "My husband and I are travel video-bloggers and have been watching you for a while, admiring your equipment. Is there anything we can help you with?"

"Yes!" God bless them! "We need to carry all this equipment to the Hephaestus temple for a photo session before we lose the light."

"Okay! Hey, Love!" she calls out.

A man as big as a football quarterback approaches and hugs the tiny stranger from the back. "What's up, Babe?"

She addresses me. "This is my husband, Luke. I'm Chrissie."

"I'm Mia." I shake their hands, then point at Ezra who's already on his way to the temple. "And that's my friend Ezra. We could really use your help."

It turns out prayers do work! Luke and Chrissie help me bring the rest of the equipment in one quick trip across dusty ancient roads and tall grass. With Luke's help, Ezra rearranges our set in record time. Meanwhile, Chrissie walks with me around the temple, offering some wise input about the best places to shoot. Wow! This team is better than Marcia and Trent.

Who, by the way, are still not answering. I've sent them messages through all social media available, but they're unlikely to see them until they reconnect to Wi-Fi.

"This is a lost cause!" I return my phone to my pocket. "We have the perfect location, but this is useless without a model!"

"*You* be the model!"

Ezra's words blow me away and I have to take a step back. "That's ridiculous! I'm not a model anymore!"

"Of course you are! Just look at you!" Chrissie waves a hand around me.

Ezra holds my shoulders. "Mia, this is a once in a lifetime opportunity. What are the chances of us getting all this equipment again tomorrow and catching the light like this?" His gaze supplicates and infuses me with reassurance as he hands me the garment bag. "Come on, Princess! Put it on."

This is insane. But we're a team now, and we didn't come this far to fail at the last minute. I'm officially the emergency replacement model.

"I'll help you!" Chrissie gestures me to follow her. "I saw a niche on the side of the temple where you can change!" (20)

With Chrissie's help, I retouch my makeup, tie my hair up in a lose bun and then change into the goddess dress. Thank God this outfit is designed to flow like a Greek tunic and fits me despite the way my body has filled out since my modeling days. It's surprisingly comfortable and stretches to accommodate me. I pick up my skirt as high as I can, to prevent the hem from touching the ground. Followed by Chrissie with the bags, I return to our improvised set. I step on the canvas rug on the ground and let my hem fall.

Standing behind the camera on its tripod, Ezra gasps and

presses a hand against his mouth. He's mute for a moment. "You're stunning!"

"You'd better get started now that the place isn't crowded," Chrissie urges us. "Some buskers are performing at the Agora and most tourists have gathered there!"

She's right. Only a handful of tourists walk around us.

"And I can help you get rid of the rest." Without preamble, Luke paces around the temple, clapping and summoning the people. "Okay, everybody. Come with me. We need this place just for a few minutes."

"Come on, everyone!" Chrissie follows him, addressing them in a singsong voice. "We appreciate your cooperation!"

I can't believe this. Without questioning Luke and Chrissie's authority, the tourists are moving away, leaving us the place all for ourselves.

Ezra starts snapping pictures before I've psyched myself up for the job. Soon, however, the sense of urgency nudges me into model mode.

This sequence of small miracles worked. For the next hour or so every picture promises to be better than the previous one, as the natural light evolves to golden, then to pinkish red. Ezra takes pictures from afar, from up close. From above. From below. And every time he clicks the shutter, he caresses me with his words. "You're breathtaking. God, you're beautiful! You're the sexiest goddess I've ever seen."

It's been so long since I've been this side of the camera, I have to remind myself that Ezra doesn't mean those words. Like any good photographer, he's just flattering his model to make her glow. If you're not careful, the artificial bond can end up feeling real.

"Give me a smile now, gorgeous!" Ezra drops himself on the canvas mat on the floor to capture me from a lower level. "Now look into the distance. You're standing on top of Olympus and all mortals invoke you. Excellent!" He springs from the floor and comes closer, constantly snapping pictures. "Now give me softness. Give me vulnerability. Aphrodite drank her own love potion. She's fallen hopelessly in love with a mortal and yearns for him."

The atmosphere arounds us sizzles and something surreal is happening. As if I were trapped in a science fiction movie, I'm flashing in and out of parallel realities. At moments, I'm back in the time when I was a model, fighting to survive in a world of wolves. I sense glimpses of the old me: the drinker, the smoker, the young woman hooked on amphetamines to lose weight. And she desperately wants this man in front of her to like her.

But at other times a different woman emerges. She's a new me, a powerful goddess who's found her strength and doesn't need anyone's approval to rise.

And that woman is also ready to jump this hot photographer.

Ezra's eyes entice me, loaded with desire. He brushes the hair off my forehead, readjusts my chin, changes the strap on my shoulder. And every time his fingers feather me, this hunger for touch I've been suppressing for a year roars inside me. I want him to keep stroking me. I want to get him in that niche where I changed, rip his clothes off and beg him to ravish me.

Ezra has forgotten about the dress. He's shooting close up of my face. We're so close to each other his hot breath wraps me. I want to drink that breath.

By the time we lose the last of the light and he lowers the camera, we're panting as if we've run for our lives for hours.

"Wow!" he says. "I think we got it!"

"Yes," I whisper. I get lost for a moment in his blue eyes.

And in a blink, we're kissing.

I mean, *for real*. Open mouth, closed eyes, lips sliding... whole-body kissing. We're practically climbing onto each other.

I should've known that the awkward kisser I remember has had sixteen years to polish his technique—but it's beyond that. This man knows what he's doing. He sucks at my lips, explores my mouth, teases me with his tongue with expertise… And I have no idea what he did with the camera but he makes exquisite use of both hands as he holds me tight against him. One holds the back of my head, locking our mouths; the other wraps around my torso, crushing our bodies together and setting mine on fire.

His contagious passion fills me with desperation. One of my hands caresses his hair while the other indulges in appraising those splendid muscles I've just recently discovered. From his arm, to his back, to that glorious, firm behind.

CHAPTER 15

Ezra

I HAVE NO IDEA HOW THIS STARTED, BUT I'M KISSING MIA. AND the most amazing part is that she's kissing me back. And did I say I was *eighty* percent over her? I must've made a gross miscalculation, because the numbers keep falling—fast.

Her honey and rose scent envelops me as I sample her lips again and again. She tastes so different, yet so similar to my memories. In flashes, I become Ezzie. I'm a seventeen-year-old kissing the girl of his dreams, uncertain of what he did to deserve the privilege, but exploding in gratitude all the same. However, the rest of the time it's me. The adult me, who's burning with desire and would give everything to guide her by the hand to the forest around us and take her right here, in the tall grass.

Through the slit in her dress, I run my hand over her incredibly silky thigh and she wraps it around me. I kiss her lips, her delicate chin, trace the soft edge of her jaw to behind her ear and relish her shuddering pleasure. Then my lips find their way back to her mouth.

We end the kiss at last, but remain holding each other, panting. As the realization of what just happened dawns on me, my jaw drops. Mia's wide golden eyes also speak of shock, but neither of us moves to release the embrace.

The sound of throat clearing brings me back to reality. "I was about to say that photographic session had so much spark, it was like watching you guys do it." In my stupor, it takes me a few moments to recognize Trent's voice.

Mia and I spring away from each other as two kids caught red-handed. When did Trent get here?

Trent keeps staring at Mia and me by turns. "Uh…the couple helping you had to run; they sent their best wishes on the project." He picks up the closest light box. "Now… after this *successful* session, let's go return the equipment." He spins on his heels and heads to the complex exit. Before he gets out of earshot some mumbled, chuckling words reach me. "Childhood friends my ass."

My brain turned into a cloud of vapor, I help disassemble our improvised shoot station while Mia changes back into her clothes.

After the equipment truck is on its way, Mia and I ride a taxi back to the hotel in complete silence. We still haven't said a word by the time we enter the hotel room. Grave-like quiet, we unpack our things; Mia re-hangs the Aphrodite dress and I set my electronics to charge. Just to kill some time, I re-awaken all my charging devices to check their battery levels.

Arms crossed, Mia eases down onto the edge of her bed. I find my way to the other bed, in front of her, and copy her posture. "Now…are we going to talk about what happened?"

She flushes and flutters her eyelashes. "And what exactly happened?"

Ezzie quivers inside me. I scratch the back of my head, avoiding her eyes. "You tell me."

"No, you tell me." She leans back.

I sink in the bed. "No, you tell *me*."

"No, *you* tell me." She tightens her self-embrace.

Damn it. I can never win an argument against Mia. "Well…" I read her features as I venture. "Maybe we just kissed because …"

Because ever since that night we kissed at age seventeen I can't let go of this dream of making you mine someday? Because long before that, since we were kids, you were everything I ever wanted?

117

This is the moment Ian warned me about. I'm taking the jump. I'm about to find out if we're all the way in or all the way out.

A strident legion of electronic devices burst out ringing at once. Mia startles, then releases a long breath and closes her eyes, as if relieved. "Your phone is ringing,"

She seems to need some time to gather her thoughts so I scramble to the other side of my bed where two computers, an iPad and a cell phone all shout deafening ringtones at once. I debate how to shut the hell out of them when the name on the incoming FaceTime call hits me. It's Walter.

"Oh shit." I take the call on the closest device, my gaming laptop. "I'm sorry. I was about to call you." In a sharper moment, I would've answered the phone and not the laptop and would've stepped out of the room for privacy. Now in my mental haze I'm having trouble figuring out how to transfer the call to my phone.

"Cohen, are you playing games with me?" His frown darkens his usually pristine complexion. "Tell me the truth, did Roger offer you more?"

"I'm not dealing with your competition, Walter." The fact that I didn't seize on his question to bargain on my price is testimony to how frazzled I am right now.

"Four million dollars is a very generous offer, Cohen. Don't play with my patience. Don't tempt me to make a few calls and start talking about your *real* business."

"Oh, come on! Cut the act." I roll my eyes. "You have more dirt to hide than me." Shoot. The impulse to deflect his threat made me forget for a moment that Mia is within earshot. "Walter, this is not the best moment to talk. I'll have to call you back."

I disconnect the call and brace myself for Mia's confrontation.

Eyes huge, mouth open, Mia stares at me. "Ezra what does that guy have on you?"

I take a second to gather myself, reconnecting the computer. Then slowly turn around. "Mia, it's nothing."

She springs from the bed and steps toward me. "I've enjoyed our banter, when I tease you about being a nerd and you tease me about being a dumb airhead model. But I am *not* stupid." She plants herself in front of me. "Ezra, what's going on?"

This is not what I would like to talk about. My hormones haven't leveled out yet and all I want is to resume the conversation the call interrupted. But I know Mia. Evading an answer would be like fighting a tornado—a volcano, a hurricane. Maybe all at once. I have to give her something; at least the less scary half.

Resigned, I signal her to take the only chair in the room and sit on the edge of my bed. "Remember when you said you couldn't understand how I make money with *Squiggles*?"

She ignores the chair and remains standing. "I can't fathom who would buy ads from you when no one has to watch them."

"The ads you ex-out are not what's important." Here I go. "The advertisement is happening constantly, in the way of subliminal messages embedded into the game's music and graphics."

Mia gapes at me. "*Subliminal messages*?" Her eyelashes flutter as she processes the news. "So, *Squiggles* is a brainwasher? The most addictive game app in America is a tool to hypnotize people to go buy or do stuff?"

I shift, uncomfortable. "The advertising industry has been doing it for ages."

"Why are they so interested in your app then?" She crosses her arms.

"*Squiggles* runs on *Cupcakes*, a next-generation cookie software I patented—"

She signals me to stop. "In English, please."

I pick lint off my jeans, avoiding eye contact. "*Squiggles* keeps track of everything you do. It records shopping habits, social media likes, websites visited." My voice trails off. "Even keywords used in email and text."

"You spy on your users?" Color drains from Mia's face, then

119

she slowly eases down onto the chair. She covers her mouth with a hand. "Ezra, didn't you learn your lesson at Stanford, when your hacker friend ended up in jail? You promised you wouldn't get involved in shady computer business again!"

"This is not the same." I raise a hand. "This is just a more sophisticated version of what social media and websites are doing all over the world. Managing cookies and storing information about your preferences and likes." A tiny scruple tugs my insides. It's much more than *just* that.

"So, *you* tell me." She frowns at me. "What makes it different and 'more sophisticated'? Why are they offering you four million dollars for it?"

I hesitate. "My program tailors the subliminal messages for each user based on their core identity and deepest longings."

She gapes at me in silence for a few heartbeats. "And how are you able to figure out their core identity and deepest longings?"

Okay, here I go. "The app transfers the data to my server where my AI uses algorithms based on the person's online activity to estimate their deeper emotions, fears and dreams."

"Oh shoot." She rakes her hands over her scalp. A sign of deep upset, as Mia would never risk messing up her hairstyle. "So basically, you made a fortune exploiting what the girls and I taught you? How to read people's cues and understand what others think and feel?"

Pretty much. I look up to the ceiling. "Mia, you're making a bigger deal of this than necessary. This is not that much different than what social media platforms do."

Mia rises from her chair and places her hands on her hips. Her tone reminds me of a stern schoolteacher. "So, if everyone else is doing it, it's okay?" She's copying my own words when I used to reprimand her about underage drinking in high school.

I'm speechless for a moment. "It's all spelled out in the user agreement. People sign it and give me permission every time they download the app."

"The fact that it's legal doesn't mean it's right, does it?"

And that was *my* reply whenever she claimed nicotine was legal.

I groan. "Mia, you're going to need to step aside and let me handle my business."

"But Ezra!" she protests. "This is not you! You've always been my example of character and honesty."

"Well, maybe you don't know me!" I snap.

She startles at my rising tone.

"Maybe you still see me as the twelve-year-old you first met. But sooner or later you'll have to admit that…You. Don't. Freaking. Know me anymore!"

Dead silence falls between us as we lock eyes for a small eternity.

I can't believe I just raised my voice at Mia. I grab my cell from the charging station and the room card from the nightstand. "I'm sorry. I need some time to think." I rush out, afraid to see the recrimination in her eyes.

* * *

I've spent the past two hours in a coffee shop, calling other potential buyers for *Squiggles*, exploring offers that I had originally rejected. But I admit I'm also dragging my feet about returning to the hotel room. Maybe if I wait long enough, Mia will be asleep and I won't have to confront her.

And now, as the day sinks in, I'm venting to Ian over FaceTime.

"I ruined it, Ian. I did the two most stupid things I could've done on this trip. First, I kissed Mia before figuring out what's really going on between us, and now I can't think clearly. And then

I yelled at her and exposed the shittiest part of me. Now she'll never respect me. This is a disaster!"

"First of all, stop talking like you're in the middle of a tragedy, when all you're facing is a minor inconvenience." Ian moves closer to the camera. "Do you even know what a *real* disaster is? It's living in a filthy *favela*, watching hungry, barefoot, half-naked children around you waste their lives."

Ouch. Ian always knows how to slap me back into perspective.

"Don't lose track of what you went there to achieve," he continues. "You're not there figuring out what *she* feels for *you*. You're there figuring out what *you* want. Are you over her—yes or no?"

"*Mostly*." I fib. I'd say I'm fifty one percent over her, forty-nine percent *smitten*. Or is it the other way around? It's too close to call right now.

It's difficult to figure out what I want when half-a-dozen different Ezras inside me contradict each other—competing operating systems and software programs. One is dying to return to the hotel room and silence Mia with kisses. Another is terrified of losing her friendship and the girls' and refuses to act. Another just wants to get her in bed and figure things out later. There's the real me, completely lost, and of course, there's Ezzie—the reason I came on this trip.

"I just want to put Ezzie to rest forever. To make sure any decisions I make from now on come from the grownup part of me."

I'm not sure I'm making any sense, but Ian seems to follow. "And what does Ezzie need for closure? What's he thinking?"

The answer emerges so loud and clear, I surprise myself. "Ezzie is happy to have kissed Mia one more time. He's glad he had a chance to show her he's not the clueless case she once knew."

Hope fills me. Perhaps our kiss is not a setback, but progress in my plan to free myself from this infatuation.

"And what else?"

It feels weird talking about myself in third person. But it's

MEET ME IN GREECE

working. "Well, Ezzie has always been indebted to Mia for having kissed him. She only did it to help him gain confidence, and her kiss turned out to be life-changing." A hundred warm memories fill me. Dang it, Ian should consider becoming a counselor or something. "The whole point of coming on this trip was to pay her back and settle that debt. Maybe there's a way I can still do that. Even if that involves confronting one of my biggest fears."

An idea solidifies in my brain. I wrap up the conversation and end the call. My hands tremble and my eyes blink in excess as I search my contacts for Paul's number. He answers on the first ring.

"Hello, Cohen? Are you calling on behalf of Mia?"

"No, Paul, I need an audience with your boss." I draw in a lungful. "I have a business proposal for him."

CHAPTER 16

Mia

"I FEEL LIKE I'VE STEPPED INTO A PARALLEL DIMENSION."

In my hotel room, I video-chat with Iris, Chloe and Sophia, trying to put my thoughts in order at the end of the day.

"I still can't understand what happened in that photo session. I was ready to drag Ezra to the closest private place I could find, rip his clothes off and—"

"Okay, we get it!" Sophia squeezes her eyes shut and waves a hand.

On the screen, Iris seems suspiciously serious. "So, you and Ezra still haven't talked about that kiss, huh?"

With the phone propped on the nightstand, I use facial towelettes to remove my makeup at the armoire mirror. "We haven't talked since yesterday. He came back to the room very late and left quite early." I omit that I pretended to be asleep when he arrived, not ready to resume either of our two pending conversations. "He texted me an apology for raising his voice and said he had some errands to run. Then I spent the whole day at the fashion shows and didn't run into him."

I should be ecstatic; the third day of AXD was just as exhilarating as the first one. I attended fashion events as diverse as a black-light display of fluorescent color athleisure—leggings and ultra-cropped tops—followed by a show flaunting the most glamorous eveningwear and bridal dresses. Yet Ezra's kiss keeps returning to my thoughts, monopolizing them.

A huge crowd packed the last show I attended—handcrafted men's suits. Several men in the audience kept shooting me flirty grins, but I didn't care to smile back out of courtesy. I should've at least admired the striking physiques of the male models—most of them as gay as humanly possible, but also gorgeous. But their perfect features only deepened this terrible hunger for that one guy with uneven blue eyes who kissed me in front of the Hephaestus temple.

I haven't even bothered to read the messages Quentin keeps sending me about his fashion show.

"I could almost justify the kiss as a mutual impulse." I set down the towelette. "We were practicing art together. We were combining my passion for design and Ezra's passion for photography. An intense bond can happen temporarily between people sharing a moment of success like that. But I can't understand why I still can't shed it!"

The image of Ezra's face when I confronted him about his call flashes in my mind, and arousal washes over me. This attraction to that new dark side of him must be another instance of my tendency to fall for bad boys.

But for goodness sake this is *Ezra*! The friend I'd never forgive myself if I lose again.

On the screen Chloe gives me a knowing half-smirk. "Maybe you do like Ezra after all."

I focus on removing my eye shadow. "That makes no sense. I told you, in my mind Ezra will always be the awkward pre-teen I met in seventh grade, obsessed with videogames and monkeys." Perhaps if I keep saying that, I'll believe it.

"Well, maybe this is just the result of you being alone for so long." Iris takes the conciliatory side. "You've mentioned that this celibacy vow is a personal record."

"That's it! The vow explains it!" Hope sparks inside me. "I've been depriving myself of sex for way too long. And now I'm back in my former world of modeling, and the old me is coming back." I'd rather cling to this theory than consider I might be lusting over my friend.

Somewhat relieved, I carry the cell phone to the restroom. "Of course this isn't about *Ezra*. This is about the floozy inside me, who couldn't keep her clothes on if her life depended on it." I prop the phone against the bathroom mirror and tie up my hair to rinse my face at the sink. "And I just need to push her back with meditation and mineral water…the same way I'd crowd out a temptation for cheesecake with damn Brussels sprouts and organic kale." I dry myself with a towel, then I whimper and drop my head in my arms on the sink edge. "Who am I kidding. I hate this vow! I'm so ready for sex again!"

Sophia and Chloe, who already renounced their vows, say nothing. Iris intervenes. "It's only one more month; you can do this."

"No, I can't," I grumble. "You guys could do it because you were practically nuns to begin with! But not *me*!" I lift my head. "I'm a reformed slut."

"You're doing a great job," Iris reassures me.

"Please girls, help me get back on track," I beg. "At another time in my life, if I were obsessing about a guy who was off limits, I'd just go find a distraction. I'd head to a club and pick up the first good-looking guy I found. But with this vow I can't even do that! Can I?" Not that any of the hundreds of men I saw today interested me.

"I usually let people interpret my book the way that speaks to them." Iris enunciates slowly. "But I'd say that hooking up with a random guy is the *opposite* of what the vow is about. The vow is meant to slow us down, to raise our standards. To make us only consider sleeping with someone worth committing to."

I groan as I carry the phone out of the bathroom. "But that's a catch-twenty-two for me, I don't open up easily. It takes me a long time getting to know a man before I decide to commit to him. And I can't tell if a man's worth investing time in until I confirm we're compatible in bed."

"I'm sorry. I never said the concept of the vow was perfect." Iris gives an apologetic shrug.

"The bottom line of the self-vow is *love*," Chloe chimes in. "That trumps all the rules. And getting to love someone doesn't have to take that long. When Max and I—"

"Wait a minute." I perk up as I sit back in bed. "Chloe, did you just say that love trumps the rules? Sleeping with someone you love is not considered breaking the vow?"

Chloe nods. "That's the main escape clause in the self-vow."

"Yes," Sophia seconds. "The vow ends automatically if you find someone you love for real and want to keep in your life."

And I do love my Big Nerd, Ezra.

It hits me so hard that I almost slide off the mattress. Of course I love Ezra. And he loves me. If I go to bed with him, I'm not *technically* breaking the vow.

Have I been blind to a solution right in front of me?

I shake myself. That's crazy. That's preposterous.

Is it?

The clicking of the door unlocking announces Ezra is back and I rush to say goodbye and disconnect the call with the girls.

I brace myself as he enters the room. Which side of Ezra am I about to encounter? Will it be the angry, dark side? Will it be my goofy friend, joking and pretending nothing happened? Will it be the seductive kisser I met yesterday?

Okay that last one was just wishful thinking.

As he approaches me, his expression is difficult to read. He extends a paper bag to me. "A peace offering."

I open the bag and peek inside. It's a cupcake. Is this a child-like bribe? Or a tempting forbidden fruit?

His lips twitch as he gestures for me to follow him. "You can have it for dessert. Let's go grab dinner."

I glance at my yoga pants and sweater. "I should change."

"We're just going to the hotel's restaurant." He opens the door. "I have to get you to sleep early, since tomorrow will be a busy day."

I study him, frowning, as I slide my feet into my bejeweled flip-flops. Does he know something I don't know?

* * *

The hotel's rooftop restaurant has an amazing view of the Acropolis at night. The Parthenon shines beautiful and golden, illuminated by electric lights (21). We order something light—definitely not the *spanakopita* spinach pie I'm craving for comfort food. Ezra's serene, casual conversation over dinner feels bittersweet, like a farewell. Somehow his air reminds me of the day Chloe and I met him at our favorite ice cream place in Greenyard and we didn't know it would be our last time. Days later, he left for Stanford to start the summer semester and I thought we'd never see him again—luckily I was wrong.

By the end of my salad Ezra's jaw clenches and his shoulders tense. I follow the direction of his focus to Quentin and Paul, pacing toward us from the restaurant entrance.

What the hell?

Frowning, Ezra rises from his seat. "As I said, a phone call would've sufficed."

"Yeah, right. And let you claim all the credit?" Paul pulls out a chair for Quentin.

Wait, what's going on here?

Wearing the eternal calm that conceals his hunger for drama, Quentin eases onto the chair and addresses me. "Darling, how would you like to come to the Mykonos fundraiser and show all ten of your designs?"

I have to hold on to the edge of the table not to stumble with surprise. "Are you inviting me to the charity fashion show?"

He bows his head as an answer.

My pulse speeds up. This could represent all eyes in Europe and the US on my designs. "All ten? Including the Aphrodite dress?"

He gives a single nod. "I'm sorry; I hadn't realized that dress was so important to you."

I could climb on the table and scream in celebration right now. But my years with Quentin taught me everything he gives comes with a price tag. What's the catch?

"Isn't it too late to add another designer to that event?" I ask, still incredulous. "And I can't afford the donation fee—" The answer hits me, and I whip my head toward Ezra as he settles back into his seat. "You sponsored me, didn't you?"

"He insisted, but that was unnecessary," Quentin rushes to answer before Ezra talks. "I was willing to cover the expenses myself. That's why I've been trying to talk to you for days."

My heart racing, I shift my attention from Quentin to Ezra. "You're paying my fifty-thousand-dollar fee?"

"One-hundred-thousand, actually," Ezra's tone is as casual as if we were discussing the waiter's tip. "And as your sponsor, I'm offering my online marketing contacts for publicity for the event worth more than that. So, rest assured, you are doing Xenakis' charity a favor, not the other way around." He smirks at Quentin.

I get it; Ezra's trying to spare me having to owe Quentin. But I'm not sure if I should hug Ezra in gratitude or slap him.

"Let it be clear that none of this would've been possible without Mr. Xenakis." Paul chimes in, as the loyal minion he is. "He has moved mountains to convince the event directors to accept this last-minute addition."

I'm too overwhelmed to answer, but there's no need. Ezra glowers at Paul. "We got it; he's the real hero. Now if you excuse us, I can take it from here."

Quentin and Ezra exchange a few murderous looks before Quentin stands up. "We'll talk later, darling," he tells me with a silky voice. Then, he walks away without saying goodbye to Ezra.

Paul pushes the chair back. "See you tomorrow at eight at Zappeion Hall for fittings. We have little time, so brace yourself for hell on wheels." He pivots around and leaves the restaurant.

I stay frozen for a moment, then turn to Ezra slowly as anger builds up. "Ezra, I could kill you!"

"And that's why I had to make sure we were surrounded by witnesses." He raises his hands in surrender, but seems amused. "Please, Princess, hear me out." He lowers his hands. "What would Chloe say? This had to be done to make amends for my bad karma." His expression sobers up. "My donation to the charity comes from *Squiggles* money. If I ever profited in less than ethical ways, this is a small penalty I'm paying."

My head jerks back. It's hard to argue with that. My voice alternates between shrieks and whispers. "You teamed up with *Quentin*?"

"As a businessman, I knew he was low-balling you to make his next offer look even more generous."

Once again, Ezra sees through Quentin's scheme better than me. Of course, that would be Quentin's pattern! He's mastered the art of demoralizing me and then appearing like an angel the next time he offers something good.

"I told him I could help overcome your objections," Ezra continues. "Your first one would be to Xenakis paying the fee." He leans closer. "The next one is that you don't believe you deserve this break."

This guy knows me so well. "I can't accept this."

"Yes, you can, because I have a debt to you I had to pay." He reaches for my knuckles across the table. "Mia, I owe my career to you."

For a moment, I have trouble following his words. His hand feels larger than I remember. It's still soft, warm and comforting, but something has changed. His touch, that used to soothe me, now leaves me restless.

I struggle to focus. "What do you mean?"

He draws in a deep breath. "Sixteen years ago, your charity kiss changed my destiny."

I shake my head, confused. It feels strange to talk about this so many years later—really talk, not mock it or joke about it. "No, it didn't. I meant for you to brag about us kissing, to shut up the bullies teasing you, but you never did." Deep inside, a hurt seventeen-year-old peeks her head out. *I wanted you to be proud of it. I wanted you to tell others I was your girl.*

"I didn't have to brag, because the transformation had already occurred inside me." He joins his second hand to wrap mine in both of his. "After you kissed me, my outlook changed from self-pity to pride. And I gained the attitude that became my trademark in life, 'I may be a geek, but I have a secret; I have it going on.'"

I start a little. He slowly releases my hands and reclines in his seat. "Soon, other people could sense my confidence and paid more attention to what I had to say. That by itself opened countless doors for me, but there was more." He points at himself. "I was Hephaestus. The impossible had happened and the goddess had given me her attention—even if only for an hour. And at once, I acquired the new belief that even when everything seems hopeless, miracles can still occur." He pauses. "Maybe that's why my life improved so much after that. You kissing me had to be a miracle. And like Sophia says, when you believe in miracles, you invite more to happen in your life."

I should thank him for his beautiful words. But it's taking everything I have not to sob like a baby. He seems to understand I need time to gather myself and remains quiet as he settles the check and we stroll out of the restaurant.

As we wait for the elevator he resumes. "See? Every bit of worldly success I have today, I owe it to you. Yes, the girls helped me by teaching me to behave like a charmer. But I wouldn't have even tried that if I hadn't had a glimpse of hope for myself. *You* started it all."

I reflect on his words as we ride the elevator down. "Maybe

there's something good in me after all. Maybe I'm not just the 'Worsest floozy in Greenyard.'"

"And that's my point." After we exit the elevator, he places both hands on my shoulders and pins me in place with his blue gaze. "You're going to accept this break in your career, because you *earned it*. This is not Mr. X doing you a favor. This is a law of nature: the kindness and compassion you once extended to me is returning to you."

"I accrued good karma," I mutter in disbelief, using Chloe's words.

"Exactly." Ezra claps once. "Repeat after me. I paid my dues, darn it! I deserve to be happy."

Despite tears filling my eyes, joy floods me. "I paid my dues, damn it! I deserve to be happy!"

He stomps a foot on the floor. "So I'm taking this offer!"

"Yes!" Laughing, I clasp my hands together. "I'm taking the offer!"

He hoots and pumps his arms up in celebration. I clap and jump like the twelve-year-old I regress to in his presence. Then I throw my arms around his neck. "Thank you! Thank you! I love you, Big Nerd!"

"And I love you, Big Airhead." He embraces me. Our forms click into each other like perfect pieces in a puzzle.

And there's nothing left of my twelve-year-old.

His strong arms hold me tight against his hard, searing body, setting me on fire. I so want that body next to mine—over mine, under mine. His masculine scent entrances me. Every inch of contact as he crushes me feels glorious—but I want so much more. I need his hands all over me, making me shiver in delight. I want his mouth driving me crazy with pleasure. I need to fill myself with him.

His tension and abrupt silence hint he's as torn as I am, but he doesn't move. I take it all in, the beating of his heart, his warmth, the wine on his breath.

He releases me with reluctance. His glassy eyes, shining with the same desire as during our photo session, cling to me for a moment before they jerk away. He clears his throat and searches his pockets for the room key.

My blown away brain can hardly grasp this fundamental change. I'm the woman who gravitates toward a-holes who treat me bad. I've never been turned on by *kindness* before.

But right this second, the knowledge is clearer than ever.

I want this man.

CHAPTER 17

Ezra

I NEEDED THIS SHOWER. AFTER HOURS NEGOTIATING WITH Mr. X, I feel dirty. Walter's multiple calls to raise his offer on the sale of *Squiggles* add to the feeling I've been contaminated. And after so many days walking among Greek ruins, I envision coats of ancient dust covering me from head to toe that my shower removes along with my previous bad deeds. I'm pleased with how my plan went. In a few days my debt to Mia will be paid and I'll be ready to move on. It's bittersweet, but I feel at peace.

I step out of the bathroom refreshed and ready for bed. Glasses have replaced my contacts; my pajamas are on, my hair still wet. I look forward to my nightly routine of catching up on emails and tech news in bed with my laptop.

Yet my bed is not empty. Immersed in her phone, Mia sits on it, her feet up, her back against the headrest.

"Excuse me?" I rest my hands on my hips. "I thought we'd established that is *my* bed."

She bats her eyelashes and sends me an innocent smile. "Really? I must've missed that."

I'm glad to see the relaxed camaraderie is back. I point a hand in the direction of the other half of the room. "You have a perfectly comfortable bed begging you to get in it. Why not use it?"

"My phone battery is dying." She indicates the charging cable plugged into her phone. "And your bed happens to be next to this wonderful charging station."

"Oh!" I fold my arms and tilt my head with a chuckle. "So now my comical charging station deserves credit, huh? Didn't you say it reminded you of a cat nursing her kittens?"

"And that's why I love it!" She pats the charging brick. "There, there. Good girl, *Luna.*"

Did she just name my station?

She lifts her phone. "Luna is nursing this kitten right now and they can't be disturbed."

It's taking all my strength to restrain a grin and fake a stern tone. "Out of my bed. Now."

"For goodness's sake. Loosen up!" She scoots to the side and pats the space next to her. "Here. I won't bother you a bit and will be out of your hair as soon as my phone charges."

I hesitate. Getting in bed with Mia would be too much temptation and torture.

"FYI. I don't have fleas or any contagious illnesses," she teases.

I don't want to advertise how much her proximity affects me. We've made so much progress on mending our friendship today. And just a few days ago we fell asleep in the same bed like two freaking platonic friends. Reluctant, I settle onto the mattress beside her, under the blankets while she sits on top of them.

It's awkward at first, this deep awareness of her body next to mine. Even if we're not touching, my entire skin can trace her form as if sensing a power field. I have to reach over Mia every time I want to retrieve one of my devices—my laptop, phone, headset. My arms can't help brushing her. Her mint-scented breath reaches my neck or my ear; and I fight fantasies about tasting it.

Then I relax into her pleasant closeness. She browses her phone, and I work on my computer, side by side. No words pass between us, yet my whole being charges from her energy as much as her phone is nursing from my station.

"Are those your pictures from the trip?" She looks over my

shoulder at the photos of the Parthenon I'm reviewing. "Wow! They turned out awesome!"

"I know." I flip through the images. The Acropolis. The Temple of Zeus. Her beautiful pictures at the Hephaestus temple.

Somehow, she wiggles herself under the blankets. She curls up and slides closer to me and soon she's practically snuggling me.

Why does this have to feel so delicious? I would gladly do nothing but this all my life.

As if echoing my thoughts, a moan of pleasure escapes her lips. "This feels so good," she mumbles with her eyes closed.

"Don't fall asleep in my bed. Go to yours," I warn, half-hearted.

"I'm just resting my eyes." She stretches and yawns and wraps a leg around mine. Inside me, Ezzie whimpers.

"I'd forgotten how good it feels to cuddle in bed," she whispers. "This is the longest period in my adult life that I've slept alone."

I desperately need a joke. Or something to bring us back to remember we're nothing but old friends. But I got nothing.

"I'm so ready for this vow to be over," she continues. "Even more than missing sex, I miss physical affection. I miss touch. I miss company."

She rolls and shifts in bed. Now she has both legs wrapped around mine and her head nestled into my shoulder. Is she doing this on purpose? Is she trying to kill me?

She takes a whiff at my neck and goose bumps awaken all over my skin. My heartbeat picks up speed. None of the responses I learned from the girls ever prepared me for this.

"I can't wait for that guy who's going to blow my mind." She casually caresses circles on my forearm. "He'll be a lucky man to collect all this passion I've accumulated during this year."

All my brain algorithms fail me. As far as I know, I'm the furthest thing in the world from someone who would "blow her mind." I'm nothing but that goofy friend she respects so little she's not even self-conscious about climbing into his bed.

But my logic offers an alternative hypothesis. Is she challenging me to prove I can be that man? Sending a signal that she wants me to make a bold move?

If half a dozen guys competed for space in my psyche yesterday, today I've added a handful more. A familiar part of me drowns in desire, screaming that I should kiss Mia right now, yet another part reminds me that I'm here to protect her—and that includes from myself. A new part explodes in euphoria with the suspicion that Mia is trying to seduce me—while another scolds me, outraged, for even thinking such nonsense.

I'm still processing the contradictory voices when Mia comments. "Is it me or is it hot in here?"

"Do you want me to turn down the heat?" Making an effort to keep my voice calm and my eyes away, I close the laptop and set it on the carpeted floor.

"I need to shed some layers." She shifts and wriggles under the blankets; a second later, her yoga pants are in her hand and she's discarding them on the floor. Then, she sits up and peels off her long-sleeved T-shirt, stripping down to a dainty silk and lace camisole and panties so brief, they're barely a triangle of fabric.

Saying that my jaw has dropped would be an understatement. I believe my jaw fell from the fourth floor to the basement.

Mia stretches, which raises the hem of her camisole exposing her flat abdomen. "Ah, this feels so much better." She spreads out like a cat, making herself at home as she lies on her side next to me.

"Mia—" When my voice squeaks, I clear my throat and try again. "Mia, what are you doing?"

Her lips quirk as she fixes her golden eyes on me. "Can you guess?"

With trembling hands, I remove my headset and scoot away

from the headboard. I give it my last try at jarring us back to safety with humor. "You're going through premature menopause and having hot flashes?"

"For goodness' sake!" Mia growls in impatience while sitting up. "Are you really *that* clueless?" Without giving me a chance to answer, she pushes me with both hands and I flop back in bed.

It happens in a flash, but it feels like slow motion. She sets a palm beside me on the mattress, swings to her knees and corrals me with her other hand. Her head moves closer and closer to mine, making my pulse skyrocket. Before I can react, her mouth is against mine.

Oh my God. She's kissing me.

The shock lasts a second or two, but then I explode in joy and excitement and kiss her back. Her hair cascades over my face and I lace my fingers through it, keeping it away from our vacuum-sealed mouths.

She removes my fogged glasses and sets them somewhere. The nightstand? I don't care. Because she's settling on top of me, sinking into me as she resumes kissing me. Her body feels even softer than before. Her rose and honey scent feels different right now. She smells of raw desire. Of woman.

The weight of her searing feminine form crushing me lights a blaze in my southern regions. It's not fair; I'm at her mercy, powerless. Her every movement, every shift make the flames grow inside me, yet leave me little control.

I apply a jiu jitsu move and now I'm on top. She giggles around my mouth, then her laughter dies, replaced by moans of pleasure as my tongue trails down her neck. She breaks contact for a moment to pull my pajama top over my head, then I help her get rid of my pants, stripping me down to my briefs.

A last residue of sanity sparks in my mind. I release her lips. "Wait. The self-vow." Panting, I look at her from my plank position above her. "Should I stop?" *Please say no. Please say no.*

"No."

Oh thank God. I kiss her again and roll her to her side. My fingers explore the silk of her thighs, her hips, her waist, then travel to the hem of her camisole.

But something stops me before peeling it off and I have to ask one more time. "Are you sure, Mia? You won't regret breaking the vow?"

Her face lights up. "That's the best part! This doesn't count as breaking the vow! Because we love each other!"

Something in the casual way she drops the words stops me cold. This is not the awkward moment when one of a couple throws around the L word when the other isn't ready. This is a matter-of-fact statement, as if she just mentioned her nail salon appointment.

"Wait. Say that again?"

"The vow has an escape clause." Her breathing is quick and shallow, her fingers thread through my hair. "You can end it to sleep with a man you love and who loves you back. Well, *I* love you. *You* love me. That's the solution."

Forty-four percent of the Ezras inside me are screaming in joy right now. Five percent are a little freaked out. Yet the other fifty-one percent point out that something doesn't sound right in her tone. "Did you just say you love me?"

"Of course, I do, silly. I've always loved you. Nothing has changed."

Nothing has changed. The biggest, most inexplicable disappointment drains me. Every other Ezra shuts up and retreats to a corner of the room.

Inch by inch, I disentangle myself from her limbs. "So, you love me...like your PMS slumber party buddy, right?"

"What's the difference?" Her fingers cling to my back, not allowing me to go far. "Didn't you say romantic love and any other type of love are the same?"

"Regardless of what I said, I'm not interested." I escape her hands and stagger out of the bed.

With abrupt movements, I rescue my scattered pieces of clothing from the floor. At once, every other memory of disappointment with Mia returns to my mind. Every time she broke up with Xenakis and used me as the friend to vent to. Every time my hopes rose when she asked me to braid her hair, or cuddle with her under a throw blanket. I'm sick of being the guy she goes to only when she has nothing better in sight.

I replace my pajama pants. "I don't want you to be with me just because you have an itch and I can help you scratch it."

She folds her arms with a frown. "You said you'd sleep with ninety-seven percent of women you meet…And *now* you decide to have a high bar?"

I might've trapped myself in my own experiment. "I'm sorry. I have standards. And the answer is no." I slid my T-shirt back on.

"Standards? Or double standards?" She settles her knuckles on her hips. "So you are a guy, so you're allowed to have needs, but I'm not."

"No. It's not that."

"So, you're a guy, so it's okay if you sleep with someone you might never see again, but it's not okay for me because I'm a woman? It's okay for you to be the hunter, but women must be passive and play hard to get?"

This is not about double standards and you know it, a wiser than usual Ezra whispers to me. *You're terrified of crossing that line with her when the two of you are in such different places.*

"You and the girls spent so many years teaching me what women want to hear from men, and it never occurred to you to ask the other way? Well, I have news for you." I mirror her righteous tone. "Men don't like to feel they're your last resource. That you're with them only because they're 'here' and nothing better is around." Maybe I'm also talking to Crystal, remembering how she used me and dumped me too. "And while we're at it, men don't like to feel they're a home improvement project!"

"Is this a male pride thing? Did I fail to stroke your ego first and remind you of how impossibly sexy you are?"

I *do* like hearing those words.

But I refuse to give into that. Even if put my pride away, I can't allow a fling with Mia to destroy our friendship, and my bond with Chloe, Sophia and Iris along with it.

And I definitely can't allow myself to get my hopes up and let Mia shatter them again.

"The answer is still no." My firm tone leaves no room for negotiation.

"Okay then," Mia takes a big breath and springs up from bed. Her cheeks are flushed, her lips swollen and her eyes glassy. "Then I'm going to...take a cold shower and get ready for bed." I try not to stare at her glorious behind as she stumps to the bathroom and slams the door behind her. At least this time she closed it all the way.

I flop back into the bed and cover my face with my hands. Ezzie sulks and pouts inside me like an immature teenager. The rest of me feels like when Ian kicks my ass in jiu jitsu practice at the gym.

Water runs. How will I manage knowing she's naked in the shower with only a flimsy no-lock door between us? If sharing a suite with her felt daunting an hour ago, now it's unbearable.

I grab my phone and Air Pods and go straight to the hotel reception to inquire if I can take another room, but due to the fashion event, not one room remains vacant in Athens.

"Are you trying to accommodate a friend?" the nice lady concierge asks.

"Yes." It's not a lie. I need a room for my friend Ezzie. And a dozen other horny adult Ezras that need to be away from Mia for a while.

"You're welcome to bring them to your suite. Since you have two queen beds, you're allowed to have up to four guests there. We can bring you a futon."

I mumble a thanks and a polite goodbye, then head for the lobby chairs. The Greek inspired columns and ceiling reliefs blur out of my focus.

I video-call Iris. It's nighttime here but the afternoon there. "Hi, Ezra, everything okay?" Her wig suggests she's somewhere in public.

I draw in a lungful. "Iris." My voice cracks just a little. "I need you to come rescue me from the garbage dumpster."

Iris nods slowly and sighs, resigned. "Okay. Buy the ticket; I'll start packing."

CHAPTER 18

Mia

A	FTER THIRTY-SIX AWKWARD HOURS BETWEEN EZRA AND me, Iris comes to the rescue. Her joyful, bubbling presence flows into our hotel room dispersing the tension like golden sunshine vanishes darkness. Ezra must've brought her in as a buffer. Or perhaps for extra support because he senses how frantic these days are about to be.

Dress fittings, rehearsals with the models, coordinating makeup and hairstyles to go with each outfit… If modeling has brought back the wild woman in me, preparing for a fashion show on such short notice summons the neurotic designer—in need of someone to shoot her with a tranquilizer dart gun. Though I bless the hectic schedule that prevents me from obsessing over Ezra's rejection.

It's our last night in Athens. Marcia and Trent want us to attend the AXD closing party at the Fuzz club. But Ezra and Iris, who can't dance to save their lives, want to retire early to rest before the trip to Mykonos. I negotiate for the five of us to join Quentin's staff for drinks and appetizers at the restaurant where they're meeting before heading to the club.

"It's such a relief to take off this wig!" Iris scratches her scalp through her short hair as we settle at our table.

"Why do you even wear it? Your hair looks cool," Trent comments.

"Yes!" I second. "Like you cut it super short on purpose."

"Nah. People with beautiful, feminine features like you could

143

pull it off, not ordinary me." She points vaguely between Marcia and me while studying the menu. "If either of you got a buzz cut, you'd look like a supermodel making a statement. Me? I look like GI Joe's butch twin sister." She puts down the menu. "Anyway. Mr. Xenakis and I talked for a long time yesterday."

Iris' main assignment has been to buffer me from Quentin, since getting ready for the Mykonos show demands that we spend more time together than usual. He's been present at most of my rehearsals, giving me excellent input that only experience can offer. Yet now I can hardly remember a time when he tempted me. It reminds me of the experience of outgrowing the childhood fondness for cheap candy, acquiring a taste for more sophisticated dishes.

"Xenakis is so much nicer than I recalled!" Iris goes on. "I can't believe he remembered me by name."

Oh my. Poor Iris is falling prey to Quentin's charm. His ability to remember people has nothing to do with caring and everything to do with his visual designer nature. And Iris has too much faith in humanity because she had an abnormally happy childhood.

"Xenakis remembered everybody from our college graduation party!"

Ezra and I exchange a quick look. He rolls his eyes and subtly shakes his head, showing he shares my skepticism.

Absorbed in the menu, Iris continues, "He remembered Chloe, Sophia and her ex-fiancé, George—he even remembered Crystal!"

Ezra puts a finger on his throat and pretends to puke.

I snort with restrained laughter. It's so hard to stay angry at Ezra for long.

Maybe I should be glad he set his foot down against my crazy idea of seducing him a few nights ago. Maybe I should be grateful he did damage control for my impulsiveness.

Agh! Who am I kidding? I am *not* glad and I'm *not* grateful. I'm royally pissed at him and quite sore in my feminine pride.

I'm still holding my grudge when the waiter brings our appetizer of olives, pita bread and *revythosaláta*—Greek hummus. Iris is making us howl, sharing her recent adventures being asked over and over by people "what her pronouns are."

"There has to be something about my clumsy, ungraceful way of walking," she says. "When I don't wear my wig, people take one look at my hair and assume I'm a transgender man." She points at her chest. "But with these fake boobs I got after my cancer surgery, when I wear my big wig and makeup, people think I'm a drag queen."

Guffawing, Ezra and I reach for the last olive at the same time and our hands bump. The electricity jolts the amusement out of me, and I withdraw my fingers as if his touch could scald me.

"Sorry, you can have it." He points at the olive with his open hand.

I'm still angry with him and don't feel like owing him any more favors. "No, you take it." I spear the olive with a toothpick and offer it to him.

"I insist. You have it." He waves a hand.

"Can you stop being a stubborn head and just take the freaking olive?" I snap. "You're not supposed to reject what someone offers you with kindness. Especially when it's obvious that you *do* want it!"

Dead silence falls around the table. I may not really be talking about him rejecting *the olive*.

Ezra tone turns edgy. "Well, only *I* decide what I want or not. And I have the right to change my mind."

"Oh, so this olive is not good enough for you?" I put down the toothpick.

His voice rises. "Or maybe this olive doesn't take me seriously and I'm sick of it."

The silence intensifies until it solidifies among our table companions. Iris wears a puzzled expression, while Trent and Marcia gawk at us.

"Uh…" Trent keeps looking between Ezra and me. "Marcia and I are going to head to the Fuzz Club early." He pulls Marcia by the arm and they pace away, throwing glances at us over their shoulders.

"Ezra?" Iris raises one re-growing eyebrow. "Last time I checked, olives can't take people seriously, so I'm going to assume what you said is a metaphor for something else." She squints, as if thinking hard. "And I'm usually good at this, but between the chemo brain fog and the jet lag, I'm going to need your help."

Regret flashes in Ezra's eyes, then he clears his throat. "It's nothing. Mia and I are a little tense because we…had a recent dis-agreement. She…doesn't approve of the way I've made money through *Squiggles*."

"Yes, of course, that's it!" I follow along. I'm dying to talk to Iris about everything going on, but not in front of Ezra, and defi-nitely not in public.

"Oh, do you mean how he advertises through *Squiggles*?" Iris dips a piece of pita in the hummus. "Ezra helped me tremendously in the marketing of the Self-Vow book, I owe much of its success to that platform."

Innocent Iris has no idea what *Squiggles* really is.

"Iris, do you remember that Christmas our freshman year when we had to fly to Stanford and help Ezra move back to Illinois?"

Ezra gasps. "*Squiggles* is not hacking!"

"I wish I could believe you," I tilt my head. "But lately you seem to be sending mixed signals and contradicting yourself over and over."

Growling, Ezra removes the napkin from his lap and rises from his chair. "Mia, can I talk to you for a minute?" He swings his head, pointing at a corner of the restaurant.

I follow him to the area in front of the single no-gender restroom typical of Europe.

"What the heck is your problem today?" he asks. "If you're so unhappy with my presence, I'll be glad to pack and return to the States!"

"Then do it!" I snap back. "You brought Iris to replace you because that's what you want, don't you?"

"I would if she could stay longer than just a few days!" He growls, then squeezes his eyes shut and points between us. "See? This is exactly what I've been trying to avoid. We're one blink away from ruining our friendship."

"Maybe we already ruined it!" I'm so irrational right now I annoy myself.

"No, we didn't yet," he contradicts. "But if we'd—" He stops and looks around. From the table, Iris stares at us while munching on pita bread, as entranced as if she were watching a Netflix series.

Ezra grabs my arm and guides me inside the bathroom for privacy. "Our friendship is still salvageable because we've survived making out before," he says, locking the door. "But if we'd crossed that line and slept together, we might lose each other forever."

His words feel like the slap someone would administer to a hysterical person. I can't believe I'd lost track of that possibility. A flashback hits me from the time after we kissed in senior year and slow terror replaces my anger.

"I...I thought things could..." Saying I believed we could return to normal would be lying. What was I thinking? That this time he'd stay with me and never leave me?

As if Ezra had exorcised a crazy spirit—perhaps a temperamental Olympian god—a sharp understanding of my recent recklessness descends upon me.

I tuck a hair strand behind my ear, looking at the floor. "Can I claim temporary insanity?"

He forces a chuckle. "Princess, insanity is your *permanent* state."

I wish I could laugh at his joke. But right now, a deep sadness settles in my soul. It's the sadness of the twelve-year-old girl whose mother shipped her to Dad and disappeared from her life. And the seventeen-year-old who kissed her best friend and then watched him withdraw from her.

I steel myself. I don't need him. I've survived on my own all my life and I can survive now. I raise a hand and give him my best prima-donna scowl. "Don't test me. I still have that footage of you singing into your hairbrush, doing that Mariah Carey impression."

"There she is!" Sighing in relief, he steps toward me as if about to hug me, but then stops himself. For an awkward moment we debate whether to shake hands or do something childish like high fives, but then decide on a half-hug keeping our bodies as far away as the tiny bathroom allows.

The insane woman inside me considers shoving his head in the toilet. Then immediately another part contemplates pushing him against the bathroom door and kissing him until he admits he wants it too.

"We're good?" Tense, he pats the side of my shoulder again and again.

I bow my head. "We're good."

We exit the bathroom and almost stumble over a couple waiting outside the door. It's Marcia and Trent, wearing the same morbidly curious expressions they sport lately. They seem to find it fascinating that Ezra and I were locked in the restroom together.

"Uh…" Marcia clears her throat. "We couldn't find a taxi soon enough so we thought we'd go to the…" Her words trail off.

"Uh…guys." Iris approaches behind them and she looks as pale as during the worst of her chemo. Her enlarged hazel eyes make her appear as if she'd encountered one of the dragons of the fantasy fiction she writes under a pen name. "Uh…there's someone at our table I wasn't expecting."

"Here you are!" Quentin paces toward us. "We have a friend joining us from London last minute. Hopefully I'll convince her to walk the catwalk for me in Mykonos."

The way Ezra's body stiffens gives the first hint of trouble before the high-pitched voice reaches me.

"Ezra! Is that really you?"

That voice would feel like nails on a chalkboard any day, but today it sparks territorial aggression inside me. No, this can't be happening.

Crystal Harrison. AKA Crystal Meth. The woman who once broke Ezra's heart.

CHAPTER 19

Mia

T HE FLUSH OF HOT ANGER HITS ME SO HARD I'M AFRAID I'LL break into a pouring sweat and ruin my makeup. Can Quentin possibly be *that* evil? Could he have brought Crystal on purpose, to derail Ezra?

And he's succeeding. Ezra's mute and frozen, blinking in excess as he does when his contact lenses bother him.

Crystal goes straight to him and hugs him and I want to rip her peroxide blond head off and throw it in the Adriatic Sea, then feed her body to the seagulls.

Never mind. She has so much Botox in her face and silicone in her body that she'd be toxic to sea life.

"Ezra, dear, it has been so long." She releases the hug but still rubs his back while keeping eye contact. "I've been dying to talk to you."

* * *

If I ever doubted that Quentin is an evil demon, I confirmed it tonight. Like an illusionist who confuses you with quick hand movements and leaves you wondering which cup hides the freaking ball, he twists all of our plans around. Before I know what's happening, Iris and I share a limo to the Fuzz Club with him while Ezra is sent away in a different car with Crystal. And we've been sitting at Quentin's table for an hour and there is no sign of those two.

I can't remember a time when I had a taste for clubbing. The music deafens me, the lights blind me, and the smell of booze and cigarettes that once turned me on, repel me. The place is so crowded I feel claustrophobic. Iris and I end up escaping Quentin's table and heading out as soon as we give up on waiting for Ezra and Crystal.

"I can't believe Quentin's nerve!" I grumble as I adjust my wrap to protect me from the chilly night breeze. "He planned this. He sent for Crystal to upset Ezra!"

"Now I understand why he asked me so many questions about her the other day. Mr. X used me to get information to find Ezra's weak spot!" Iris gives a guilty wince. "I can't believe I fell for the guy's charm."

That's going below the belt. That's messing with Ezra's psychological stability. And mine too.

"If that witch Crystal convinces Ezra to take her back, I swear I'm going to claw her eyes out!"

"Whoa!" Iris jerks her head and her wig goes askew. "Where is this intensity coming from?"

I wish I knew the answer to that. I flag an arriving taxi. "Let's get out of here."

Over the cab ride back to the hotel, I open up to Iris about the past few days, including my moment of insanity when I threw myself at Ezra and he turned me down. Thank God, she's the least judgmental person I've ever met. The story sounds crazy to my own ears and, as I retell it, I come across as such a scuzzy character.

I held a faint hope that Ezra beat us to the hotel, but the room is empty. He still hasn't answered my texts by the time Iris and I are in our pajamas and ready for bed.

I sit on my bed, hugging my pillow while Iris lies on her side on the futon, drinking in every word as I finish the story.

"Well, I don't blame him for telling you to slow down! You don't risk a twenty-one-year-old friendship on an impulse like that. What were you thinking?"

It feels strange to be reprimanded by her. "Aren't you supposed to be my most supportive girlfriend?"

"But this concerns me too!" She reaches closer to give me a small slap on my arm. "If you do something crazy here, *I* might lose Ezra as a friend."

Another reason to stay away. If Ezra and I ever got involved and then split, the girls would be like children in a broken marriage. "I just thought it was the perfect solution. But he has a point." I groan.

Iris pierces me with her hazel eyes. "Mia, are you *sure* you don't have feelings for Ezra?" I open my mouth to protest as usual, but her no-nonsense look stops me. "It's time to confront the demons you've been ignoring."

"What do you mean?" I hug the pillow tighter. Iris leaves the futon and joins me on the bed. She sits with legs crossed and motions for me to put down my pillow and imitate her.

Like a mime, Iris stirs an imaginary witches' brew, scoops some into a non-existing jar and waves a hand around it. "Here's the magic potion—the Truth Concoction. The moment this touches your lips you won't be able to speak anything but the truth."

I refrain from chuckling and rolling my eyes. Over the years, Chloe and Iris have enjoyed recreating this symbolic ritual. What a team they are. Chloe, who I joke is an amateur witch with a doctor's day job, and Iris, who has the wild imagination of someone who writes fantasy stories about wizards and enchantresses.

I humor Iris by pretending to drink the invisible potion. And as happens every time, I feel the sudden urge to cry.

"Mia, I'm going to ask you this again," Iris starts. "Why did you kiss Ezra your senior year of high school?"

The question jars me. Besides our jokes over the years, I hadn't allowed myself to dwell on that night until Ezra's reference to it a few days ago.

I can't believe this imaginary potion still works. But psychological or not, my brain releases its hold on the truth and it spills through my lips.

"Chloe and Ezra were the first friends I made when I first moved to Greenyard with my father and stepmom. Maybe I clung to them because I desperately needed to belong somewhere. I was twelve, heartbroken about my mother ditching me, and adjusting to living full time with a father I barely knew."

"That was when your mother moved away for that job in another city, right?" Iris frowns, trying to recall.

I shrug. "That was the excuse. My grandparents had been pressuring my dad for years to take over custody because my mother wasn't a 'good example' for me. She had a revolving door of boyfriends."

Iris' hazel eyes are full of compassion without showing any pity. "Did you ever make peace with her about leaving you?"

"We talk regularly now; I never blamed her." I hesitate. "Yes, a part of me might've felt abandoned, but most of me knew in a way she was giving me an example of a woman who fights for her happiness."

"Anyway, my relationship with Roxanne, my stepmother, was strained from the beginning. And my father withdrew emotionally from me. So, through middle school and high school I practically lived at Chloe's and Ezra's houses. More than once, Roxanne kicked me out of the house for some rebellious behavior; the first time, I was just fifteen." The rawness inside me turns to tenderness. "Ezra would sneak me into his house and feed me. He would let me sleep in his bed while he dozed in a sleeping bag on the floor. If his mother had found me, she would've killed us both!"

"Wow!" Iris presses a hand to her chest.

I nod once. "So, *I* knew what an amazing human being Ezra was, regardless of what the stupid school bullies said to torture him. And I envied Ezra for the way he faced the harassment, fighting the bullies with wit and not aggression. He was my hero." My voice trembles. Damn it. No tears again.

I'm re-discovering truths as I express ideas aloud. "So that night, studying at his house before that science test, when he told me how bad he felt about being unpopular, I couldn't help it. I had to show him the part of him I saw that he didn't see. I had to prove to him he was not only likable, but lovable."

"Wow!" Iris shimmies. "So, it wasn't true that you were just 'doing him a favor.' You did kind-of have a crush on him."

I startle. "A crush? I wouldn't call it…" I stop to consider it for the first time. I'd never associated that warm, softer type of love I felt—and still feel—for Ezra with romantic attraction. It's very different from my pattern with all the boyfriends I ever had: I chased them and clung to them when they didn't want me, drawn by their coldness. Then, if they showed too much interest, I pushed them away. *Obviously*, for a man to be truly interested in me, something must've been wrong with him.

"What happened after you two kissed?" Iris asks.

"Ezra started avoiding me. He skipped school for several days, using asthma as his excuse. I didn't see him again until prom night." I relive my disappointment when he didn't ask me to the prom. "At prom, I gave him a chance to brag to our classmates about making out with me, but he didn't. And it kind of hurt. It confirmed what Roxanne used to say: a floozy like me was a quick thrill for any guy, but not the woman someone would choose for the long term." The words still sting sixteen years later.

"You know that's not true, right?" Iris crosses her arms.

I don't answer. It was a relief to hear Ezra's version of why he didn't speak out. Yet, an unreasonable part of me still wishes he would've told the world I was his girl. It's ridiculous. What would I have won with that?

And regardless of what he now says, he passed on me for the long term, like he's doing now. Just like my mother did. Just like later on Quentin refused to formalize our relationship. It's the story of my life.

I wrap my knees with my arms and continue. "Shortly after that, he headed out for the summer semester at Stanford, and you know the rest."

"No, I don't," Iris shakes her head. "I know about our adventure flying to California and helping him transfer to our college. And I saw four years of strange interactions between the two of you, that's it."

I reflect on the memories from college. "By the time he came back from Stanford I was dating someone else. Ezra never gave any sign of being interested in me, so I just pushed everything away from my mind. Then between my break ups and make ups with Quentin, and Ezra's three years with Crystal, we were never available at the same time for long. And you saw what happened after she broke up with him. He turned into a player. He denies it, but I've always been afraid it's because he never forgot her." I groan. "And now she's back!"

The deep sense of dread returns. Where the hell is Ezra? Is he with Crystal right now? Is she kissing him, is he loving her the way he refused to do with me?

Sensing my distress Iris pats my arm. "Mia, just talk to him."

"I tried! He claims he's afraid of losing our friendship…and he has a point." I whine and drop onto bed. "Is it worth it risking so much?"

"If that means living without regrets—hell yes." Iris pulls me by the wrists and makes me sit back on bed. "Take it from me, Mia, life's too short. Don't wait until you get a terrifying diagnosis to start doing what you really want to do."

It's the first time it occurs to me that Iris, with her happy childhood and her pristine past, might have regrets about wild adventures she never took. "You wish now you'd been less cautious, don't you?"

Iris' expression carries a gravity I'd never seen before. "I wish I could turn back the clock and be a little more reckless in my life— especially regarding love." She swallows and her eyes dart away. "Especially regarding a certain man."

Now that's a surprise. Iris has dated a few guys, but as long as I've known her I've never seen her swept off her feet by anyone. Sounds like there's a story she hasn't told me.

The familiar sound of the door unlocking reaches me. Ezra is returning to the room. "Finally!" Without thinking, I spring off the bed and run to him. My first thought is to hug him but instead, I slap his arm.

"Ow!" He rubs the spot.

"Where the hell have you been? And why didn't you call us?"

"Crystal insisted on deviating from the route to talk." He goes straight to the charging station to plug in his phone. "We spent an hour catching up on the past eight years."

I point at the alarm clock on the nightstand. "Uh…you left *three* hours ago."

"And I've spent the last two hours on the phone with different buyers for *Squiggles*. I talked for so long my phone battery died." He points at his cell's black screen.

"What's Crystal doing here?" Iris asks.

"Yes!" I add. "And what did you guys talk about?"

Ezra stretches in a yawn that seems forced. "Can we talk tomorrow? I'm really tired." He grabs his pajamas from his suitcase on the floor and heads to the bathroom, closing the door behind him.

I stare at the closed door wondering if he has something to hide.

The powerlessness weighs on me with the heaviness of my entire luggage set. Ezra's slipping through my fingers. And if I'll lose him forever either way, perhaps risking it all is my only choice.

CHAPTER 20

Ezra

T HE SUN SHINES AGAINST A BRILLIANT BLUE SKY AS OUR PLANE approaches Mykonos. The moment I glimpse it from the plane, I fall in love with this surreal town of white, flat-roof houses against rocky cliffs and ocean. Bougainvillea and occasional red or blue church domes offer splashes of color (22 a-e).

So much beauty distracts me from ruminating on yesterday's fiasco. I'll say it again: Mr. X is worse than the Devil. Bringing my ex-girlfriend from London just to upset Mia and me is pure evil. I didn't want to worry Mia and Iris by sharing that Crystal tried to seduce me last night and continues to harass me. Could she be following orders from Xenakis even in that?

"Oh, my goodness, I love it!" Iris claps, as we get the first close impressions of the town through the taxi window. "The houses seem built of white cake frosting!"

"Or melted marshmallows," Mia adds.

My clever girls! I never would've come up with those words, but the minute they say it, I see it.

I have to hand it to Mr. X. Coming to this island in November, during the off-season, means avoiding the usual crowds, and having it practically to ourselves—it's worth dealing with lower temperatures and shorter days. And the weather is quite pleasant, warmer than San Francisco. Slow season also allows me to get Mia and Iris their own room, separate from mine—I wouldn't risk Mia staying with Mr. X and his crew in the luxurious Cavo Tagoo hotel.

Almost upon arrival, work swallows Mia. I'd love to explore this beautiful island, but instead settle for indoor rehearsals and dress fittings at the resort where the fashion show will take place. Our first two days in Mykonos I end up working harder than I expected, helping with light tests and last-minute errands. I don't mind. My friendship with Mia is a critically ill patient on life support and I'm fighting for its survival.

Thank God for Iris, who takes over the chaperone role each time I get pulled away. What am I going to do when she returns to the States in a couple of days?

It's a relief to call it a day and retire early. I looked forward to the privacy of a suite to myself, yet I suspect that, just like last night, I'll fall asleep the moment my head touches the pillow.

My phone rings as I remove my contacts in the restroom, getting ready for bed. Thinking it's one of my buyers, I let the call go to my Air Pods.

To my dismay, it's Crystal. "Hi, baby. I miss you."

The voice that once upon a time I loved now irritates me like a slow-to-load webpage. But if the girls taught me anything it was always to be polite to a lady. "Hey. I expected you to be asleep after all those rehearsals."

In fact, Crystal never seems to rehearse. She's a leech, following me around, her flirtation less and less subtle.

And apparently, she just removed the last string of subtlety. "I can't sleep. Would you come over and keep me company?"

I freeze with my hands on the towel, knowing exactly what that invitation means.

Sex-deprived and stirred up from my close call with Mia, a small part of me feels tempted to take the offer. After all, Crystal has no chance to entangle me emotionally after how bad she treated me in the past.

But I'd never touch the woman who spread all those rumors about Mia. "Sorry, I can hardly keep my eyes open. But thanks."

"You're still hung up on Mia, aren't you?" she blurts. "I always knew I was just a substitute for *her*."

I tense at her words, which ring truer than ever today.

"See?" She huffs at my silence. "You used me just as much as I used you. Let's stop pointing fingers, put all this behind us and start over."

Like I didn't know the only reason Crystal claims to want me back is because now our leagues have come closer. She's eight years older and I'm twenty-million richer. I grab my phone from the vanity. "I'm heading to bed now—"

"You should take my offer." Her sugary voice hardens again. "You know, it's a matter of time until Mia returns to Xenakis."

Her statement hurts like a stabbing dagger. It brings back the feeling of raw inadequacy Mia revived when she tried to use me like her temporary fix. "Goodnight, Crystal." I disconnect the call and turn off the phone.

Maybe that's why I've poured every free minute into exploring other offers for *Squiggles*. As if three or four million more could plug the void that the first twenty couldn't fill. It sucks. I'm the guy women seek out when there's nothing better around. I'm the placeholder until they find what they really want. Like Crystal did. Like Mia tried to do.

I turn off the restroom light. *Mia.* As I head to bed in the dark, I relive our kisses at the Hephaestus temple and in our Athens hotel. The memory is so vivid, it's like having her in my arms again.

As I get under the blankets, I can almost feel her warm body and sense her honey and roses scent. I can almost hear the soft sound of her breathing.

Wait. This may be *too real*.

I reach for the lamp on the nightstand and turn it on. My pulse races as I confirm my suspicion. Mia lies sideways, stretched out on my bed, carrying an expression between daring and frightened. Despite not wearing my glasses her proximity allows me to admire her beauty in soft focus. She wears next to nothing—black satin-and-lace lingerie.

"What the hell? Mia, how did you get in here?"

She silences me with a kiss. An exquisite invasion of my mouth that sends a rush of blood below my waist. As her plump lips entice me, her soft, warm body climbs on me, enveloping me with her scent and flooding me with desire.

This is wrong, my mind says. Yet my tongue darts to meet hers and I respond to the kiss eagerly, desperate, while my fingers thread into her silky hair. Straddling me, she guides my hands over her body, encouraging me to caress her; they gladly oblige, tracing her shape like they had a mind of their own. Her moan of delight echoes my thrill.

A flash of rationality enters my mind. "Stop." My ragged voice sounds alien to my own ears. "I told you I didn't want to do this."

Above me, her darkened eyes search mine and she smiles. "But you lied." She claims my mouth again.

Oh, God. My half-hearted attempt to stop her doesn't fool her. I so want this, and she knows it. Her luscious lips move to my neck—dang it, she learns fast what I like. My disobedient hands cling to her hips and crush her against me. The pleasure might kill me.

"Double standard alert!" I manage to say with a broken voice. "If the situations were reversed, and *I* were the one not taking *no* for an answer, the whole *Me Too* movement would be here protesting."

Mia grumbles a curse word and releases me. Every circuit in my body cries in protest as she disentangles herself from me and flops against the pillows. Her chest rises and falls in fast, shallow gasps. My own breathing is short and my heart is racing. And it takes every megabyte of my will not to bury my face in those beautiful breasts, pushed up and forward by her balcony bra.

"I've seen you with Crystal," she murmurs. "I've seen her tempt you, and I've seen your reactions: you've considered taking her offer."

I tense in bed. I hadn't realized she'd been paying attention.

"The bottom line." She moves her hand between us. "You need this as much as I do. And if you're about to make a mistake with an airhead bimbo tramp—" She points at herself. "I would rather you make it with *this* one."

Anger and disappointment rise inside me, I sit on the bed and cross my arms. "So, once again you're doing me a favor."

"Oh my God, can you be more impossibly stubborn!" Mia pulls chunks of her hair. "Okay. You win." She sits up in bed and her expression sobers. "I'm ready to admit it. I do want you. I don't want you just because you're…*here*. I want you because…you're…*you*."

I stiffen at her words. Is she saying she has feelings for me? Is she leaving open the possibility that this is not only a fling? A blast of joy nearly knocks me over, but I immediately hold on to caution.

"So…you want *me*."

Her eyes dart away. "Hell yes I do."

I repeat the question, changing the intonation. "You…*want* me?" Am I too picky to complain because she's said that she loves me and that she wants me…but not in the same sentence?

Her cautious eyes return to me. "And you…*want* me too, don't you?" She seems to ask more than her words reveal. She's challenging me to give a name to this new strange energy between us—where our friendship and our desire walk hand in hand.

We're two gangsters in a negotiation. I have the money and she has the contraband I want to buy, but neither party trusts the other. We're both holding onto the goodies, refusing to surrender them, convinced that the minute we do, the other will run away with both the merchandise and the cash and we'll be left with nothing. And negotiation remains stalled.

But for how long will her interest last? Here I'm exciting because I'm her only choice. What will happen when we return home? When the vow expires? Am I the man she'd choose if she had endless options?

"Three months," I declare, grabbing my glasses from the

nightstand and sliding them on. "We'll talk after we return to the States, your vow ends, and you've had time to reintegrate to dating life. Then, if you're still interested, I'll look into whether I'm interested too."

"For crying out loud! For all I know in three months I might be dead!" She jumps off the bed, picks up a silk robe from the floor and slips it on.

I extend my hand. "And however you got it, give me my room key back."

She picks a card key off the floor and hands it to me. She must've tricked me and kept the duplicate when we checked in. "I'm going to let you be for now, but sooner or later we're going to need to resume this... talk."

"Three months," I repeat as I take the card. "Nothing that comes out of your mouth can be trusted right now."

She makes the thinking-hard face she used to make during my math tutorials. "Lucky for you, I'll be extremely busy with the fashion show for the next couple of days. But I do not agree to wait that long. We're having this conversation soon. Even if it is the last thing we do together."

Her head up, she sashays away full of grace and determination and leaves the room with a slam of the door.

I flop back onto the bed with a groan of frustration, while Ezzie scolds me for being such an idiot again.

CHAPTER 21

Ezra

MAYBE MY NEXT CAREER SHOULD NOT BE IN WEB DESIGN, but in teaching men how to survive when their women go through a crisis. Over the past few days, as Mia prepares for the fashion show, I've needed to tap into every kilobyte of data I collected during a decade with four female best friends.

In the chaotic dressing room, the air smells of hairspray and airbrush makeup. A loud rumble of urgent conversation rises over the noise of hairdryers and blowers. Rollers in their hair, stunning models run around barely dressed, showing no shyness about it. And the vibe screams of such professionalism it would never occur to me to stare. Some models sit on the floor re-applying their makeup, overriding the work of professional makeup artists. Hairdressers tweak hairstyles with such grave expressions, one would've thought they're handling radioactive material.

Yes, the stakes are high. But I'm proud to say that I have male support down to a three-principle system.

"This is a disaster!" Mia yells while zipping a stringy blonde who looks thirteen into a sequined evening gown. "The hairstyles are too stiff, the makeup has too much glitter! I have a sequin emergency and I can't find my sewing kit!"

Principle Number One: She doesn't want advice or solutions; she just wants to vent. Nod. Pat. Support. Repeat. While she vents, do not speak unless she requests it and if you do, the only words you must pronounce are how amazing she's doing.

"Where the hell is my sewing kit! I had it a minute ago!" Mia helps the girl climb onto a low table while studying the gown losing a pixel of its bling. Then, she claps twice in front of Iris' face and mine. "You two! Stop daydreaming and help me find that sewing kit before my whole career is destroyed!"

Iris and I rush to help in the search.

Principle Number Two: Duck the blows and don't take anything personal. If your woman engages in catastrophic thinking, or becomes convinced the whole world conspires against her, it doesn't mean she hates you or that she's lost her mind. She's just a woman in distress.

"The show begins in twenty minutes and I can't find my freaking sewing kit!" Mia yells at the top of her lungs. "Someone do something, please!"

Okay, I guess this time she *does* want solutions. Which contradicts Principle One, but it's okay. Because the next principle is all about flexibility.

Principle Number Three: The perfect man is unshakable and determined, but also *flexible*. To be perfect, you need to be strong and tough, but also vulnerable and sensitive. And especially, you must learn to read minds to anticipate requests before they're formulated. In summary, it's *effing impossible*. Just do your best and keep going until the storm blows by.

I check the emergency kit I carry with my photographic equipment. No luck. I didn't pack needle and thread this time. But I do find a bottle of crazy glue that I extend to Mia. "Can this help?"

Mia gasps and winces as if someone had punched her in the gut. "This is sacrilege. I can't believe I'm about to use glue on one of my gorgeous creations!" She keeps her eyes closed and pinches the bridge of her nose with one hand as she extends the other to accept the glue bottle. Then she opens her eyes, sighs and gives a single nod.

I'll take that as a thank you.

In a snap, the sequin emergency is repaired, but when I'm

about to excuse myself and return to the audience, Marcia and Trent approach Mia. By their alarmed expressions I predict they don't bring good news.

"Mia, we have a problem," Trent says with a weak voice.

He points at Marcia, wearing the famous Aphrodite dress. Even if I lack the language to describe what's wrong, the way the dress hangs from her body doesn't seem right.

Mia screams—literally. She covers her mouth with both hands, trembling in silence for a moment, and when she finally speaks, her voice quivers. "What's this?"

Marcia's starting to hyperventilate. "It doesn't fit the way it did before. And I don't understand why, I haven't lost any weight!"

"Mia, you didn't do a fitting on the most important dress of the whole collection?" Trent's tone rings accusatory as he waves a hand around Marcia.

"I had nine other dresses to adjust, and I had just tailored this one to fit her perfectly days ago!"

Color and life draining from her, Mia holds her forehead. "It must have stretched when I wore it for the photo session in Athens! I ruined the dress!"

"You didn't ruin it!" I take a step forward, forgetting about Principle One. "I bet you can fix it again with a few stitches!"

Mia covers her cheeks and denies with her head. "Even if I could find my sewing kit right now, I won't have time to fix it before the show starts! This is a disaster!"

I have the vision of a giant tower crumbling down and turning to dust. Burying her face in her hands Mia eases down to the floor and pulls her knees against her chest. "This is the end of my career! Of my dream!"

Iris and I exchange a worried look. "Quick! What would Chloe do?" I ask between my teeth.

"I don't know; let's find out! Call her!"

Thank goodness Chloe came off her long strike against

technology. She still believes Wi-Fi and cell phone waves are poison-
ous, but at least she now owns an iPhone. She answers the FaceTime
call on the third ring from her medical office—It's around 2:00 pm
in Chicago—and I summarize the situation for her.

"Let me talk to her," she says.

I hand Mia the phone and stand behind her.

On the screen, Chloe sends Mia her hypnotic dark stare. She
reminds me of a firefighter attempting to talk someone out of jumping off a building. "Mia, take a few deep breaths. Let's find your
energy center."

Iris and I inhale and exhale along with the two of them and have
the vague impression of a Lamaze class.

"This is a sign!" Chloe declares. "There's a message from the
Universe hidden here and we're going to find it."

Is that all Chloe has? I want to crawl out of this place.

"Maybe the dress doesn't want Marcia to wear it," Iris chimes in.

Oh boy. We're really desperate here.

"Uh… the dress is an inanimate object," Trent deadpans, pointing out the obvious.

The fact that Mia hasn't exploded calling out how ridiculous the
idea sounds is testimony to how overwhelmed she feels.

"No, the dress is not just an inanimate object!" Chloe argues.
"The dress represents an archetype, a way of life. And that universal
force energy will find ways to communicate with us."

"So…" Iris offers, caution showing on her uneven eyebrows. "If
the dress could talk, what would the dress say?"

"The dress is saying, I belong to Mia," I blurt. I don't know where
the words come from. Perhaps I'm doing what Chloe claims she does
and channeling universal intelligence. Or perhaps I'm projecting my
own feelings onto the dress. "The dress says, Mia's everything that
represents who I am, and I don't want any other woman to wear me."

Dead silence seems to fall within our small bubble despite the
chaos around us. From the floor where she sits Mia looks up at me

and we lock eyes. She remains still for the longest time, as if processing my words.

"Three minutes!" Someone enters the dressing room clapping her hands. "Everybody get ready! And everyone who doesn't belong here, out!"

Iris and I find ourselves dragged out of the dressing room and into the audience. There, Paul signals us to follow him to the VIP section. A buff security guard lowers a rope and lets us in and Paul brings us to the first row.

Mr. X rises from his chair and signals Iris and me to take a seat at his right.

Every circuit in my body clenches in dread. "That won't be necessary, Mr. Xenakis. I'll be with the other photographers, snapping pictures."

"Everything is taken care of," he insists ushering me toward a chair with a hand on my back. "You've worked tremendously hard and deserve to sit back and enjoy the night."

Oh boy. I hate it when he hides his evilness and goes all nice. But I can't refuse without making a scene, so I take a seat next to him in front of the elevated catwalk. This is certainly an exclusive event, judging by how small and well-dressed the audience is, but the press is well represented.

After an introduction, the announcer informs the audience that the show will start with Mia's designs—you could say she's an opening band to a set of much bigger performers. Generic rock music plays, and model after model emerges from behind curtains, swaying in that unnatural walk that characterizes them. They swing their long legs and stringy arms while keeping a blank face that seems learned from a black and white French movie. I catch glimpses of studded leather, and lace, and sequins, but I can hardly focus on anything. My own words keep resounding in my mind. *The dress is saying I belong to Mia.*

Deep in my thoughts, I almost miss Xenakis' words when he

leans toward me and nearly whispers. "Sorry about bringing Crystal over; it was my last shot at distracting you so I could get closer to Mia."

Whoa. We're confidants now? By preservation instinct, I lean a little away from him.

"I want you to know I consider you a worthy opponent and you have all my respect," he continues. "You and I have more in common than you think."

No, we don't, sleaze, move away from me. His kind tone truly creeps me out.

"You and I have one big thing in common." Xenakis pauses and something softens in his eyes and his voice. "We both love Mia."

Ugh, it's so difficult not to fall for this con artist's charm. I gesture toward Iris' chair. "Yes, all three of us love Mia."

"That's not what I mean." He denies with the head while keeping his piercing eyes on me. "You and I *love* Mia. We both have seen her true essence beyond what anyone else knows." He gives a faint smile. "It takes a man in love to recognize another."

He pats my shoulder and just like that, as if he'd just made a comment about the weather, he returns his attention to the catwalk.

My heart pumps faster than the beat of the music playing on the stage. Soon, the lasts model steps onto the runway and I would know that body anywhere. It's Mia, the simple lines of the Aphrodite dress hugging her every glorious curve. Chloe was right: the gown is alive; it beams at me. The dress is in heaven because it's against Mia's soft skin, wrapped around her body. And it's true, Mia represents every bit of the strength and passion the design is meant to share.

The unstoppable woman walking the catwalk is Mia at age twelve, picking herself up from her parents' emotional abandonment. It's Mia at age fifteen, applying for jobs when she got kicked out of her house. It's Mia walking with her head held high in school, ignoring the gossip of the jealous girls in our class.

But it's also Mia at age seventeen, defending Chloe and me from the school bullies. It's Mia embracing charitable causes through her designs. It's Mia picking herself up from disappointments, leaving the diet pills behind, emerging a stronger woman.

For one moment I'm able to see her as a whole, in all her different parts—those individual pixels that make up that amazing human being I've had the honor of loving for two decades.

And I feel like crying. Every lesson the girls ever gave me on how to be a tough masculine man is swirling down the drain right now. I want to throw myself at Mia's feet and beg her to wear me like that dress. If I ever made any progress on denying it, the truth erupts inside me, unstoppable as the force of nature woman on the catwalk.

I'm *zero* percent over Mia; I'm *one hundred* percent smitten with her.

It's too late for precautions. If my heart will be smashed into pieces—so be it. I freaking love that woman and now I'm doomed. No other woman in the world will ever measure up.

CHAPTER 22

Mia

E XHILARATION COURSES THROUGH ME, KEEPING MY MIND awake and sharper than ever despite the long day. It's the rush of adrenaline after a successful fashion show. Now I remember how I managed to party all night when I was a model.

The unconventional take of the designer who became a model in her own show has attracted tons of attention from the press. Now changed into my silver party dress—another of my designs—I delight in being surrounded by reporters and answering questions. Now I can relax; after the stress I've been under for the past week, I look forward to a few days exploring Mykonos.

Done with the last reporter, I approach Iris and Ezra, who remain in the audience chairs, chatting, after almost everyone else has left.

"Thank you so much, guys! I couldn't have done it without you!" I hug Iris from the back and plant a kiss on her cheek, then do the same with Ezra. He holds on to my arms, wrapped around him, and doesn't release them. Excitement fills me. Am I over reading him?

"Can we go sleep now?" Iris yawns. "I'm exhausted."

"Sleep? The night is young!" Quentin approaches us. "We're all going to celebrate at Paradise Beach, my treat. And the three of you should join us."

"We all need to rest." Ezra releases my hands and rises from his chair, forcing me to undo my embrace. Inside, I whimper in protest.

"I will not take no for an answer." Quentin places a hand on Ezra's shoulder. "You deserve a break, my friend. I know how hard you've been working." They exchange a look that strikes me as too friendly, and then Quentin paces away.

I study Ezra, confused. "Why is he being so nice to you?"

Ezra doesn't reply. "Mia, I need to talk to you." He summons me with a hand gesture, and I follow him in the direction of the backstage.

We stand in front of the dressing rooms and he hesitates for a long time before he speaks. "Mia, are you absolutely sure you're over Xenakis?"

I widen my eyes and step back. "Uh…was Coco Channel a goddess? Duh!" I shudder. "I can't believe you're still asking me that!"

I'm having trouble recognizing this man in front of me. He shows nothing of the levity and good-natured goofiness he usually carries and that makes him more attractive—while contradictorily, it makes me miss the other him.

"I just…I don't want to find out that I…that the girls and I imposed our bias on you and stopped you from following what you really wanted to do."

"My goodness, what is it with you?" I dig my fingers into his shoulders and stare right into his eyes. "I. Am. Over. Quentin. No doubt about it."

Ezra exhales a long breath. His shoulders drop and his brows un-knit. A mixture of relief and caution fills his countenance.

"What's going on with you?" I ask.

His grave expression returns. "I'm about to take a big risk. The cause is worth the fight, but I need to know where I'm standing. This could mean fulfilling the biggest dream of my life—or losing it forever."

Seeing Ezra this serious is starting to freak me out. "Are you talking about selling *Squiggles*? Did you find a more ethical alternative?"

He doesn't answer.

"We have to talk," he says. "Is there any way we can ditch this party Xenakis is dragging us to?"

I'm about to answer that we should say we'll ride our own taxi there, and then not show up, but Paul approaches us and interrupts. "Ms. Kostopolous! There's another reporter who would like to interview you and Mr. Xenakis during our ride to Paradise Beach."

Before we know it, we're shepherded out of the building and Paul's dragging me to Quentin's limo.

"Ezra, are you coming?" Crystal's screechy voice sounds from another car's door.

Ezra looks between her and me. He glances at Quentin, then to Iris nearby. "Iris, would you keep Mia company until I come back?"

My world plummets. No, it's not possible. He's choosing Crystal over me?

As if noticing my silent panic, he fixes his gaze on me and lifts one finger. "I'll be back right away. I promise."

He gets in the car with Crystal and I hold my breath. Abandonment clamps my chest as the chauffeur drives away.

* * *

Paradise Beach is Mykonos' party central and famous for its perennial celebration. It might've been ambitious to plan an outdoor party in this brisk weather. But firepits and torches in strategic locations make it doable, along with the heat generated by dancing human bodies. It also helps that most guests are too drunk to feel the cold. Upbeat electronic music plays, but dancing couples hardly follow it, and use the music as an excuse to hold each other and make out.

The beach's barren landscape, nude of palm trees, echoes the desolation in my soul (23). Fear and dread spin inside me as Paul guides Iris, Quentin and me to our table in the beachside restaurant. I barely pay attention to the jokes of the tipsy staff or Quentin's flattering comments beside me.

When Ezra mentioned risk, did he mean he wants to give Crystal another chance? Is that why he rejected me a second time? My current panic makes the pre-show chaos in the dressing room seem like nothing. Maybe Ezra had a point about not crossing lines. If he slips away from me after this, it will be like someone amputated one of my limbs.

A bubbly waitress with a haircut similar to Iris' approaches our table with our drinks and beams at her. "Here!" After setting the tray on our table, she removes a rainbow pin from her apron's pocket and extends it to Iris. "Your drink is free. Today the bar is holding a special event honoring the LGBT community."

"Uh…" I lift a finger. "Actually…uh, her hair is just short because—"

"Oh, thank you!" Iris attaches the pin to her blazer while grinning at the server. She takes a sip of her drink and pumps a fist. "Go Rainbow Pride!"

When the waitress walks away she takes another sip and shrugs. "I gave up. I just go with it."

I wish I could joke along, but I can't. I keep staring at my bracelet watch and scanning the area, hoping to see Ezra arrive. Every minute stretches to infinity as the party continues with no sign of him.

Quentin rambles something by my side about how beautiful I look, but I don't pay attention. Diligent in her work as chaperone, Iris puts down the mirror she was using to reapply her makeup and cuts in right away. "Oh, look at that, Mia! The moon is rising!" She slides her wig back on. "Let's go take a look!"

Iris drags me by the arm and we step toward the water. Away from the torches and crowd, a chill settles into my bones, and I brace myself against the breeze.

Iris sheds her blazer and offers it to me. "Here. My chemo hot flashes keep me warm."

I thank her and slip the jacket on, studying her. With her wig on, and after re-doing her makeup, she seems unrecognizable from an

173

hour ago. Her self-deprecation may be endearing, but I hope some-day she drops it and embraces her beauty.

"Thanks," I repeat.

"Don't mention it." She flicks a hand. "I only wore it to hide my fake-looking boobs."

"Speaking of fake boobs. Where do you think Ezra and Crystal are now?" I grumble.

"Who knows?" Iris flails her arms while rocking out to the music with zero self-consciousness about her lack of grace. "Ezra behaved so weird after the show. He kept saying that maybe Xenakis wasn't such a bad person as he thought."

Please no. I hope Quentin didn't find a way to brainwash Ezra so he'd agree to get out of his way.

I must've sunk really deep if Iris' attempt at cracking me up with over the top, goofy dancing is failing. When a head bang makes her wig fall off, a pair of cheerful drag queens nearby pick it up and hand it to her.

"Hey!" One of them summons her with a hand gesture. "Come join us for the Pride dance on the stage."

Oh shoot. Please don't tell me they think she's a cross-dresser like them.

Iris gasps in excitement while straightening her wig. "Do you mind?" Her expression transmits pleading. "It sounds like fun!"

I bow my head, and she prances away with them to the stage.

Not interested in returning to Quentin's table, I join Marcia at hers. Finished with her fashion show duties, Marcia is returning to the States with the Aphrodite dress in her custody. Trent will stay a couple more days and leave when it's time to go to Santorini.

"Hey, look who's joined us!" Trent returns after his own dance with the rainbow crew and reclaims his seat. His face is flushed and he slurs his words. "Mia, are you ever gonna cut the BS and tell us exactly what's going on between you and your geeky hottie?"

"Yes!" Marcia taps on the table. "What's the deal with Ezra?"

Trent counts on his fingers. "You guys share a hotel room, play tonsil hockey after photo shoots, and lock yourselves in the restroom together…but you're *just friends*?"

Today I don't feel like giving a witty response, perhaps because I'm not sure of the answer myself.

The sudden weight of a hand on my shoulder should've startled me; instead its pleasant familiarity announces the newcomer's identity even before he speaks. "Of course we're just friends!"

My chest expands with relief and joy at the sound of Ezra's voice. I whip my head toward him and my heart jolts at the sight of his smile. He's back! He kept his promise!

And the best part: Crystal is nowhere to be seen.

He drops onto the chair next to mine and wraps one arm around my shoulders. "Mia and I are *just* friends. Friends who like to kiss each other from time to time, and sometimes fall asleep spooning in bed." He sends me an adoring look. "Right, my dear?"

His mischievous smirk encourages me to play along. "Yup, guys, we're just friends who've seen each other in their underwear." I squeeze Ezra's knee and return the loving gaze. "Did you like my new lingerie, darling?"

He pinches my cheek. "I loved it! Just as much as I love *you*, Big Airhead."

"I love you too, Big Nerd." Our usual playful words feel different tonight.

Ezra returns his attention to gawking Marcia and Trent. "But no, we're nothing but platonic friends. We're *not* sleeping together—" The pause seems to whisper, *yet.*

"Uh…I need another drink." Trent staggers away from the table and signals Marcia to follow; they stumble off, turning from time to time to stare at us.

Ezra and I laugh together. I'm so grateful to have him back.

"So…where did you and Crystal go?"

"We went for a walk down the pier." He tucks a strand of hair behind my ear and it takes conscious effort not to tremble at his touch. "I had to explain she wasted her time trying to get me back."

I should clap and cheer, but I can't move. There's something new in the way Ezra looks at me; electricity flows from his eyes to mine. Did his genius IQ invent some form of implantable brain device? One that entangles my brain waves and puts all sort of sexy images in my mind?

"Well…good."

With a chuckle, Ezra points at Marcia and Trent, still watching us from a distance. "Do you think we've puzzled them enough about what's going on between us?"

"Oh, those two could not be more baffled than they are." It feels good to project my own confusion on someone else—no one's more lost than me.

Ezra rises from his chair and crooks a finger. "I think they could."

He guides me to the dance floor where couples squeeze each other. He then wraps his arms around me and crushes me against him. Every inch of my skin in touch with his hard body shivers. He rocks me to every other beat of the music, slowing our dance to a pace of our own, our movements an excuse to hold me tight.

Is this the magic effect of the beach? The drinks? The scent of the crowd reminds me of my old party days and serves as an aphrodisiac. But the best pheromone is the scent of Ezra's sweat. End-of-day stubble gives his features a flattering angularity that makes him more attractive than ever.

"Wait a minute." Entranced by his sight and smell, I've missed an important detail. We've begun to follow the musical rhythm way too well. "You're not supposed to know how to dance."

His eyes darken. "There's a lot about me you don't know."

He brushes a stray wave off my forehead and runs the back of his finger over my cheek. My breath hitches; I know exactly what he's about to do.

And I have no intention to stop him.

He kisses me with premeditation and intent. If every other kiss we've shared has been a knee-jerk reflex of automatic sexuality, this one comes from another realm. It carries a weight that's heavy on me, grounding me in place.

I did not remember Ezra's lips this soft or his touch this silken. He takes his time tasting me, and alternates between gentle sucks on my lower lip and prying my lips open with the tip of his tongue. A warm tingle spreads over my skin, and hunger for him springs inside me like a fountain. I part my lips, he deepens the kiss, and the fountain inside me turns into a geyser.

By the time the kiss is over, I'm not sure I'll remember how to walk.

"So…what does this mean?" I ask, chest fluttering, as I hold onto his shoulders for balance. "Are we sleeping together tonight?"

His gaze radiates adoration as he touches my nose with the tip of his finger. "No."

Wait, what? "*No?*"

"Instead, I'm going to do what I should've done when we were seventeen." He plays with my hair with a soft smile. "I'm going to take you out on a date. I want to get to know you better—the new you. And I want you to get to know *me*. The *real* me. No shenanigans. No false saintly appearances." He looks up as if considering something. "And then we'll see what happens."

This is terrifying and exciting at once.

My head floats in a haze as we wave goodbye to Iris dancing and sneak out of the party. We kiss madly in the taxi all the way back to our hotel. Ezra tortures me with searing touches as he guides me through the hotel lobby to the elevator. He kisses me senseless—ravishes me—against the door to my room and I don't believe he can resist my offer to let me join him at his suite. But he does. He pecks the top of my head and leaves me in front of my room, breathless and witless and aching for more.

CHAPTER 23

Ezra

I RIS HAS RETURNED TO FLORIDA AND MIA AND I HAVE BECOME high school sweethearts exploring Mykonos together. Every time we hold hands as we stroll down the pier, she heals my wounds of adolescent rejection. Each time we steal a kiss in front of the windmills, my whole life story shifts and my adult disappointments hurt less. And as we get lost in labyrinths of marshmallow walls and narrow cobblestone streets, my future feels as bright as a batch of cupcakes waiting for me in the oven (22 a-e, 24 a-b).

Some would say that I *am* engaging in shenanigans, because my refusal to take Mia to bed keeps her enticed—when she taught me rule number seven, "always leave her wanting more," she never thought one day I'd use it against her. But the truth is that the stakes are too high to rush. I'm giving her a chance to get to know me— the adult me. And I also hope to reprogram her brain like she once worked on mine. I'm showing her that I can be the goofy friend who makes her laugh, and *also* the man who makes her shudder with desire. I'm teaching her that she doesn't need me to be a good guy to love me, or a bad boy to want me—love is much more multi-dimensional than that.

But she sure does tempt me as we tour Delos Island on an excursion Xenakis put together for his VIP mastermind. Instead of networking with everyone else, we've ditched the group and have been exploring the island's famous ruins and great natural beauty. We've cackled, making up cat superhero stories next to the famous Delos

Lions statues. We've discussed feminism while admiring the temple of Isis—an Egyptian kick-ass goddess honored in ancient Greece. And now we sit in the wild grass, on a hotel bedsheet I brought in my backpack, taking in breathtaking views of ocean, islands and the mountainous Mykonos coast (25-27).

Kneeling behind me, Mia wraps her arms around me and nibbles at my neck. I hide how much her touch affects me by keeping my eyes on my phone. It's a small miracle we have cell phone reception to keep us in touch with the rest of the tour.

She whispers in my ear, "Wouldn't it be an amazing story to tell if our first time together were on this magical island?"

"Actually, there's a legend that says that this island can curse you. If you try to steal something from it, you'll have bad luck until you return it."

Ignoring my attempt to distract her, she sits on the blanket behind me and wraps her legs around my torso. While she massages my back, she continues kissing my neck, filling me with goosebumps and throwing off my focus. "Uh…and…I can only imagine what the curse would be if… if we desecrated the island by…"

Like a contortionist, Mia shifts and circles me until we're face to face. Her legs still wrap around me, but now she sits in my lap and kisses my jaw, brushing the edge of my mouth but never claiming it. The phone falls from my fingers.

It's been like this for days. Like a rebellious teenager testing boundaries, she tempts me any moment she can. But I suspect deep inside she's grateful for my decision to take things slow. A part of her begs me to prove I'm not just here for a quick sex fix.

As she licks my neck, flushing me and flooding me with pleasure, her hands caress my chest. "Young lady." My attempt at a warning tone doesn't sound convincing. "You'd better stop that right now, or I'll make you pay the consequences."

"That sounds promising." She kisses around my ear while her hand inches south. Yup, she's trying to kill me.

"I'm warning you; you'd better stop that or you'll regret it."

She titters. "What?" She gently nips at my lower lip. "Are you going to lock me in a jiu jitsu submission hold?"

This requires an emergency intervention. The moment her lips return to my neck, I reach for my phone on the grass and search for the FaceTime app. I find the number I wanted and dial it. "Hi Mom!"

Mia slides off my lap, springs up and staggers back. "Ezra!" she protests.

I restrain a snicker and gather myself as my mother greets me through the screen. Before she launches into her usual reprimand to me for never calling her, I blurt, "Mom, did you ever tell Mia that story about when you auditioned for a commercial?" I place the phone in Mia's hands, ignoring her silent plea to spare her.

Mom gasps. "Oh, didn't I? Let me tell you!" And she launches into a detailed story of those long-gone glorious days, before she traded her narrow waist for kids. Mia politely listens, while sending me murderous glares.

Yes. That was below the belt. But I was desperate to break Mia's influence and Mom has always been the best at shaping people into behaving.

On the yacht ride back, we seek the quietest corner of deck, near the bow, away from everyone. A part of me is afraid that the presence of others could threaten our still fragile bond. I cling to Mia's hand the entire time, sending Xenakis the wordless message that he's as much part of the past as those ruins we've just explored.

From his chair on deck, where he nurses a Margarita, Trent scrutinizes us. "So…" He smacks his lips. "You two are holding hands all the time, giggling code words to each other, and disappearing, getting lost together throughout the trip…" He raises one eyebrow. "But you're *not* sleeping together."

Mia spreads a hand, then slaps herself on the forehead. "Exactly my point!" She shoots me a defiant smile. "Isn't that completely senseless? I mean, don't you think we *should* be sleeping together by now?"

I smirk right back. "We've managed not to do it for twenty-one years. I think we can keep going not-doing it one day at a time."

"I give up! I don't want to play this game anymore!" With a grunt, Trent flicks a hand and walks away.

Mia and I guffaw and exchange a high-five, when Paul approaches and shushes us. "Please! Would you guys stop it! Your cheerfulness is giving me a headache!" He finishes his drink in one large gulp.

Over the trip, I've grown used to Paul's high-strung nature. But today he seems particularly jittery.

Mia has noticed it too. "What's the problem, Paul? Is the boss in a bad mood again?" she asks.

Paul releases a loud sigh and looks up to the sky. "Yes," he mumbles, "the boss is in a *mood*. Has been for days." He points at me with his empty glass. "And it's all *your* fault." With one last annoyed look toward me, he marches away.

I admit I almost pity Xenakis now. Yes, he's played dirty trying to get Mia back—but wouldn't I have done the same? Ever since that brief, weird moment when we bonded over our love for Mia, I've been wondering if I've been biased against him. That's another reason why I've insisted on taking it slow with Mia. I need to be completely sure she's over him.

"Why did Paul say Quentin's bad mood is your fault?" Mia asks.

I kiss the top of her head. "Because he wants you, but I won't let him have you."

"Actually, from what I've recently learned, that's inaccurate." Trent approaches with a new drink. "Apparently he's not that much into Mia after all."

I frown at Trent. "What are you talking about? Didn't you watch Xenakis all trip, scheming to get close to Mia?"

"Well, Paul and I were talking the other day." Trent takes a sip and glances on the direction where Paul left, making sure he's not in earshot. "Ezra, you're making the situation worse. Xenakis is only interested in Mia because of the competition you've become. If you stepped out, he'd let her go."

That makes no sense. "Why would he say that?"

Trent lowers his voice, "Because, according to Paul, there's a woman joining Xenakis at his house in Santorini. A woman booked to stay with him."

Am I imagining things? Mia has turned suddenly quiet, and as pale as those marble columns we admired in Delos.

"Another model?" Her voice is barely audible.

"No. Apparently a respectable lady. Someone he's serious about."

Mia's face falls and with it my heart. Is that expression surprise? Is it disbelief?

Is it disappointment?

Dread fills every megabyte of my brain, overloading my RAM and soaking into my hard disk memory. Is Mia jealous? Does she still have feelings for Xenakis?

She still hasn't said a word as the yacht arrives at the port, and her silence hurts like a hard drive crash as we stroll from the pier back to our hotel. Panicky thoughts swirl inside my brain. Am I nothing but a placeholder for Mia? Am I just her "better this than nothing?"

As we approach the hotel, I can't stand the silence anymore. "The news about Quentin's new girlfriend seemed to upset you."

She avoids my gaze as she gives a weak shrug. "I confess the news affected me more than I expected."

Ouch.

I'm doomed.

Mia's eyes glimmer with tears, and every victory I've achieved until now threatens to crumble. Evil Quentin Xenakis got away with his last blow. I'm about to become Mia's shoulder to cry on again— her *sister*. I'm about to be shoved back into friend zone territory. And this time I might not be able to crawl out.

CHAPTER 24

Mia

T HE TWINGE OF DISAPPOINTMENT ABOUT QUENTIN'S NEW
girlfriend caught me off guard. It's not that I'm jealous; it's my
hurt female pride. Maybe a small part of me felt vindicated
that Quentin wanted me back and enjoyed the pleasure of rejecting
him.

Wineglass in hand, I sit cross-legged on my bed, while Ezra sits
on what used to be Iris' bed, across from mine. "Can you believe
Quentin's nerve? All trip, the guy kept scheming ways to be alone
with me—he faked a mix up with my hotel room; he flirted with me
every minute Iris looked away; he even recruited Crystal to distract
you!" I squeeze my eyes shut and shudder. "And he's had a serious
girlfriend all this time?"

Ezra nods in silence as he refills my wineglass. I'm amazed he's
not showing more anger about everything Quentin put us through
just for a stupid competition with him.

"And I was convinced he planned the New Designers Awards
fiasco to appear like my savior in the end." I sip my wine. "Why would
he do that if he didn't care about me? It just doesn't make sense."

Ezra sets down the wine bottle on the nightstand and puts the
cork back on. "He's pure evil. Let's send him the gaslighting virus."
As he repeats his usual joking lines his tone and gestures remain flat.
His magnetic energy seems to have left him.

I'm grateful for his friendly support, but I'm also a little scared.
Will I wake up any minute realizing all my infatuation is gone and

this guy is only my friend? Maybe that's why I've been in such a hurry to "seal the deal" and take Ezra to bed. A part of me feared that if we didn't act on this desire fast enough, it would evaporate.

"Taking over Iris' role as our self-help guide." Ezra returns to sit on the bed edge. "You realize the main reason why this hurt you, don't you? It's your old pattern; the more someone pushes you away, the more attracted you feel."

It's scary how much this guy knows me. "First of all, I'm *not* attracted to Quentin—"

"Are you sure?" The skepticism in Ezra's voice hints this conversation is affecting him more than I thought.

"Yes, I am sure." I set my glass down, leave the bed and pace toward him. "Ezra Daniel Cohen," I search his eyes. "Are you jealous?"

"Maybe *defensive* is a better word." His dropped shoulders and air of resignation show his fatigue. "I haven't enjoyed hearing how hurt you are about Xenakis' new girlfriend."

My head jerks back in surprise. "I never said I was hurt."

"Are you going to deny you became tearful when Trent told us the news?" His jaw and fists clench. "A part of you still dreamed Xenakis would someday admit to the world he never valued you enough and regretted losing you."

I flinch at his words and the pain in his voice. "Tearful? You must've misinterpreted—"

"We swore brutal honesty, Mia." He leans an inch away.

I may have overestimated what my friend could take now that he's more than that. Cautious, I sit on the bed next to him. "Okay, maybe a tiny part inside me did get tearful," I confess, reluctant, with a grimace. "But that wasn't me; it was the last residue of my old, wounded self. The woman who dreamed someday Quentin would ask her to marry him—or at least have the courtesy of introducing her to his family." I wrap my arms around his neck. "But I *am* done with him. I'm done falling for men who treat me bad."

"I wish I could believe you." Ezra has still made no effort to reciprocate my hug. "Do you have a clue how frustrating it's been to see you with jerk after jerk who never deserved you?" He groans. "Whether it was Xenakis, or Brad the Beef Blob, your senior prom date. Or that underwear model—who I still doubt was straight."

"They're all ancient history—especially Quentin." I tighten my embrace. "I swear those tears were nothing but my ego, which enjoyed an ex's attention I had no intention to reciprocate." I tilt my head and slant him my no-nonsense look. "Are you going to deny you felt the same when Crystal came back?"

His knotted eyebrows relax and his expression softens. "I would've needed to be an idiot, crazy, *and* drunk to want that Medusa ever again." Little by little, his lips curve. "But I admit it felt good to see her come back, just so I could say, 'no, thanks,' and 'how do you like me now?'"

I chuckle and look up to the ceiling. "Thank you! Yes! That's exactly what I mean!"

Palpable relief descends over Ezra. He inhales deeply, his posture improves, and his fists unclench. Crisis averted.

"Okay. So, are we officially done with Quentin Xenakis?" he asks.

I frown in fake concentration. "Let me think about it for a— HELL YES!" I slap a hand on the bed beside us.

His face lights up, and a mixture of love and fear twinges in my heart. This is not the mischievous smirk that made me mad in desire. This is the smile of the boy who used to hide me in his house and feed me, and who slept on the floor to let me have his bed when I had nowhere to go—and I love that boy so much. He's so generous that he just put up with me venting about my ex, while my words were killing him.

I hug him tight. "Thank you for listening to my rant. I love you, Big Nerd."

His arms give in at last and wrap around me, and he holds me against his chest. His warmth and his scent encase me and, like a knee-jerk reflex, my body reacts. The sensations hit me all at once, jolting me.

I thought for a moment that our friendship's sweet love had drowned the passion—but no. My hunger for his body is alive, and stronger than ever.

I'm fascinated with this new discovery that I can hold both images in my mind at once. The friend and the lover. The man who treats me well and the man who drives me crazy with desire.

Almost to myself, I repeat in a whisper, "I love you, Big Nerd."

He gently pushes away just enough to make eye contact. "And I love *you*, Mia."

I startle. It's the first time he's dared to say those words without hiding behind nicknames and banter. The reply clogs my throat at first, unable to come out after so many years, but it's crystal clear in my mind. The words eventually flow out in a quivering thread of voice. "And I love *you*, Ezra."

Joy flashes in his eyes but then I see no more, because he's kissing me. He kisses me with gentleness and I mirror his softness as I kiss him back. It's different from any other kiss we've ever shared. And what simmers inside me is not the fire that burned me that night I ambushed him in bed. It's a mixture of tenderness and eagerness that feels both jarring and comfortable.

While his mouth explores mine and his hands appraise my body, he coaxes me to lie in bed. And I have no doubt we're about to cross that irreversible threshold. For so many fantasies I built, this is different—and way better. And it's so wonderful I'm terrified of moving, as if our new love were an exquisite porcelain that could break any minute.

I'm two different women kissing two separate men right now. First, we're a very hungry, adult couple, way overdue for this. A couple that's eagerly helping each other out of their clothes while showering every inch of each other's bodies with touch and kisses. But we're also two seventeen-year-olds again. We're two innocent kids discovering the magic of love.

The memories from the night in his room I've suppressed all these years return at once. I relive the miracle of kissing the man I love so much I didn't dare to imagine I could desire him too.

The tremor in his hands as he helps me out of my last piece of clothing reveals he's just as overwhelmed by emotion as I am. As his fingers delight me with a taste of new talents, restlessness rises inside me.

And then, everything is a blur. A blur of hands and lips, and softness and hardness, and roughness and satin and *life*, and golden light infusing my cells. And then all our sub-parts and archetypes vanish. Our own identities disappear in an explosion and we're one. One together. One with the entire universe.

CHAPTER 25

Ezra

I HAVEN'T SLEPT THIS DEEP AND THIS WELL IN AGES. MY BODY feels as light as if it were hollow; as weightless as a microchip.

My eyelids rise reluctant, and I blink to lubricate my dry, blurry contacts—I fell asleep with them in. As my focus adjusts, the visage of a goddess with golden eyes sharpens. Mia sits at the edge of the bed studying me.

"Are you watching me sleep, you creep?" I joke.

The truth is that I'm flattered. I did my own share of stalking while she slept, around three in the morning.

Her expression is more serious than I've ever seen her. "I'm still trying to assimilate all these new sides of you. That was..." She stops.

As memories of last night return, many words come to my mind to fill in the blank. That was unbelievable. Life changing. Every bit as wonderful as I ever dreamed.

She leaves the idea hanging and resumes, "Never in a million years would I have imagined that my goofy friend would be so... amazing in bed."

I could explode with pride, but instead, I chuckle and wink. "Yeah, a guy picks up a skill or two in a decade and a half."

I sit in bed. Mia must've been awake for a while, because she's dressed and has made coffee in the room coffee maker. Perhaps a little caffeine will help me get rid of this clouded mind. I claim her mug and steal a sip. It's hot, strong and unsweetened—just like my woman.

The thought of Mia as *my woman* makes my hands tremble in excitement and I almost spill the cup.

She takes the mug back and sips from it, then sets it down on the nightstand. "So…what exactly happened last night?"

I blink. "What do you think happened?

"You tell me." She braces herself and leans a little back.

"No. You tell *me*." I cross my arms.

She considers it. "We crossed the bridge of no return for our friendship. Where do we stand now?"

Like she doesn't know I'm not standing anywhere. I'm on my knees. At her feet. "I don't want to jinx us by trying to define it with words." This is a huge step for me, the algorithmic thinker who needs to classify everything.

Her expression softens. "The only words I had to say, I already did. I love you, Ezra."

I swear it's not that I'm still trying to play it cool. It's just that if I didn't restrain myself right now, I'd make a fool of myself, blabbering with emotion. I give a single nod. "Same here."

We exchange a coffee-flavored kiss that makes me wish I could have *her* for breakfast. Then she hugs me and buries her face in my shoulder.

"F.Y.I," she whispers. "The only reason I went to senior prom with Brad the Beef Blob was because I got tired of waiting for *you* to ask me."

Ezzie could cry right now.

Damn it, who am I kidding? *I* could cry right now.

I tighten our embrace. "We'll have to make up for that one of these days."

And the craziest ideas jump into my mind. A big engagement party-slash-high school reunion, where we could recreate the prom dance we never had. A destination wedding. A life together. Children—grandchildren for my mother.

My thoughts race. We're leaving for Santorini tomorrow, which is famous for its jewelry stores. Should I surprise her with an engagement ring? Should I take advantage of these phenomenal locations and plan the perfect proposal?

Whoa, Ezra, slow down; you'll freak her out! Being turned down once, by Crystal, was bad enough—if *Mia* said no, that would kill me.

"What's up with the silence and the pensive face?" She scrutinizes me at arm's length.

"Nothing." Clearly a new crazy Ezra has sprouted inside me and joined the legion. I need to cool down, return to the US. Give us time to acclimate to each other as a couple.

Figure out what I'm going to do with *Squiggles*. Mia still doesn't know the whole story. I need to leave behind the part of me I'm not proud of before I can offer her my best.

"Have you ever felt as if you're not *one* person, but there are many parts inside you?" I ask.

She lights up. "Yes! All the time! It's like different sub-personalities inside take over from time to time. Perhaps archetypes, like mythology gods."

"Or like alternate operating systems." Nodding, I lace my fingers with hers while circling her with the other arm. "Well, there are some parts of me I'm not proud of. But I swear I'm working on them." The unsaid words are, *please don't give up on me in the meanwhile.*

She shifts in my arms. "It's the same with me. You know sometimes I can be a witch—or a *bitch*. Hopefully you'll cut me some slack when that happens."

"Bring it on." I pull her closer and nuzzle her neck. Tiny hair at her nape tickles my nose.

"Guess what," I whisper. "You've only made love with one

Ezra. There's a dozen more inside me who want to give you a sample of something new." I nibble at her silky neck. She tastes better than any cupcake she ever fed me. "Should we start testing them all?"

Goosebumps rise on her skin. "Can't wait to try them on."

We kiss again. Thank goodness our boat for Santorini doesn't leave until tomorrow. It's going to be a long time before we make it out of here.

CHAPTER 26

Mia

TRENT HAS GIVEN UP ON HIS INTERROGATIONS. BY NOW, Ezra and I must have a neon sign above our heads advertising we're sleeping together. Our last night in Mykonos, we're the most daring couple at the party in Paradise Beach. We kiss all night, unapologetic, our dance an excuse to hold each other tight. The perfect foreplay in preparation for the night ahead.

And the minute we arrive in Santorini we break away from the group and do our own exploration of breathtaking Oia. (My Yaya's voice returns to me, correcting me: "It pronounces *ee-ah*"). Where Mykonos impressed me with its all-white houses, Oia adds gorgeous pastel color buildings against amazing backdrops of blue sky, ocean and riffs. So much beauty makes my inner designer spin, envisioning new spring palette ideas. But Santorini is much more than dreamy buildings; it's a collection of geological wonders, such as jagged mountains, volcanoes and exotic beaches (28-29c).

And I wouldn't have chosen to enjoy this beauty with anyone but him. The mischievous accomplice who's still the best slumber party buddy in the world, yet also makes me tremble when he touches my knee under the table.

Did I ever fear I'd be bored with Ezra because we knew each other too well? He's right; he's many men at once. He's made of different parts, and each one calls for a different part of me. Big

Nerd and Big Airhead have tremendous fun teasing Trent or joking about our host's fake tan. Bad Boy Ezra reaches for Bad Girl Mia for the most passionate lovemaking of my life. And now Deep Ezra calls to Mia-after-the-Self-Vow—or maybe *she* calls *him*. We revel in deep conversation over dinner, contemplating the most mind-blowing sunset over ocean and rocky islands that seem to float in the sky (30).

After a succulent meal of fish and famous Santorini vegetables—the volcanic ash where they grow gives them a distinct sweet flavor—we enjoy a baklava dessert. Our serious conversation topics unwind, and Ezra seems distracted by his phone.

I swipe the phone away. "Do I have to confiscate this, so you don't forget I exist?'

"Hey, give me that!" He tries to get it back but I hold it away from him.

"What's so interesting in that phone anyway that can compete with this stunning sunset?"

I might be fishing for compliments, hoping he replies with the automatic response I taught him, "nothing can compete with *your* beauty."

However, Ezra skips the usual pleasantries. "This is about the *Squiggles* sale." He recovers his phone and thumbs on it, frowning.

I don't like to think that, just because we're now sleeping together, Ezra can take me for granted. It reminds of every time Quentin stopped appreciating me once he lured me back. It brings back my stepmother's voice, warning me that boys didn't take "easy girls like me" seriously. That men "screwed the bad girls but married the good ones."

Ezra lowers the phone and reaches for my hand. "Sorry if I seem distracted. On top of all the work emails, Paul doesn't let me be. He keeps sending me messages to make sure we join Xenakis' party tomorrow night."

We've been absorbed in our bliss and ignored all the

networking gatherings for days, but tomorrow Quentin is closing the VIP event with dinner at his villa for his mastermind members and their staff. "And that bothers you?" I ask.

"Yes." Ezra's jaw tightens. "I suspect Mr. X is trying to make you jealous by showing off his new girlfriend."

It's not impossible. Even if Quentin were serious with this woman, it wouldn't be beneath him to rub her in my face, just to pat his own ego. "It's okay; I'm not going to hide."

"We should skip it."

I shake my head. "I owe it to his staff to show up after all they've done for me this trip." I slide my second hand on top of his. "Ezra, for as long as I work in the fashion world, we'll likely run into Quentin from time to time. We have to learn to see it as normal." I sigh through pursed lips. "And, knowing his addiction to drama, yes, he may do something to provoke us sooner or later. But we won't give him the satisfaction of responding. Promise me that no matter what he or his new girlfriend do to upset me, you'll stay put, say nothing and let *me* handle them."

Looking away, he grumbles. "Okay, I guess."

"Pinky swear." I extend my little finger.

Reluctantly, his lips curve. "Okay." We hook fingers. "But if he hurts you ever again, I'm castrating him."

Chuckling, I reclaim his hand. "Nothing he does can hurt me now. I have *you*."

He kisses my knuckles. "And I'm here if you need me, but I trust you. I promise to let you handle him."

He seals the promise with a kiss and then silences the phone. I smile, proud of having averted another crisis. Maybe we do have hope as a long-term couple after all.

* * *

After the VIP event ends, Quentin is staying one more week in

Santorini. Everyone else will either board ships to other Greek islands or fly back to Athens to catch flights back home. Ezra and I still debate about whether to delay our return and explore nearby islands like Milos, Paros and Naxos.

For tonight's dinner, as facing an ex's new woman dictates, I've slaved over my hairstyle and flawless makeup. I don my own take on the little black dress, the perfect design to look casually elegant. And I flaunt the best accessory a woman can have: a handsome, impeccably dressed man on my arm. I should feel unstoppable. But when Ezra and I exit our taxi, apprehension fills me.

As we approach the impressive villa perched in one of Oia's hills, I can hardly focus on the breathtaking view of the town basking under the late afternoon sun (31a-d). "Is it too late to change my mind? I'm nervous about facing Quentin's girlfriend." I confess.

Ezra tightens the grip on my arm. "Do I have to get out the jealous gorilla?"

"No, silly. I don't mean I care for him." I lightly punch his side, then sigh. "But if history repeats itself, she'll be a smashing, barely legal supermodel who will remind me I'm past my prime for the catwalk."

"First of all, no model in the world is more beautiful than you."

I beam. There he is: my favorite AI of appropriate male responses.

"And second, you heard Trent; she's supposed to be some high-class lady."

"Worse!" I grumble. "She's probably an heiress."

Ezra narrows his eyes, pensive, as we climb the stone steps at the entrance. "He's so evil that I wouldn't rule out something shocking. Like he's dating Crystal."

I giggle. "You're right. Or Marcia? Something really weird, to mess with both of our minds?"

Ezra fakes a dramatic gasp. "Maybe it's not a lady, but a man! Maybe he's dating Paul!"

I laugh again, grateful for the tension release. "Whatever evil surprise he's planned, I'm so glad I have you there to hold my hand."

We stop at the top of the steps to exchange a quick kiss. I love this man so much. How was I so blind not to see he's all I've ever wanted?

"Mia, Ezra, I'm glad you're here." Paul greets us at the entrance. He summons us with a flick of the head and hand. "The boss needs to talk to you for a minute."

Oh boy. Here we go.

I catch a glimpse of the dinner table, already set against a glass wall that reveals the most unbelievable view of Oia set against riffs and ocean (32a-c). We follow Paul through the lavish house that seems even bigger inside than it appeared. Soft music and the murmur of other guests chatting hum in the background.

Paul takes us to an office where Quentin waits for us, sitting at a desk. I relive the feeling of going to meet the boss and wondering if I'm about to be fired.

"Thanks for coming, this will only take a minute." Quentin says as Paul closes the door. He picks up a folder from his desk and hands it to Ezra. "This is a wire transfer receipt for the refund of your donation. I'm deeply sorry, but the breast cancer foundation can't accept it."

Ezra blinks at the document, frowning. "Why?"

"Because it could affect my reputation." He pauses. "I had a conversation with Walter Tolstoi and he filled me in on some details about the way you make money through *Squiggles.*"

"Stop it." Ezra's skin flushes and his nostrils flare. Clenching his fists, he glares at Quentin. "Don't go there."

"Don't get me wrong, I'm not judging you," Quentin continues with extreme calm. "My charity deeply appreciates your generosity. But I hope you understand I can't risk bad press by accepting your money."

I seriously doubt Quentin would stop himself from accepting money made in unethical ways. He must be doing this to provoke Ezra. And he's succeeding.

"You scumbag!" Ezra snaps. "How did you even know I was in business with Walter? Have you been eavesdropping on my phone calls?"

I hold Ezra's arm to calm him down while addressing Quentin. "You're wasting your time if you're trying to start a fight between us. Ezra told me everything about *Squiggles*. Right, Ezra?"

I turn toward him and my heart drops. I'm the world's top expert at reading Ezra's expressions. And the one he wears right now screams of guilt.

Quentin's eyes dash toward me, then dart away to fix on Ezra. "So, he's told you *everything*. He's told you how his program is a dream come true for cyber-hackers and bot spreaders?"

Dread fills me. It was bad enough when I thought that app was a way of influencing young people to buy stuff.

"He's lying, isn't he?" I beg Ezra to defend himself. But he's mute, blinking fast as he does when his contacts are bothering him, not making any attempt to contradict Quentin.

Despite his efforts to appear neutral, Quentin can't conceal his satisfaction. "I will let you two speak." He rises from his chair and steps away. "Please join us at the dinner table when you're done."

The door closes behind Quentin and I stand in front of Ezra, breathing fast, my shoulders back and my chin up. "Are you going to tell me what's going on or not? Why is he saying *Squiggles* is some form of hacking app?"

Apparently resigned, he leans on the desk, still avoiding my eyes. "*Squiggles* is not just a way to deliver subliminal advertisement while you play; it extracts personal information from all your devices linked by cloud—which includes the parents' devices in the case of minors. Then it allows my AI to continue targeting you with tailored subliminal messages even when you're not using the app—through email and through bots interacting with your social media accounts."

Oh God. I ease down onto the nearest chair. All of a sudden, my dim model's brain understands the dangerous implications of selling *Squiggles*. "So, it could be used to spread rumors? To manipulate news? To influence voters in elections?"

He lifts a hand to signal me to stop. "And that's exactly why I decided not to sell it to Walter. I couldn't trust him."

"I can't believe you even considered it!" I hold my forehead. "It doesn't matter if you trust the buyer or not—once you sell the program you have no control who they share it with. How long have you been doing this?"

He hesitates and his rapid blinking resumes. "I started designing the software at Stanford."

My hands slide from my forehead to my cheeks and stop over my mouth. "So you've been lying to me for fifteen years. You never quit your hacking business."

"This is not technically hacking. And I did quit for years." His eyes dart away. "But after Crystal dumped me, I vowed to make as much money as I could, to rub it in her face."

I don't know what makes me angrier, that we're still mentioning her name, or realizing that Ezra treated me like the airhead he always joked I was; he gave me a sliver of information to pacify me, assuming I wasn't bright enough to infer the rest.

And he was right.

"I can't believe you hid this from me!" I rise from my chair and push his shoulder. "You lied to me."

"I didn't!" He scowls, taking a step back for balance. "I didn't want to worry you giving you all the details until I could fix the situation."

"There's nothing to fix. You have to get rid of that program!" My voice is getting high-pitched.

"I've spent my adult life perfecting that program." He shakes his head. "And I'm sure it can be used for good if I find the right buyer. I'm working on it."

I get right in his face. "I don't believe you!"

"Then that's your problem!" he snaps, startling me.

I stare at him in disbelief as he continues, "Mia, you need to accept that I'm no longer the little boy you used to boss around. There are lines you cannot cross. And one of them is my work."

I wince at his harsh tone. The same hardened expression that used to turn me on is terrifying when it's directed at me. My goodness, I don't really know this man. And it's scary. "I don't know what to say. I don't recognize you."

"You wanted me to be real, didn't you? Now you take it or leave it. Yes, I've been scum. I've made terrible mistakes in my life. It comes with this package."

We lock eyes. Outside the room, the sound of clapping announces the activities of the night are beginning.

Knocks sound and Paul's voice comes through the closed door. "Mia, Ezra, your presence is requested."

I pivot on my heels. To hell with this dinner. I just want to return to the hotel and put my thoughts in order.

Blind in anger and hurt, I leave the office and head to the exit but as I pass the dining room, Paul catches up with me.

"Sorry, we have instructions that no one is allowed to leave until Mr. Xenakis finishes his speech." Before I can escape, Paul has ushered me to my site at the table where Quentin addresses his guests, about a dozen people. I breathe deeply, trying to calm myself, hot blood waves crashing on my face.

Ezra appears in the dining room entrance and searches my features, his expression full of regrets. I'm too angry at him right now, so I avoid his eyes.

"Here he is!" Quentin says. "Please everyone, give a warm welcome to Ezra Cohen. I want to thank him for his generous offer of arranging for publicity at our charity event. Give him a hand."

All attendants clap and I taste sour bile in my throat. Quentin's friendly tone would fool anyone. Like he hasn't just thrown a bomb at Ezra and me.

Ezra inches toward his seat next to mine at the table and takes it. His hand reaches for mine and I pull it away. I fixate on the head of the table where Quentin speaks wonders about Ezra's generosity, but I don't listen. Stopping myself from crying consumes all my energy and concentration.

In how many other ways has Ezra lied to me? Said only what I want to hear? Did the years of training him to give "the right answers" backfire against me?

As Quentin thanks people for the success of the event, the most amazing view appears through the glass wall. The sun is setting, and the golden and pink colors bathe Oia's pastel-colored buildings, transforming their palettes (33). In any other time of my life, this would've been a sight to relish, but I'm unable to enjoy it, lost in my disappointment.

Ezra's attention is also fixed ahead, but he doesn't give up. He searches for my hand and I pull it free. Relentless, he does it again and again, each time slower and gentler than the previous time. His soft touch wins me over and I give in, allowing him to lace his fingers with mine.

"And I want to thank one more person tonight for her wonderful participation," Quentin continues. "Mia, would you please come closer."

The hair on the back of my neck stands up. Whenever Quentin has been this nice to me, terrible things happen. Against my own instinct, I release Ezra's hand, rise from my chair and step in Quentin's direction.

"There's a special woman I want to introduce to everybody

tonight, but especially to you, Mia. She's the woman I love the most in the world."

How evil can this man be? Now he's going to flaunt his new girlfriend in front of me? He probably planned my fight with Ezra, to leave me vulnerable for this moment.

Ezra springs from his chair but I gesture him to stay put and raise my chin. Bring it on, Quentin. I already know you're the worst lowlife on earth. You can't hurt me anymore.

A woman enters the room, but she's not a young model. She's a stubby lady in an all-black outfit who limps my way with the help of a cane. Once she's closer, the lines on her tanned face reveal she's elderly.

"Mia, please allow me to introduce you to Anastasia Xenakis, my mother."

My head jerks back in surprise, but I recover in time to accept the hand the lady offers me. Ezra eases back down into his chair.

"I know this is something you always wanted." Quentin's eyes soften as he addresses me. "So, I'm trying to make up for lost time."

I'm baffled. But before I can react, Quentin resumes talking. "I planned the whole trip for this moment." He sighs and throws a glance toward Ezra. "And things didn't turn out the way I wanted, but I'll carry on anyway." He gestures to a small group of elegantly dressed people I hadn't noticed at the table. They stand up and approach. "Mia, this is my aunt Olga, my brother Atticus, and my sister Cassandra."

I shake one hand after another, still struggling to understand what this is about.

Quentin turns to me. "Mia, I was blind for the longest time. I am so sorry I never valued you enough to give you the place you deserved in my life. It may be too late right now. But life's too short to live with regrets. So, here I go."

He retrieves a black box from his pocket, and flips it open, revealing a ring. It's a blinding, cushion cut, diamond solitaire, so large it must be at least five carats. The world seems to stop as Quentin gets down on a knee. "Mia—would you marry me?"

I'm frozen and mute. Flabbergasted. The earth resumes turning, first in slow motion, then speeds out to terrifying levels. Everything around me seems to spin. I'm screaming inside, but no sound comes out.

CHAPTER 27

Ezra

MY WORST NIGHTMARE HAS COME TRUE.

First of all, evil Mr. X just stole my thunder for the rest of my life. No proposal to Mia I ever plan will match this. The Santorini sunset. His luxurious house. The relatives she always wanted to meet. The most gigantic freaking diamond in the world.

But second of all, I'm doomed. I promised—I pinky-swore to Mia that I would not intervene and would let her handle anything Xenakis threw our way. If I make a scene right now and go punch this bastard like he deserves, I'll be humiliating Mia in front of all these people she's worked so hard to network with. I have to grind my teeth and hold my breath, powerless.

And third of all, a small part of me always knew this would happen—like Hephaestus must've known Aphrodite would not last with him.

Please send him to hell, I beg quietly. Please tell him to disappear. Please tell him I'm your man now.

Instead, Mia pivots in her heels and runs out of the room without giving any answer at all.

Swallowing my humiliation, I follow her.

At the closed entrance, a frantic Mia pushes and pulls at the door, grunting, unsuccessful. It takes me a few moments to find the deadbolt holding it locked. The moment I open it, Mia rushes outside.

As we descend the steps, she braces herself against the chilly wind, her face pinched with disturb. A taxi is dropping off some late guests and she waves at it without saying a word.

We climb into the car in silence, and I fish the hotel card from my suit jacket to extend it to the driver without words. Then, we proceed to have the most painful, silent cab ride of my life.

A while into the ride, the anger and frustration boil inside me, and I'm unable to hold quiet anymore. "You didn't say no."

Mia stirs from her trance and turns to look at me. "What?"

I clasp my fists, feeling like the loser nerd who used to only get breadcrumbs of her attention. "You didn't say no when Xenakis asked you to marry him."

Her eyes widen and she slowly shakes her head, but it's not convincing. "He just took me by surprise."

This is not what I want to hear. I need to hear that she has no doubt that I am what she wants. I need to hear that I'm not her *better this than nothing*.

"I can't believe you didn't shut him up immediately. That you didn't tell him you're taken."

She lifts her hands and huffs in exasperation. "Ezra, this is no time for your insecurities. I've just been emotionally highjacked. I need more support from you."

"I'm sick of being the man who's always there giving you support!" I shout, startling her. "It hasn't gotten me any acknowledgment so far. Or any respect."

"Excuse me? Are you raising your voice at me—again?" She rests her knuckles on her hips. "*I* am the one who's supposed to be angry here. You're the one who's been hiding things from me!"

"Don't change the subject, damn it!" I punch the back of the passenger seat in front of me. "Is it too much to ask for you to open your mouth and say, 'I'm sorry I cannot marry you, I'm with someone else'?"

Her head jerks back and her eyelashes flutter. "I was just confused and overwhelmed."

And that hurts even more. "This is exactly what you wanted, isn't it?" I ask with a ragged voice. "It's like the bastard had us wired that day you admitted you always dreamed of him asking you to marry him; introducing you to his family."

"I agree, this was surreal." She shudders. "That's why I couldn't think clearly and had to step away."

Pain pierces me. "Oh my God; you *are* considering it."

The silence probably lasted just a few seconds, but in my mind, it stretches like an eternity.

"Of course not," she says at last in a weak voice.

Too little, too late.

I've been an idiot. Of course, I could never have been her man. I'm nothing but the emergency guy. The guy she goes to when she has no other choice. Her nicotine patch for men.

The taxi has arrived and I drop a bill in the partition window, fingers clumsy and trembling with anger. I yank at the door handle, kick the door open and step out without waiting for change or helping Mia out.

I'm suffocating as I march to our hotel room. I could cry right now, except that my eyes feel dry like marbles. I blink and blink, my contact lenses burning me like acid. This is high school and college all over again. I'm Ezzie on the sidelines, watching the unreachable girl leave him behind and run toward some other jerk.

CHAPTER 28

Mia

I FEEL LIKE SMACKING EZRA ON THE BACK OF HIS HEAD. How can he be so insecure? Why can't he see that Quentin is no competition for him? That it was shock and not temptation that kept me mute at the villa? But I also want to smack myself. How didn't I see it coming that Quentin's revenge would be to try to break us up? And that he'd follow his pattern and jar us in the most dramatic possible way?

Today of all days, Ezra broke his custom of overpaying taxi drivers. In his hurry, he handed over a bill smaller than our cab fare, so I have to dig out my credit card, hidden in a secret pocket in my dress, to pay the difference. The card reader is slow, and it takes forever until I can follow Ezra into the hotel.

By the time I arrive at our room, he's halfway packed. He's busy wrapping cables and putting away his multiple electronic devices. I panic; is he really leaving me?

"Listen to me, you, stubborn head!" I pace toward him. "I never said I was considering Quentin's proposal."

He rotates his wrist and looks at his Apple watch. "And it took you all this time to come up with that answer?"

I pull chunks of my hair. "You have to stop reading rejection everywhere!"

He finishes packing his devices in his backpack and moves to the next suitcase, dumping his clothes in it. "Oh, don't worry. I am done being rejected. If a man learns something in a decade and a half, it's not to stay where he's not valued."

"How can someone with an IQ of a thousand behave like a clueless teenager!" I look up to the ceiling. "I'm tired of being the understanding friend who lifts your self-esteem." And perhaps I'm tired of being the chaser, running behind him and begging him to give us a try. I'm reliving that time after we kissed when he withdrew from me. I managed once again to fall for the man who pushes me away.

And worse, is he giving up on me so easily—again? I'm only the girl who's good for a fun time but not worth fighting for?

In the restroom, he washes his hands with angry, abrupt movements. He removes his contact lenses and throws them in the wastebasket, then slides on his glasses. "I'm too furious to talk right now. I'm out of here."

"You can't leave the island at this time of night!"

"I'll pay a private boat."

What I really want to do is cry and fall on my knees and beg him, *Please don't leave me like you did sixteen years ago. Please don't abandon me like Mom did.*

But no. I'm done being that fragile woman who desperately sought love. I make my voice glacial. "If you're going to be this idiot who can't see that he's throwing away something really good, then I don't want you in my life."

We lock gazes, and for an instant, doubt and fear flash in his eyes giving me hope.

But he recomposes himself and recovers his cold mask. "Fine."

He swings his backpack over his shoulder, drags his suitcase out and disappears with a slam of the door.

It takes me a moment to react, then panic floods me. "No, wait! Come back!" I run after him, but he's gone. I rush down the stairs to the lobby and out. The sound of a car door closing makes me whip my head on the direction of the street. Our cab driver had the business sense to stay, guessing one of us would need him soon.

I run toward the vehicle, but it's too late. I watch the taxi drive away, tears brimming in my eyes.

I can't believe I managed to lose Ezra again. This time forever.

CHAPTER 29

Mia

THE RETURN HOME BLURS IN IN MY MEMORY. I BARELY RECALL the flight bringing me from Santorini to Athens. And my flight back to the US—layover included—becomes a big void of darkness. I only remember the pain that hit me midair as denial wore off and the realization of what happened with Ezra sank in. Yet, my tears clog in my eyes, refusing to come out.

I've been traveling for a whole day and I'm still not close to home. Bad weather has caused a cancellation of the Newark-LA leg of my trip. On an impulse, I ask the airline employee trying to accommodate me if I could exchange my ticket for a trip to Chicago and, to my surprise, they agree. I need Chloe. As the other leg in our old tripod, she's the best person to understand how miserable I feel about losing Ezra. Chicago also houses Sophia, and I can use her support too.

Chloe's old apartment is the perfect place to throw a pity party, but it won't be for long. She's putting it on the rental market now that she's moving in with Maxwell. The girls have been trying to cheer me up, but they're torn too. They love Ezra as much as they love me, and seeing our love story end before it even started seems to have shaken them as much as it has me.

"It's the eternal story," I mutter as the three of us snuggle under a blanket on Chloe's big floral couch. "Guys just want to sleep with me. But then, when life gets real, I'm not worth the trouble and they'd rather high-tail it." My mind whispers, *Like Mom did.*

"Don't say that," Chloe rubs my back. "Ezra loves you."

I keep my eyes fixed on the bay window. A mixture of drizzle and ice falls from Chicago's brooding late November sky. "I know that. But he's always loved me as a friend. *I* was the one who shoved myself into his life, trying to become more than that." I remember that night I threw myself at Ezra, arguing that our friendship love was enough to justify breaking my vow. I was bluffing, I already had feelings for him. Should I have taken a hint from his rejection that he wasn't really interested? I whimper and sink deeper in the couch. "I did exactly what I used to do with Quentin: I chased Ezra with desperation. Why am I even surprised to find out he wasn't truly invested in us? That he'd only been taking what I offered because it was free?"

"That's not true!" Chloe insists.

Of course, it's a sensitive issue for Chloe. Ezra has been her friend even longer than mine. And now she'll be torn between defending him or me. I spoiled our friendship with him for all of us.

And then, of course, there's my sweet Sophia. "I'm sorry, Sophia," I hold her knuckles. "You've always been so squeamish when I tell the story of Ezra and I making out—and now I'm forcing you to listen to all this."

"It's okay." Sophia sniffles. "Once you add love to it, the story stops being yucky."

Love. Oh yes. Love had always been there. But just like all those sub-parts of us we discovered during the trip, it seems I also have hundreds of variations of my love for him. Like different shades on a color wheel.

"But I insist, Mia. You need a good cry." Chloe squeezes my arm. "Until you can process what happened, you won't be able to heal."

Chloe has been trying to get me to open up, even threatening me with a marathon of tear-jerker movies. "But I can't," I repeat for the tenth time. "The tears are stuck behind my eyeballs. Maybe I'm done crying for the rest of my life."

Chloe moves the blanket aside and gets off the couch. "Well, I didn't want to have to do this but this is an emergency." She disappears into her room, and after a few moments, reappears with something in her hands. It's an ancient photo album I recognize from our high school years. Chloe's family must've been the last clan in the world to embrace digital photos.

Chloe deposits the heavy album in my hands. It smells of mildew and thrift store. When I fail to move, she opens it and turns the pages herself.

This is supposed to be the ultimate torture to force me to cry. But I'm so numb not even the image of Chloe at age twelve, hugging four-eyed, rail thin Ezra touches me. Sensitive Sophia bursts into tears immediately. In a way I feel thankful for it. It's like she's doing the task for me and now I don't have to. She's crying for the two of us.

I stare at the image as if seeing it through a telescope, from a long distance. Or perhaps as if seeing it through thick glass. "Maybe it's just the jetlag; but I feel nothing." I set the album down and reach for the hot chamomile tea Chloe made for me, still on the coffee table. "I'll be fine. After so many times picking myself up from heartbreak, I'm an expert on the system." I sip the hot liquid and it burns me, but I don't flinch. "I'll mope for a little while, then I'll distract myself with work and time will do the rest."

"You have to call him," Sophia sobs. "You guys can't throw away your chance to be happy together. What's worse, you can't throw away over two decades of friendship—of history."

"I'm too angry with him," I groan. "It's bad enough he lied to me. I can't believe he's such an idiot that he really thought I would take Quentin back. Who does he think I am?" I punch the cushion with the edge of my fist. Maybe the numbness is finally breaking. "I can see Quentin's plan now with excruciating clarity. He prepared the ground ahead of time, keeping my nerves on the edge about the awards. He presented himself as the savior, by helping me get into the Mykonos show...I wouldn't doubt he made Paul tell Trent about his 'new woman' to make me jealous. Then he provoked that fight with Ezra, to break us up and weaken my defenses."

"I can't believe he had the nerve to propose in public, knowing you were with Ezra!" Chloe hisses. "Why would he do that? Revenge?"

"Worse! Quentin claims he wants me back for real!" I point at the table where my phone has been lighting up with messages from Quentin, begging me to talk to him—I so need to block him, but don't have the energy right now. "I can't believe I ever cared for that drama-seeking bastard."

For a moment, I think Chloe will get her wish of making me cry. But I quell the gush of sadness and anger rising inside me.

My phone ringing interrupts us. Sophia gasps and Chloe stiffens, and their eager eyes show their hope this is Ezra calling. But it's not the *Squiggles* theme ringtone. "It's just Trent."

Poor Trent must be wondering how come I didn't return to work today as planned. I seem to have abandoned the *atelier* and dumped all the work on him. I brace myself for a reprimand and pick up. "Hey, Trent, what's up?"

"Mia, you'll never believe this!" The excitement in his voice takes me by surprise. "We have an offer for the Aphrodite dress!"

"What?" I straighten myself on the couch.

"Some billionaire's wife saw it at the fashion show in Mykonos and asked the price. Thinking she'd bargain us down, I told her it was a hundred thousand dollars and she accepted!"

I try to reply, but no sound leaves my mouth.

"Do you have any idea what this means?" Trent's joyfulness is out of character for him. "The money is the least of it. She wears that dress at a gala, she talks about it to her club friends, and you'll have the rich and famous knocking at your door! You might have a future in *haute couture* after all!"

I should be happy; this is exactly what I said I wanted. Then, why do I feel so miserable?

Perhaps because I was wearing that dress the day Ezra kissed me at the Hephaestus temple? Maybe because I still remember his adoring gaze the day of the photo shoot, and again at the fashion show?

As I wrap up and disconnect the call, the suppressed memories break free. I relive the night I cried myself to sleep in Ezra's arms; the times he protected me from Quentin's schemes. I see him again soothe me when I panicked before the fashion show.

I open the album randomly and a photo from our senior prom springs into my sight. It's the exact same picture I once burned—me being crowned prom queen. Next to me stands not Ezra, but Brad, the star quarterback. And the seventeen-year-old me fakes a smile but cries deep inside. Because a few nights back I'd kissed Ezra and now I couldn't stop thinking about him.

My eyes slide to the white, flowy dress I'm wearing—the first design I made, using my grandmother's sewing machine. An idea crystalizes in my mind and for the first time it hits me that the Aphrodite dress was inspired by it.

"Only now do I realize the Aphrodite dress was never about honoring the Bad Girl," I mutter when I can talk again. "It was my attempt to return to my innocence; to reclaim who I was before the world wounded me." The stubborn tears flow at last and I dissolve in sobs. "I lost my dress!" I wail. What I'm really saying is, I lost my innocence. I lost my Ezra.

God bless Sophia and Chloe, they immediately embrace me, hold me and let me cry forever with great patience. But it's not the same. I want my best friend's arms around me. The man who could snap me out of my misery with a gut-busting joke. The boy I really wanted to take me to prom.

A long time later, I raise my head from Chloe's shoulder and accept the tissue she offers me to clean my eyes and nose.

"This is excellent!" Chloe says, but tears also hint in her voice. "The moments we touch bottom in our lives are worth celebrating. They are when our old wounds are closest to the surface, and therefore, easier to heal."

I blow my nose. "What good can come from remembering old wounds?"

"Well, that's a good question." Chloe uses a fresh tissue to finish wiping the tears from my cheeks. "And it's very convenient that we happen to be ninety minutes away from Greenyard, Illinois, where your story with Ezra began, and also where your deepest wounds were born."

"What do you mean?" I ask, tense, knowing the answer.

With tenderness, Chloe places her hands on my shoulders. "It's time to confront the past you've been avoiding and go make peace with your father."

Near panic descends over me. "I can't possibly go visit Dad...I have to get back to work right away and I have a lot to catch up with."

Chloe picks up my phone from the coffee table and extends it to me. "Well, it doesn't hurt to say hi."

Damn it. As usual, Chloe has a point.

I accept the phone and search my contacts for that number I haven't dialed in over a decade, the contact labeled as "Dad." My fingers tremble as I tap on it and let it ring.

CHAPTER 30

Ezra

A FTER A DEPRESSING OVERNIGHT BOAT RIDE TO ATHENS, twenty-four hours in transit and two stops, I'm back home in San Francisco, drowning my misery in coding work.

I've picked up the phone to call Mia a dozen times but stopped myself. Sometimes because anger convinces me *she* needs to apologize first. And other times, because I'm so overwhelmed by desolation I can't imagine she'd ever want to hear from me again.

After all, Mia has never waited for a man to take the first step; the way she pursued me during the trip is proof of that. If she really had any intention to get me back, she'd be all over me already.

Sunk in my black recliner, I stalk her *Instagram*, *Twitter* and *LinkedIn* accounts hoping for an update about her life. Her vanishing from her social media worries me; that used to happen every time Mr. X. reappeared. Is she considering his proposal—maybe even talking to him?

To make matters worse, the stupid cookies on my phone browser must've registered my recent whereabouts. My social media ads keep suggesting vacation places in Greece and fashion design lines. When an ad appears for evil Quentin Xenakis' label, I'm tempted to throw my phone against the wall, but instead just curl into a ball and sulk. From the side table, my beer-drinking monkey figurine reproaches me for losing not only Mia, but probably all our girls.

And this late afternoon I'm at the gym, venting some aggression during my jiu jitsu practice with Ian. But I should know that the whole point of jiu jitsu is using the opponent's strength against himself.

Ian has just slammed me onto the mat and locked me in a pretzel-like hold.

"Ow, Ow!" I tap the mat signaling my surrender.

He frees my neck but makes no effort to let go of my legs or get his weight off me. "Dude, what's up with all this anger today? That's the opposite of what you want to channel in a fight."

"Still having trouble breathing here." I point at his knee on my chest.

Once he releases me, I cough a few times and sit on the mat, legs crossed, imitating his posture.

"What the hell is going on with you?" Ian asks. "Did something happen on your trip with the famous Mia?"

"I don't want to talk about it," I grumble.

"Well, good, because I'm not your freaking therapist. If you're so upset, you should call a bunch of friends and go drink." He tilts his head. "Or call your beloved girls."

My voice is barely audible. "The girls' loyalties are with Mia."

"Your girls deserted you?" Ian rises his eyebrows.

"They keep texting, to check on me. Texting!" I groan. "No more calls, no more video chat. I knew this would happen: our friendship has turned awkward."

Ian frowns. "So…you're offended because they're *texting* you." He clicks his tongue "This has to be the ultimate example of a First World Problem."

I ignore his veiled reprimand. "The point is that I lost all four of my best friends in one sweep. And now I'm miserable and don't have anyone to talk to."

"Man, you're spoiled. You think you know what being miserable is?" He leans forward to get his face closer to mine. "Remember I have *real* misery stories from jail and Brazilian *favelas* to traumatize you for life; don't test me."

Ouch. Ian's always ready to slap me into perspective.

But no, today I'm too sunken into despair to be reasonable. My voice rises. "I've been dreaming of Mia since age *twelve*; now I can say it without censoring myself. And when I finally admitted it… when I thought I could die of a joy overload because she'd accepted me—her stupid celebrity ex-boyfriend had to appear to claim her back." I punch the mat with the edge of my fist. "And of course, she'd choose him over me! I was nothing but her fallback guy! The man who's good to scratch an itch, but then she's happy to ditch him if she finds something better!" The anger and hurt from the memory returns to me. "The man she doesn't take seriously enough to declare in front of everybody that she's with him!"

Ian must've tricked me with a mental jiu jitsu move. Because I just vented to him as if he were my *freaking therapist*. I growl. "And why am I even talking to you? Your advice didn't work. You told me to be all the way in or all the way out. And I tried being all the way in and *this* is where it got me." I scramble to get off the floor, intending to leave. But I've barely risen to my feet when Ian pushes my legs and makes me fall back on the mat.

"You know what you just did wrong?" he asks with eerie calm.

Once again, I forgot his eternal jiu jitsu advice. "My stance wasn't wide or stable enough."

He nods. "You always have to stand on a solid base. No matter what your opponent does to get you off balance, you return to base—to home."

I'm sure there's a metaphor here, but my algorithmic brain has trouble grasping it.

"I repeat. Stop talking like you're in the middle of a tragedy, when all you're facing is a minor inconvenience." Ian rearranges on the mat to sit with one knee bent, one leg extended. "Let's start all over with your story. Why are you *inconvenienced*?"

I draw in a lungful and then proceed to thoroughly spill my guts.

But there's something different now. Under Ian's no-nonsense scrutiny I'm forced to tell the story without any embellishment. I tell him how Mia and I grew closer during the trip. How I struggled with the dilemma of risking our friendship for a temporary fling. How I realized she was worth any pain and decided to bet it all for her. How finally having her was the most glorious moment of my life. And then how I blew it.

"So…if I'm getting this right," Ian's Portuguese accent is getting thicker as the day approaches its end. "You knew from the beginning that her drama-junkie ex-boyfriend would do everything possible to de-stabilize her and sabotage you. Yet, when he found a way to do it, you acted all surprised, blew things out of proportion and pushed away the woman you claim is the love of your life…" He squints. "All because she *hesitated* for a second or two before answering a question?"

Dang it. All of a sudden, my romantic drama sounds ridiculous. As if Ian slammed me back onto the mat in another submission move, it hits me what an idiot I've been.

"I must've regressed to the times when Mia was the popular girl and I was the nerd." I mumble to myself. "When she didn't reject Xenakis, I felt like the biggest loser in the world."

"A loser?" Ian shoots me a blank stare. "Says the man who's a gazillionaire and works only for fun."

I open my mouth to clarify that I'm only a penny-millionaire, but he lifts his hand to stop me. "And please, spare me the need to praise your good looks. My super-macho Brazilian ancestors would turn over in their graves if I ever flattered another man."

A memory I haven't shared with Ian haunts me. How Mia only pursued me because I didn't count as breaking her vow. "I'm only the guy people seek out because they want something. Mia became my friend in school mostly because I helped her with homework. Most women who ever dated me did it out of interest. Most guys who ever befriended me just wanted me to use *Squiggles* to promote their products."

Speaking of *Squiggles*. I finally found a buyer Mia would've approved of. But what's the point now?

I'm stuck in self-pity. "I don't even know why *you* are my friend."

Silence falls for a few breaths before Ian talks. "Well, about that… there's something I've been meaning to confess." Ian's gaze falters for a moment. "When I first approached you, I knew I couldn't afford your rates as a marketing consultant. All I wanted was an excuse to talk to you in person because…" His dark eyes seem apologetic when they meet mine. "Because I wanted to break your neck."

It takes me a few moments to assimilate that. "You what?"

He plays with a loose thread in the hem of his gym shorts, while avoiding eye-contact. "I'd seen you on online news with a certain woman I've been trying to track down for the longest time. I needed to find out if you were the reason why she rejected me—you know, before beating the crap out of you."

My jaw hangs low.

"But halfway through that first interview, I figured out you were a good guy and not who I needed to beat up. Then you called me back the next day and asked me to be your trainer. Since then, you grew on me."

I haven't had a chance to react when Ian resumes. "The bottom line is: it turned out to be great. I got an amazing new friend, and you got one in me too." He uses his index finger to tap my forehead. "So never worry if people seem to approach you for the wrong reasons. Give them time and they'll learn to dig you, like I do now."

I wonder if Ian's ancestors heard that, but I consider it quite flattering. In fact, I'm a little moved right now.

The song Baby Shark bursts from a distance and I jolt. That's the ringtone I assigned to Mia on my phone, just to tease her, when I installed the *Squiggles* song as my ringtone on hers. I spring off the mat so fast that not even Ian has a chance to stop me. I dash across the training room into the shelf area where I've left my gym bag and

219

fish my phone out. My heart explodes in excitement when I confirm her name displays on the caller ID.

"Hello! Mia!"

It's too late. The call has gone to voicemail.

I rush to call her back. But it's going straight to voicemail. She must be trying to call at the same time or leaving a message. Growling in frustration, I search for other numbers I have from her but find only her office, which is unlikely to be open on a Saturday evening.

"Wow, dude," Ian comments from his spot on the mat. "You're going to need to teach *me* that jump."

I wave at him, signaling the session is over, while picking up my gym bag. As I cross the gym and hurry to the parking lot, I keep trying Mia's number over and over with no success.

Once in my car, I give up on connecting and check my voicemail. As I hoped, there's a new message from Mia.

"I'm so royally pissed at you!" Mia's words slur a little, suggesting she's gotten into the wine. But her angry voice sounds like an angelic chorus to my ears. "Do you know where I am? I'm in freaking Greenyard. Right now, I'm with Chloe at Mrs. Smith's B&B. Across the street I can see the park where you, Chloe and I met. And it freaking hurts that you're not here with us."

Pain stabs my chest. I know exactly the place she's referring to.

"I've been waiting for you to pick up your sorry ass and call me for days now, damn it!" Mia continues. "And every second that goes by, you're digging yourself deeper in the hole. But you know what? Forget it!" Slurping sounds indicate she's sipping her drink. "I've been sitting here like a stupid seventeen-year-old again, holding my breath for a call from you. I've been dreaming of the moment when you and I would finally crawl back to each other and melt away in a puddle of ridiculous puppy love." She pauses. "But I'm sick of being the hunter. I'm done chasing you, mister. It doesn't matter how much I effing love you and how miserable I am for losing you, for the first time in my life I'm going to play hard to get."

"I love you too. I'm also miserable," I mutter, even knowing she can't hear me.

The slurping sounds mix with sniffling. "If you ever realize what an idiot you've been and come get me, it's going to be too late. You're going to need to lure me, beg me…crawl on your knees. But I'm going to turn you down over and over again like you did to me."

My pulse quickens. She can't be serious. Can she?

"And the very first thing I'm going to do now is block you on my phone. No more GIFs and funny videos. No more texts. If you want to talk to me, you come get me, so I can reject you face to face."

She disconnects the call, leaving me staring at my phone, speechless.

CHAPTER 31

Mia

RENT SEEMS TO HAVE FORGIVEN ME AT LAST FOR DELAYING my return to work—things are crazy at the *atelier*, as holiday sales season just began. But the trip to Greenyard, my first visit in fifteen years, is something I needed to do.

What a shock to learn Dad had a stroke last year and became wheelchair bound. He's just recently made enough progress that he's balancing with a walker. Like me, he's non-sentimental. But his expression, and the long hug we share in our re-encounter reveal he's relieved to see me, and regretful for the years lost.

My stepmother left him a long time ago. His new caregiver and girlfriend, Luz, has only wonderful things to say about how lovingly he talks about me. I like her at first sight and I'm glad she takes such good care of him. I wouldn't have minded the chance to confront Roxanne: I would've loved to flaunt my success as proof that she was wrong to believe me a hopeless case. But I guess not all loose ends can be tied up.

That first visit with Dad, reminiscing about the past and exchanging wordless forgiveness, felt therapeutic. But the visit to Greenyard heals me beyond that. Over the weekend, Chloe and I roam around our old town, hunting for memories. Or better said, we drive around it. After living in LA for years, I'd forgotten how freaking cold the Midwest can be in late November.

The ice cream parlor has been remodeled into a diner, but Mr. Thompson's barbershop still looks the same, sporting its eternal red and white pole. Chloe's old home, the "witches' house," has been demolished, but luckily The Willows family's naturopathic store still stands, and it smells the same—a mixture of fresh herbs, incense and vitamins. Chloe's grandma still runs it with as much energy as two decades ago. It's awesome to sit in the store with Chloe, chatting and watching the town pass by through the large glass window—just like in the old days.

But it's not the same without Ezra.

This trip has been torture, because every corner of this town reminds me of him. My Ezra at age twelve, obsessed with videogames and monkeys; so pathologically shy, his parents were convinced he had autism. My Ezra at age fifteen, winning the school math contest, wearing glasses as thick as binoculars. My Ezra at age seventeen, who only showed his brilliant wit to Chloe and me. I've purposely avoided our middle school and our high school, because I couldn't stand to wander those venues without him.

It's so frustrating that when I finally worked up the nerve to call him to apologize, he didn't answer. That made me furious, because Ezra is *never* more than inches away from that phone! He must've sent my call to voicemail on purpose.

The past few nights I slept with my phone in my hand, waiting for a call from him—even after I'd blocked his number. After all, if anyone could hack his way out of a phone block, it would be Ezra. Every time some stupid phone around me plays the annoying *Squiggles* theme song, I jump off the ground, mistaking it for his ringtone.

Sunday evening, Chloe decides she wants to visit Ezra's mom before she returns to Chicago—I plan to stay with Dad for a few more days, catching up. She even bought her some herbal supplement Mrs. Cohen likes from Grandma Willows' store. No wonder Chloe has always been Mrs. Cohen's favorite.

"Can you go without me?" I grumble as I zip shut my Louis Vuitton weekender on the B&B bed. "Ezra's mom has always hated me."

"No, she doesn't." Chloe hangs her green and orange woven bag from her shoulder. "Besides, her house is on the way to your dad's."

I've always liked Mrs. Cohen—more than she's ever liked *me*. It's not that I wouldn't enjoy seeing her. But now every time I hear her New Jersey accent, I'll think of Ezra. Especially of the teasing we did to each other calling her while in Greece.

I try to convince Chloe to let me stay in the car, with the engine running and the heat on. But of course, the environmentalist in her won't hear of it. And there's no way I'll stay in the car freezing, so I'm coming in.

Chloe parks her Mini Cooper in front of the immaculate driveway, flanked by piles of symmetrically packed snow—Mr. Cohen has always had a fixation on shoveling snow. The sloped-roof blue farmhouse must be the least changed place in town. Even if I can't see the second story deck from here, an avalanche of memories from the night Ezra and I kissed overcomes me.

Fortunately, the arctic wind doesn't allow me to indulge in nostalgia too long. My stylish light trench coat might look dashing, but it does a poor job of protecting me from frostbite as we wait on the front porch until someone answers the door. The instant Mrs. Cohen lets us in, I make a beeline for the fireplace.

"Hello to you too, young lady." Mrs. Cohen has finished hugging and kissing Chloe and lifts an eyebrow at me.

Darn it. In my hurry for warmth, I forgot to greet her. Here I am, committing the same impolite mistakes that earned me her dislike as a teenager. "Oh. Hi, Mrs. Cohen."

She wrinkles her nose as if something stank and clicks her tongue. "I see someone *still* hasn't learned to behave like a lady."

I consider giving her a smirk and replying, *I'll take that as a compliment.* But somehow, after making peace with Dad, I feel less inclined to snark.

And also, there's something I have to do. Not for Ezra; not

even for Mrs. Cohen. But for me. "Mrs. Cohen, I think I owe you two decades of apologies."

She startles as if I'd thrown a firecracker at her feet. "You what?"

Chloe, who took a seat on the couch, sends me an encouraging look. She clears her throat while rising, mumbles something about saying hello to Mr. Cohen, and disappears into another room.

I resume before Mrs. Cohen can speak. "I'm sorry for all the torture I submitted you to through the years. I'm sorry for feeding Ezra cupcakes and sabotaging his special diet—even if he wasn't really allergic to gluten, sugar, and dairy. And I am sorry about the incident with the blue food dye; I didn't know he really *was* allergic to that."

It's liberating to say all this. "And I'm sorry I taught Ezra to cut class, and that I gave him his first and last cigarette. And I'm sorry I offered him his first beer and…" I wince. "His first joint."

Mrs. Cohen stares at me with a blank expression for the longest time. I hold my breath, waiting for her reply.

She finally blurts, "My nephew is now a niece."

That was the last thing I expected to hear. "Excuse me?"

"Yup. My nephew George now calls himself Shantal and has long hair and boobs. Oh, and my other niece cooks meth in her garage and grows hallucinogenic mushrooms for sale in her garden."

My eyes turn huge. "Uh…I'm missing your point."

"My point is," she moves closer to me. "I've come to understand cupcakes, cutting class, and a little experimenting weren't the end of the world."

Her words sink into me slowly, as does her soft smile. Am I hallucinating? Mrs. Sarah Cohen is *smiling* at me?

"Uh…I thought you hated me."

"Of course I didn't!" She snorts and wheezes a laugh very

similar to Ezra's. "I was delighted that you were Ezra's friend despite how awkward he was. Why do you think I kept looking the other way every time he let you sleep here whenever you had a fight with that witch Roxanne?"

Wait! She knew about that? "But you kept saying I was a bad influence on him…and Roxanne said you both thought I was a floozy."

She raises her eyebrows and tilts her head. "Did it ever occur to you that a woman as dim as that might not have been a reliable source?"

I'm out of words. At once, every hurtful word Roxanne ever told me is exposed as nonsense and hateful lies. As silly as her ignorant grammar when she used the word "worsest."

"Hon, someday I'll have to tell you the *real* stories of my youth I don't share with Ezra. You were not the first girl in the world to sneak through a window at night to party with friends or visit a boy." Mrs. Cohen's eyes dart away, and she chuckles. "In a way I was using reverse psychology. I was relieved that Ezra had such a huge crush on you and listened to your fashion and socialization advice. This may be coming too late now. But you've always had my blessing."

She offers her hand and I shake it, feeling about to cry. Then she takes one step forward and hugs me. I want to wail, sob and slobber. This is even better than having had a chance to rub my success in my stepmother's face.

It takes huge effort to keep myself together. By the end of the hug, I feel like I've ridden a time machine to the past and changed my history of being the "Worsest floozy in Greenyard."

I hardly register when we say goodbye, and this time don't feel the freezing wind when we head back to Chloe's Mini Cooper. Chloe remains silent for the longest time, letting me process my encounter.

And bit by bit, like a thousand little jewels in an evening gown coalesce into an image, my history with Ezra comes into sharp focus. He might be behaving like an idiot right now, and I might feel like smacking the back of his head a thousand times. But my love for him still shines intense, excruciating, both immutable and ever transforming. And his love for me persists, solid and relentless, reliable as the sun over the decades. Nothing in the world can take away our love for each other. Not a stupid fight, not our idiocies combined. Not even death.

It's not a matter of *if*, it's a matter of *when*. Ezra and I will reconcile and share the rest of our lives together—even if I have to slap common sense back into him.

CHAPTER 32

Ezra

I'VE DIALED MIA'S NUMBERS SO MANY TIMES IN MY PHONE THAT now Siri whines in protest at the command. Mia must not have been kidding when she said she was blocking me.

I'm starting to panic. How will I convince Mia to give me another chance? For all the charm my girls ever taught me, nothing I can think of seems good enough. Decision paralysis makes me drag my feet for days.

And now I've had to leave on a business trip to Arlington, Virginia, followed by a stop in Chicago. Maxwell has connected me with some of his contacts in research and the military who are interested in the *Squiggles* app and the *Cupcakes* software.

The half day of meetings at the National Cybersecurity and Infrastructure Security Agency (CISA) felt successful. Maxwell's contact is eager to learn about *Cupcakes* and use that knowledge to help improve the country's resilience against cyber-attacks. He also believes my AI could be used to help in profiling criminals and predicting their movements. He promises to get back to me soon, but knowing how slow government bureaucracy can be, I'm ready to wait awhile. Tomorrow I leave for another meeting at Midwestern University in Chicago, where Maxwell works. I'll be talking to some pediatric neuroscience researchers who are interested in studying *Squiggles* as an educational tool. Forfeiting financial gain is worth it for the peace of mind. This is my best chance to close this chapter and present myself to Mia as a changed man.

But of course, unless I do something soon, I'll never know if this was worth it—because I'll lose her forever.

When I return to my hotel after my last meeting at the CISA, the distance from Mia hurts more than Ian's jiu jitsu holds. And my own brain entangles me more than any pretzel-twisted submission Ian ever put me in.

How will I get Mia to take me back? How can I show her how sorry I am for my stupidity?

Apprehension tightens my chest and I end up reaching for that asthma inhaler I haven't used in ages. My eyes burn so much, I have to ditch the contacts in exchange for my glasses. Desperate for help, I create an iMessage group with Chloe, Iris and Sophia and send them a FaceTime request.

I hold my breath while the call rings. Will they ignore the call, proving that I've ruined my friendship with them too?

My agony soon comes to an end. Sophia answers first, followed immediately by Chloe and Iris.

"Finally, you reappear!" Sophia says, eager.

"I was so worried when you weren't answering my texts!" Iris speaks at the same time.

Chloe wags a finger at me. "I can't believe you've been talking to Max and not calling me!"

Their reprimands feel great. "I thought I'd put you in an awkward position if I called. You know, that your loyalties would be with Mia."

The simultaneous protesting grunts and eyerolls delight my spirit.

"Sweetie, I should smack you for even thinking that nonsense!" says Chloe.

"We'd never stop being your friends!" Sophia and Iris say at once.

I'm so relieved and grateful I could cry.

The second they've reassured me of their eternal love, Chloe proceeds to scold me. "Ezra, you and Mia are behaving like stubborn teens, making the same mistakes you made sixteen years ago."

She twists her long braid. "She's waiting for you to call and ask her to the prom—to take the next step and apologize. And you're stuck in your low self-esteem assuming you won't be welcome if you do."

Iris and Mia must've filled Chloe in about the events surrounding our senior prom.

"I've tried to come up with an idea to surprise Mia. But I can't even track her down on social media anymore." I hesitate forever, but I finally burst out the words that have been strangling me. "Is she talking to Mr. X?"

"Oh karma!" Chloe slaps her own forehead.

Sophia shivers and whimpers. "Of course not, you silly!"

"Why would you think that?" Iris throws a hand in the air.

Now I've also outraged my other girls. This proves how unreliable my brain is at this time. "She's blocking my calls. And she disappeared from her social media, like she used to every time she got back with him."

Chloe huffs and sighs at once. "She's just hurt. And going crazy, catching up with emails and work messages after four weeks out."

Hope bubbles inside me, but I still have to ask, "So… she never considered Mr. X's proposal, right?"

A suspicious silence falls, and the girls exchange looks as they seem to muse on the question for a moment.

Sophia speaks first. "I'm sorry, it's against the sisterhood code to team up with the guy who broke one of our hearts—even if it's you." She drums her fingers on her desk and her lips twitch. "So, I'm not supposed to tell you she had her lawyer warn Xenakis that if he ever approaches her again, she'll sue him for harassment."

The relief expands my chest better than my inhaler. "She did?"

"Yes, you, clueless man!" Chloe adds. "And also, I'm not supposed to tell you that she misses you like hell."

Overcome by emotion, I ease onto the bed. "She wasn't serious when she left that message, right? Is she really going to punish me if I approach her now?"

"You can bet she'll make you suffer a little, mister! You've pissed the diva off." Chloe chuckles. "She'll definitely take you back—eventually. But as of the last time we talked, she first plans to make you beg for a while."

My eyes plead through the screen. "Please help me, girls. I'm out of ideas. What can I do to win her back?"

"Wait!" Iris lifts a hand. "I think we should all step back and not interfere."

My stomach plummets along with all my hopes. "What?"

"We're too invested in this outcome to be reliable," Iris adds. "And I'd never forgive myself if we gave you a wrong idea and made things worse."

Chloe and Sophia second with a nod and a mumble.

Shit. I'm in trouble.

Iris shoots me a loving but concerned look. "Ezra, this is going to be your graduation from everything we taught you about how to be an irresistible man. We love you, we're here to help you. But you have to come up with the plan yourself."

This has to be the hardest challenge anyone has ever posted to my rigid brain. "Can you at least give me some intel? Answer some questions for me?"

The silence that follows feels like the longest wait of my life, but then a bow of the head from Chloe is followed by agreement from the girls.

I prop the phone against the wall and pull out my work computer.

CHAPTER 33

Mia

WHO WOULD'VE THOUGHT THAT EVIL QUENTIN XENAKIS would ever pay me back—if indirectly—for all the pain he caused me? Whatever his real intentions when he invited me on the Greece trip, it all turned out for good. The press attention after the fashion show in Mykonos has boosted my website visibility to the sky. I will be busier than ever and have to recruit more staff when I return to work Monday.

Yes, the future looks promising—but I feel miserable. Losing my Aphrodite dress to a billionaire's wife hurt. I played with the idea of rejecting the offer, but my hesitation only enticed the buyer to raise her bid.

And today, Chloe offered to pick me up from my Dad's house and drive me to O'Hare airport, so we can spend a little more time together before I leave. She surprises me by showing up also with Sophia, the two of them holding up a large sign with my name, mimicking a taxi company. After a dozen hugs, they help me carry my bag to the door.

"How are we going to fit in your Mini Cooper?" I ask, remembering that Chloe was supposed to bring the rest of my luggage from her place in Chicago.

"I hired a taxi company and a driver. I'll go get them."

A blizzard rages outside, so Sophia and I stay in until Chloe makes sure our taxi is at the curb. After I've said goodbye to Dad and promised a future visit soon, a text from Chloe signals us to come out.

But what I find in front of the house is not a taxi. It's a limo.

With the temperature hanging around the freezing point, I wait until the three of us are nestled inside before I ask, "A *limo*?"

"Yes, this limo company belongs to one of my patients." Chloe appears distracted, texting on her phone. "Since I needed to rent transportation, I thought I would support his business."

I've traveled in a limo many times, but always on my way to some stressful event. It turns out riding one with two of my best friends is awesome. That way, someone else does the driving and the three of us can focus on calling Iris to share one of those moments when we're reunited, mostly in person.

Iris must be out of her house today. I don't recognize that green wall in the background. The moment the greetings are completed, she asks. "So, have you heard anything from Ezra, Mia?"

"No. I unblocked his number a few days ago, but he hasn't called. I'm starting to get angry with him *for real*." I remove my gloves with a growl. "I almost regret that drunken voicemail I left on his phone."

"What did you say?" Sophia asks.

I replay the message in my mind. "I picked up the phone to mend things between us. But then the call went to voicemail and it made me furious. Because Ezra's never too far from his phone—he even brings the damn thing to the shower! It had to be that he sent my call to voicemail on purpose." I stop, and another more worrisome thought reveals itself. "Or that he's already with another woman."

"Oh, come on!" Chloe rolls her eyes. "You know you're talking nonsense, don't you?"

I cross my arms and jiggle a foot. "No, I don't! Obviously, his brain is not reliable right now. Otherwise, how could he even believe that I might consider dumping him and going back to Quentin? For all I know, right this minute, he's soothing his bruised ego with another ditzy blonde."

Grimacing, Chloe fiddles with her quartz bracelets. "You forget that Ezra's brain works literally. You told him you were mad at him and he'd ruined everything."

"Yes!" Iris adds. "And he's trained to give a woman space when that happens. I know, because *we* trained him."

"I didn't mean to make it sound as if I was pushing him away." I pinch the bridge of my nose and close my eyes. "All I wanted was for him to take the first step. All I want is for the first time in my life stop being the chaser and letting him chase me." A twinge of sadness rises inside me. Maybe a naive part of me believed I'd changed the past by returning to Greenyard. I thought that from now on I didn't have to be the easy floozy anymore, but the lady playing hard to get.

The ride to Chicago takes forever. Apparently, the snowstorm has caused some accidents and the driver is taking a different route to evade traffic jams. I really hope I don't miss my flight. As my conversation with the girls winds up and Iris yawns a goodbye, my hands twitch with an urge to dial Ezra. The fact that they didn't suggest adding him to our videocall with Iris proves how awkward things have turned with him.

Between the blizzard and the darkness, it's hard to see what's outside the window when the limo finally takes a highway exit. But these low buildings don't look at all like Chicago.

Then we pass a boxy, three-story brick building that looks very familiar. It's Greenyard High School.

"What the hell? Are we back in Greenyard?" Shoot. Did the driver's GPS fail and we turned around? "Now I'm definitely missing my plane!"

"This is crazy, isn't it?" Chloe seems unconcerned about the mix up.

The shock of seeing the school leaves me witless for a while. We pass a football field that flaunts the same outdated lighting as before, and the limo stops in front of a side entrance.

"Well, now that we're here, we might as well go in." Before I can demand an explanation, Chloe and Sophia have dragged me out of the limo by the arms. My surprise almost makes me forget about the freezing temperature as they usher me inside the building.

I should be protesting, but I'm still in shock. The school has changed even less than the Cohens' house. We cross hallways and classrooms that have barely had a coat of paint since the last time I was here.

"So, this is the high school you guys attended? Wow! It reminds me so much of the one Iris and I went to!" Sophia also appears suspiciously cheerful as she helps me out of my coat.

"And if memory serves me well, this is the way to the gym." Chloe guides me to an adjacent building, connected by an enclosed walkway.

The minute I enter, a retro wave slaps me. Avril Lavigne's "Fall to Pieces" plays from an old-fashioned DJ station. The place is decorated with purple and golden balloons and cheesy banners I've seen before.

I saw them at my senior prom night.

A small crowd has gathered inside and person after person comes to greet me with a hug, starting with Chloe's grandma and Ezra's parents. Then, a handful of high school classmates I barely recognize. Even a couple of our chaperones from that night gather here: Mr. Thompson the barber, and Mrs. Collins, the owner of the old ice cream parlor. Then the sight of my father in his wheelchair, beaming at me, adds to my puzzlement. He knew about this?

I believe I've reached my limit for bewilderment when another person lines up to hug me.

It's Iris.

"Iris!" We embrace, and I struggle to understand what's going on. So, a few minutes ago, when we video-chatted…she was here?

Soon my three best girlfriends and I are linked in an embrace I haven't experienced since the night of the beach ceremony a year ago.

I shoot Chloe a baffled glance. "Chloe, are you going to explain—?"

"May I have your attention, please." The voice coming from the stage makes me jump. It's Ezra! He stands in front of a microphone

235

wearing his glasses and a replica of the outfit he sported for our prom: a gray turtleneck and ripped jeans. He holds a corsage box.

The crowd at the gym claps and whistles as he approaches me. My pulse speeds up as he extends his arm and offers to pull me up on the stage. The zing of his fingers on my elbow reminds me of how long it's been since I had access to those delightful hands.

"Hi," he says when we are close, sounding as shy as he did six-teen years ago.

"Hello." I'm trying to play it cool, but my squeaky voice resem-bles that of the twelve-year-old who first met him.

He turns off the microphone on the stand and whispers, "My first plan was to declare in front of the whole town that you're my girl and I'm so proud of it." His hands holding the corsage box tremble. "But then I realized, first I have to apologize for being an idiot and ask if you still *want* to be my girl."

A warm trickle of joy spreads through my soul. I want to kiss him and tell him how happy I am to see him. But when he planned this grand gesture, he didn't take into account that I'm not a fan of public displays of affection.

I control the grin taking over my face to retro-fit it into a smug expression. "Well…I may need to think about it for a little longer. If anything, to enjoy seeing you beg."

His glorious smile shows that, despite my restraint, the love in my eyes has answered for me.

He turns the microphone back on. "Mia, I wanted to bring you here, in front of all these people to say aloud what I always kept quiet. That you're the most wonderful woman I've ever met and I've been deeply honored to have you as one of my best friends for two decades…but now I want you to be more than that."

I want to cry. Okay, maybe I won't make him beg too much.

He shifts his weight and uses a shaky hand to pull at his turtle-neck collar. "It's a little late for us to go to the prom. But I thought we could put together our own party." He waves a hand around the room. "This one is just a small proto-type; a beta test for a much larger celebration I want to throw for us. In that party I would like to invite our friends and all our high school classmates. And all of our family."

He paces away from me and toward something in the middle of the stage I hadn't noticed before. A sheet is draped over what seems to be a sculpture, but when he pulls it off, it reveals a mannequin. It's wearing a white gown I recognize, and my jaw drops in recognition.

It's the Aphrodite dress.

"What the hell?" I gawk at Ezra.

Ezra lifts a finger. "Wait, I don't want to forget my lines." He takes a deep breath and continues. "Someone once told us that this design looked 'too much like a wedding dress.' So, it occurred to me that maybe we could throw that party...and you could wear it. And maybe Iris, Sophia, and Chloe could wear matching dresses you design?" He shoots me an eager look.

My heart races. I know what he means but I have to make him say it. "What are you talking about?"

"I mean that I'm all the way in. No more indecision." The sexiest geek on earth steps toward me and his intense look gives me goose bumps. "And if I had to choose someone to spend the rest of my life with, you're it, hands down. I'd rather be with that person who knows exactly who I am, who can call me on my bullshit. Who gives me comfort because she's my steady home, but also keeps me on my toes because no matter how much I think I know her, she keeps surprising me with new facets."

If he makes me bawl my eyes out in front of the entire town, he's going to pay.

He's not done. "And every facet of her, brings out a new aspect in me. So, we'll never be bored with each other. What I mean is..." He opens the box he holds and extracts something from it. But it's not the flower corsage showing through the clear window. It's a diamond solitaire. He pinches it between his thumb and his index and gets down on one knee. It's like a flashback of the night in Santorini, except today the right guy holds the ring.

"Mia, would you…"

"YES!" I don't let him finish. I throw my arms around his neck and kiss him, making him lose his balance and stumble to the floor with me. In my emotion, I've practically tackled him like a football linebacker—so much for playing hard to get.

I want to take this kiss far beyond PG, but the cheering family and friends around us force us to keep it clean. I so want to get this man alone. It's like all the accumulated hunger of the celibacy year has come back with a vengeance all for him.

He scrambles off the floor and helps me rise. He cleans his foggy glasses using the edge of his shirt before he picks up the ring from the floor and slides it on my finger, earning the applause of the small crowd. We seal the moment with another chaste kiss, and then the disc jockey plays slow music, and soon couples fill the improvised dance floor.

"What took you so long!" I gently slap Ezra's arm a little later, as we rock to the music.

"My operating system froze after that voicemail you left," he replies with a grimace. "I was terrified of blowing it and had to make sure I brought you an offer you couldn't refuse."

My eyes wander to the Aphrodite dress on the stage and my soul sings. Hell yeah, that's my wedding dress.

"Ezra did you really spend *one hundred thousand dollars* on a dress I made myself?"

"Two, actually, I had to outbid the other offer."

I stare at him, speechless.

"It's the last extravagant purchase for a while." He scrunches his face. "I'll have to become more conscious of my spending, since I just turned down four million dollars." He pauses. "I'm no longer selling *Squiggles*."

At my inquiring look, he adds, "I'm stripping *Squiggles* of ads and separating it from *Cupcakes*, the data extraction program. Eventually, it will become an educational app. I'm teaming up with a group of neuroscientists who are studying embedding math lessons in videogames as subliminal messages, to enhance learning."

Wow. I can't believe he found a way to use *Squiggles* for good. "What are you going to do with the *other* part?" I don't want to refer to data extraction and privacy invasion aloud.

His crinkled eyes carry an enigmatic air. "Sorry, I've signed an NDA on that. I'll just say I'm donating it to a government entity that hopefully will make better use of it."

"Oh, wow!" I don't know what to answer to that. I'm so proud of him.

It takes me a few moments to digest everything and resume talking.

"Actually, when I asked what took you so long, I didn't mean now," I clarify. "I meant I can't believe it took us sixteen years to make it to prom together."

He chuckles and winks. "I had some tricks to learn before I was ready to be in your league."

I get he's joking about our clumsy first kiss and our amazing first night together, but his words get me thinking. "I also had some things to figure out before I was ready for you. I had to acquire a taste for love that treats me well—instead of love that puts me down, that I have to chase."

He glances in the direction of my father, slow dancing with Luz while keeping one hand on his walker. Then he returns his attention to me. "I can't wait to show you every day that the only love worth having is the one we don't have to chase, because it's there for us, reliable, unconditional and loyal. Love that can see the best part of us, even when we've forgotten it. Love that doesn't walk away when we show our worst sides, because it knows what's real, hiding underneath."

We dare to kiss a little deeper this time and I shudder with emotion and relief. I can't believe I almost lost Ezra. I will never again let him go.

And then an idea hits me. I end the kiss and pull my head back just enough to look him in the eye. "Ezra, I'm pretty sure Trent told me he'd already accepted the first offer…how did you get the Aphrodite dress?"

He gives a guilty wince. "I may…have hacked your store's eCommerce site so it would reject the other buyer's payment again and again, giving me time to present my bid."

I gape at him. "Ezra!"

"And I may have also hacked Trent's email account to monitor the communication between them and keep the buyer from making a counter offer and…" He flinches. "And possibly yours, too, to make sure Trent didn't spill the beans about me being your new buyer."

I release him and take a step back, gawking at him. "Ezra!" I whisper. "I thought we had a deal that you would stop hacking—"

He pulls me by the wrist back into his arms in a pretend dance move, then holds me against his chest. "Let's not ruin this magical moment. How about you nag me about this later and we find another outrageous way I can make it up to you?" He seals the offer by taking a nibble at my neck and my brain melts.

Okay, we can resume this talk later.

I relax in his arms, and get lost in his familiar warmth and delightful smell, feeling like the luckiest girl in the whole world. I finally get to dance at prom with the guy I'm smitten with. And he's also the man I love most in the world.

EPILOGUE

(Three months later)

Ezra

P EOPLE CLAIM MIA AND I ARE MOVING TOO FAST, BUT I LAUGH at that. We've known each other for *twenty-one years*, and I've known she was the one for me since our first kiss at age seventeen. That's why we've decided we only want the most important people in our lives to take part in this special occasion. And to keep away any press, or any old, undesirable friends, nothing is better than a destination wedding.

We're now in Gibraltar, sitting at a restaurant table overlooking Morocco, across the Mediterranean Sea. Our parents are scheduled to arrive tomorrow, so we have one last night to be foolish and silly with our best friends before the celebration turns grownup and serious. To our left sit Sophia and her fiancée, Trevor, who barely forgive us for stealing their thunder and beating them to the altar. To our right sit Chloe and Max, who've worked miracles to be here despite all their recent travels. Across from us sit Iris, Marcia and Trent. Besides the few new additions to the clan, it's like time hasn't passed and I'm having fun with my best friends from college again.

"I'm curious, why did you choose Gibraltar?" Iris asks. "I expected you two to get married in the Greek islands, where your love story blossomed."

"Our memories from there are unbeatable, but we wanted a fresh start." Mia straightens the V neck of her ivory and gold cocktail dress that brightens her eyes—another of her designs.

"And, like the day we found the Hephaestus temple," I add, "we decided we'd find a mind-blowing option that would please our very different tastes without either of us compromising,"

"That's so sweet," Sophia presses a hand to her heart. "And, yes, I remember you saying you liked Gibraltar in the past, Mia. Why was it?"

Mia's face lights up. "Gibraltar has the glamour of having been the place where John Lennon and Yoko Ono got married."

"And it also has monkeys!" I clap, giddy in excitement. "I've always wanted to have a monkey in my wedding pictures!"

With solemn coolness, Mia continues. "Gibraltar is also a very unique place. It's geographically located in Spain, but it's British territory. It's right in the middle of Europe and Africa. We felt it represents that undefined place we were in for years."

"And it also has monkeys!" I pump a fist.

Mia shoots me the same warning look as when she was my fashion-and-coolness-police. "What's more, the Rock of Gibraltar is a symbol of solidity and stability," She continues. "That's what we've been, and hope to be, for each other for the rest of our lives."

I beam at her with adoration. "Yes. Mia is definitely the rock-solid base where I want to build my life. As steady and durable as the Acropolis—as the rock of Gibraltar. Of course, this was the best place to tie our lives together." We exchange a sweet kiss, but then my urgency to goof around becomes stronger than me. "Plus, Gibraltar has monkeys."

Mia groans in fake annoyance and pushes me away, suppressing her amusement.

A text message chimes on my phone and I reach for it. "Oh, great! My friend Ian made it and is on his way here! You're finally going to get to meet him."

"This is the famous Brazilian jiu jitsu trainer you mention all the time, isn't it?" Mia asks.

"Wait! Brazilian jiu jitsu?" Iris turns paper-white. "You don't mean Innacio Silva, by any chance?"

Now this is interesting. "Why yes, Iris. Do you know him?"

Instead of answering, Iris springs from her chair so abruptly she knocks her glass off and her honey-blond wig goes askew. She staggers out of her chair, knocking it over in the process, and stumbles against the waiter, almost making him drop his tray. "Uh...uh...I just remembered I have to make a phone call to my editor in the States!" She scurries backward.

Mia frowns. "Iris, it's six am in Florida."

"Uh...that's perfect." She inches out, her hazel eyes growing gigantic. "Uh...because my editor likes to brainstorm in the early morning when she's inspired. "Bye, guys!"

Iris takes off literally running.

What the heck?

I'm still trying to process Iris' strange reaction a while later when Ian approaches our table. I stand up and greet him with a hug. I'm so freaking happy lately I'm becoming a leech.

Ian's unusual smile makes him look much younger as he shakes Mia's hand and goes through the introductions at the table. He slaps my back a little harder than necessary as he takes a seat. "So, you did it, *desgraçado*! You're marrying the girl of your dreams!"

Marcia—who's already shooting Ian flirty looks—answers for me. "Yes! Finally those two are going to stop pretending they're just friends!"

I give Marcia my best impression of confusion. "What are you talking about? Mia and I *are* just friends."

Marcia's face falls. "No, you're not. You're getting *married*."

Quick to realize what I'm doing, Mia plays along and shrugs. "That means nothing, Marcia; friends get married all the time." Her lips quirk. "Our relationship is strictly platonic."

Marcia's baffled look is comical. "Uh...you're kidding, aren't you?"

243

"Of course they're kidding!" Trent rolls his eyes.

"No, we're not kidding. Me? Sleeping with this nerd? Please!" Mia points at me with her thumb. "This is the same geek I met when we were twelve, who couldn't pick a good outfit if his life depended on it."

I tease back, "And she's the same airhead who couldn't balance an equation if it had two digits."

"See? Nothing has changed," Mia flicks a hand.

I suppress a smirk as I wrap my arm around Mia's shoulders. "We're just two PMS-synchronized girlfriends who now will be throwing slumber parties every night."

Marcia looks at Mia and me in turns, frowning as if thinking hard. "Trent, they're just messing with me, right?"

Trent sighs in exasperation and looks up to the sky. "Yes, Marcia! They're just messing with you!"

We all laugh and I pull Mia closer. "Okay, okay, Marcia. I guess it's safe to admit it publicly. We're in love. We're elated with happiness." I throw a glance at Ian. "And we're *all in*. We're getting married *non-platonically*, and we intend to live happily ever after with our five children, a dog and two cats."

Mia elbows me. "Ezra!"

"Okay, okay." I huff and grumble, "*Two* children."

She lifts one finger. "And *five* cats!"

I grin at her. "And maybe a monkey?"

We guffaw again as Mia circles my neck with her hands and pretends to strangle me, and we seal the banter with another long kiss.

As the waiter brings our desserts and asks Ian if he'd like to order something, I remember Iris' strange exit, and something sparks in my brain circuits.

"Hey, Ian," I raise from the table and signal him to step away with me for privacy. I lower my voice. "You mentioned you had initially approached me because you were trying to track down a woman. Is she someone I know?"

He casts a glance around the restaurant. "I had hoped she'd be here. Yes, you do know her. Iris Kent."

Ooh. This is *more than* interesting.

Mia must have the sharpest ears in the world when her girlfriends are involved. In a snap, she's abandoned her dessert and joined us. "You and Iris know each other?" she whispers.

Ian nods and turns to me. "I saw you two hugging and holding hands in a video from her book launch party, and I thought maybe you were her boyfriend. You know, before I met you and figured out she was just your friend."

Oh. That explains his constant curiosity about my relationship with "my girls." To avoid worrying Mia, I gloss over his original intent to beat me up. "And you wanted to track down Iris because…"

Ian drops the words with a flat tone. "She's the one who got away."

Moved, Mia gasps and places a hand on her chest.

Ian's quivering lips suggest he's overcome by emotion. For an instant, his eyes glimmer with tears, then a worrisome flash of rage sparks in them. "And I mean that *literally*. She swore she'd love me forever, then ran away from me—more than once. The most infamous time she jumped through a window and hid in a garbage dumpster."

I distinctly remember pulling Iris out of that dumpster and promising not to ask any questions.

"I'm furious with her," Ian's voice shakes and his nostrils flare. "And just like the day my pet goat ran away, I'm going to lasso her and tie her up to a fence until she hears what I have to tell her."

I'm just a tiny bit worried right now. This tough guy needs someone to teach him that getting a girl requires honey, not vinegar. But I'm more worried for him than for Iris. If he doesn't watch out, my girls are going to lasso *him* to defend her. It's a miracle protective Mia hasn't tackled him yet.

"And even if you're not going to tell me, I know Iris is here somewhere." He scans the restaurant. "So I'm just going to walk around the hotel area until I run into her. See you in a bit. Nice meeting you, Mia."

He paces away and Mia and I gawk at each other.

"Wait a minute. Did he say Iris *swore eternal love to him*? How come she never told us about him?" Mia bites her lower lip. "Dang it. I can't wait to find out what happens next. But I'm afraid this might complicate our wedding."

I wrap her in my arms and kiss her head. "Bring it on. You and I are immunized against drama."

She giggles. "Hell yeah, that's true." Her hug communicates we have nothing else to be dramatic about. We're set for life.

We seal the silent promise with a kiss that makes me want to escape all celebrations and steal her for the rest of the night.

Don't Miss Iris and Ian's Love Story in the Next Book in this Series!

Would you like an opportunity to read that book and others for free? Sign up for my Newsletter! You'll also be able to download the companion photo book for this novel. Enhance your reading experience by immersing in the beautiful images of Italy.

Get your free Photo Companion book Here.

https://mailchi.mp/b53552c75f09/meet-me-in-greece

And keep reading for a sample of an entrancing book you can enjoy for free when you sign up for my Newsletter.

JUST FOR JOY:
BEYOND ACHIEVEMENT

October 2016

JOY CLAYTON'S HEART RACED AS THE TAXI APPROACHED THE white-trimmed yellow cottage, but she couldn't ask the driver to stop there—God forbid the FBI was tracking his GPS. Instead, she asked to be dropped off two houses down. She paid in cash and, after adjusting her blond wig, beach hat, and large sunglasses, she hung her weekend bag from her shoulder and exited the car.

She waited until the taxi had disappeared down the road before heading to her real destination. As she walked toward the cottage, she wondered one more time how on earth she had ended up there.

Never before had she done something this wild and crazy. She'd been the best-behaved little girl in the world—the teacher's pet, the model citizen, the exemplary physician, and, of course, the perfect lady. This was the closest thing to a crime she'd ever committed.

Shivering despite the steamy temperature, she rang the bell. Abruptly, the door opened. Her breath stole away, her heart jumped in her chest, and all second-guessing disappeared from her mind.

There he was, standing at the door. Special Agent Richard Fields. Six foot, three inches of self-assurance and wits. Two hundred luscious pounds of temptation. There he was, with his gorgeous laugh lines framing his hazel eyes, and that elusive daredevil smile she always longed to see break through.

In a flash, he pulled her by the hand into the house, closed the door behind her and clasped her in his strong arms. He made eye contact for a second before kissing her ravenously, his eagerness only matched by her own.

Freeing her from her glasses, hat and wig, he let the brunette waves cascade down her back, then ran his fingers through it. Her knees threatened to buckle.

"You're sure no one followed you, right?" he asked in between kisses. His hot breath smelled of wine, but his mouth tasted of paradise.

"Yes, I changed cabs at the coffee shop and had the second taxi circle town before heading here, like you told me," she mumbled in a hoarse voice while nibbling at his lower lip. He claimed her mouth again, deepening the kiss, and she trembled.

This three-day trip to a borrowed vacation house was exceptional. For Joy and Richard, a date usually meant a secret passionate encounter in the middle of the day, stolen during a lunch hour. With luck, "dining out" meant having takeout in his fenced backyard, under the stars. "Going dancing" meant playing ballroom music on her phone while she gave him dance lessons in the bedroom.

They couldn't risk being seen together in public—always afraid that someone would recognize them and notify the FBI of Richard's unforgivable fault: Getting involved with one of his murder suspects.

She realized he was walking her somewhere and assumed he'd take her to the bedroom first, as usual. Instead, he opened a back door and, holding her hand, guided her to the backyard.

Beaming, he said, "You're just in time! The show's starting."

His hand pointed to the west and she turned speechless. In front of them, the sunset painted the sky with fire, and the boundless Indian River lagoon was an iridescent mixture of gold, orange, and mauve.

He guided her to sit on a blanket he'd laid on the grass and sat behind her, rubbing her shoulders. As he massaged away the aching tension from the past hours, he engaged her in light conversation to help her relax.

"I have the most amazing weekend planned," he said sending her into a trance with his skillful fingers. "Tonight after dinner, we'll ride our bicycles to the beach to watch the full moon rise. Tomorrow, if you'd like, we'll go snorkeling and kayaking. It will be great to spend time outdoors after so much seclusion."

She couldn't help teasing him with their usual inside joke. "It beats jumping off a running truck and racing through the woods chased by gunmen."

He laughed. "How to forget our delightful fifth date?"

"For the hundredth time, sweetie," she tittered, "that was *not* a date."

"Of course it was a date." Without stopping his massage, he wrapped his long legs around her and whispered in her ear. "It was the first time we slept together."

She gasped. "We *fell asleep* next to each other—*in an ambulance!* That doesn't count as sleeping together!"

His thumbs massaged circles down her back. "Surviving a brush with death is the ultimate orgasmic experience. Plus, I sprayed you with my blood when you gave me first aid for my stab wound. I'm counting that as *unprotected* sex."

Joy threw her head back and laughed wholeheartedly. In a flash, the world was all right, and they were no longer forbidden lovers hiding from the FBI, but just a man and a woman in love, enjoying a Florida sunset in their shorts, T-shirts and flip-flops.

After months of terrifying nightmares, the fact that she could now joke about that night—the night when the *Lords of the Universe* tried to eliminate her as a potential witness—was testimony to how healing Richard had been in her life. That was Richard's greatest gift, the ability to pull her out of her brain and back into her body.

And suddenly the joy was too much to bear, and the fear of losing him soon washed over her soul sending her into a near panic.

Covering his hands with hers to stop the massage, she turned slightly to face him. "Did you talk to your bosses already?"

His fingers stiffened. "Angel, it's complicated."

Disappointment pierced her heart. She felt the last of her energy leak out with her sharp exhale. "Why should it be? They caught the real murderer. Michael's case is closed! Isn't it?"

He didn't answer. She didn't expect him to—his job would always come with secrets. She rotated to sit facing him. "I'm not asking for much. All I want is for us to have a date without constantly having to look over our shoulders. All I want is being able to call my man to ask about his day—without fearing someone bugged our phones."

He seemed torn. When he didn't answer again, she avoided his eyes. "I don't mean to be difficult—" her voice cracked. Even years after her husband Michael's death, she still couldn't help apologizing constantly.

The usual playfulness had disappeared from his expression. "You're not. Angel, you're the lowest maintenance woman I've ever met."

He guided her to sit on his lap and cradled her in his arms. "There's more at risk than losing my job. There's more than you know going on. But I'm working on it. You have to trust me, angel."

Could she trust him? This was the man who'd entered her life wrapped in a fake identity—undercover—and lied to her for months.

But this was also the man who'd saved her life. And the man who healed her soul every day with his patience, with amazing tenderness he hid under a stern façade.

(Continue Reading)
Get it for free by signing up for my Newsletter.

NOTE FROM THE AUTHOR

Dear Reader:

It is an honor to me that you took the time to read this story. I hope you've enjoyed it.

My goal is to write romance stories that are not only entertaining, but also enriching for the soul. I created this romance sub-genre because I couldn't find what I wanted anywhere. My books bridge the gap between "Wholesome" and "Sexy"; and between "Inspirational" and "Irreverently Funny."

My books are designed to leave you with an after-taste of Joy and Hope. They inspire without preaching They reinforce values such as authenticity, tolerance, compassion, and self-empowerment—and, of course, love.

I'd love to hear from you. What did you like in the story? What did you not like? What would you like to see more in future books? I would really appreciate if you could take the time and leave a review at Amazon, Goodreads, your blog or any other venue of your preference.

Please visit my website and sign for my email list for free short stories and sneak-peeks in future releases: www.pichardo-johansson-md.com

Please also feel free to email me at pichardojohanssonmd@gmail.com— I'm a busy lady, but I'll do my best to answer all emails.

Thank you again for reading me.

Love,
Diely

OTHER BOOKS BY THIS AUTHOR

Love Me in Paris: A Travel Romance (Trevor and Sophia's story)

Kiss Me in Italy: A Travel Medical Romance (Chloe and Maxwell's story)

Sunshine State Series
Book 1: Hope for Harmony: Baby Makers vs. Peter Pans (Hope and Tom's story):

Book 2: Just for Joy: Beyond Achievement (It intersects with the Beyond Romance series): **You can get this book for free by joining my Newsletter.**

Book 3: Faith is Fearless: Normal is Overrated.

Book 4: Grasping for Grace: Never Grow Up.

Book 5: Longing for Love: A Funny, Sweet and Sexy Romance with a Medical Twist

Check my website www.pichardo-johansson-md.com/books for more details.

Love,
Diely

ABOUT THE AUTHOR

Dr. Pichardo-Johansson is a retired physician, a Life Coach and author of ten books. She's also a happy wife to her soulmate, a mother of kids with special needs, and a cancer survivor.

After fifteen years practicing oncology, and after becoming a cancer survivor herself, she decided she no longer wanted to make a living fighting death. Instead, she now teaches people to fully enjoy life.

As a Fiction author, she specializes in romance that is "Connection of the minds and the souls, more than only the bodies" while her Mystery specialty is "How to murder someone and ensure a negative autopsy."

As a Non-fiction author and a Life coach, she specializes in helping professional women find authentic joy and love, and helping clients reinvent themselves after life-shaking events.

She is a mother of four children, including twins and a child with special needs, and adoptive mother to two cats, Ice and Rain. She lives in Melbourne Beach, Florida with all of them and her Soulmate-Husband, David, a reformed eternal bachelor turned into happy step-father. He is her inspiration for writing and the main reason why she deeply believes in romantic love.

www.ingramcontent.com/pod-product-compliance
Lightning Source LLC
Chambersburg PA
CBHW020055180626
46812CB00006B/2332